CHANGE HORIZONS

THREE NOVELLAS

What Reviewers Say About
Gun Brooke's Supreme Constellations Series

Protector of the Realm
Supreme Constellations: Book One

"*Protector of the Realm* has it all; sabotage, corruption, erotic love and exhilarating space fights. Gun Brooke's second novel is forceful with a winning combination of solid characters and a brilliant plot. The book exemplifies her growth as an inventive storyteller and is sure to garner multiple awards in the coming year."—*Just About Write*

"Brooke is an amazing author, and has written in other genres. Never have I read a book where I started at the top of the page and don't know what will happen two paragraphs later…She keeps the excitement going, and the pages turning."—*MegaScene*

Praise for Gun Brooke's Romance Novels

Fierce Overture

"Gun Brooke creates memorable characters, and Noelle and Helena are no exception. Each woman is "more than meets the eye" as each exhibits depth, fears, and longings. And the sexual tension between them is real, hot, and raw."—*Just About Write*

September Canvas

"In this character-driven story, trust is earned and secrets are uncovered. Deanna and Faythe are fully fleshed out and prove to the reader each has much depth, talent, wit and problem-solving abilities. *September Canvas* is a good read with a thoroughly satisfying conclusion."—*Just About Write*

Sheridan's Fate

"Sheridan's fire and Lark's warm embers are enough to make this book sizzle. Brooke, however, has gone beyond the wonderful emotional explorations of these characters to tell the story of those who, for various reasons, become differently-abled. Whether it is a bullet, an illness, or a problem at birth, many women and men find themselves in Sheridan's situation. Her courage and Lark's gentleness and determination send this romance into a 'must read.'"—*Just About Write*

Coffee Sonata

"In *Coffee Sonata*, the lives of these four women become intertwined. In forming friendships and love, closets and disabilities are discussed, along with differences in age and backgrounds. Love and friendship are areas filled with complexity and nuances. Brooke takes her time to savor the complexities while her main characters savor their excellent cups of coffee. If you enjoy a good love story, a great setting, and wonderful characters, look for *Coffee Sonata* at your favorite gay and lesbian bookstore."—*Family & Friends* magazine

Course of Action

"Brooke's words capture the intensity of their growing relationship. Her prose throughout the book is breathtaking and heart-stopping. Where have you been hiding, Gun Brooke? I, for one, would like to see more romances from this author."—*Independent Gay Writer*

By the Author

Course of Action

Coffee Sonata

Sheridan's Fate

September Canvas

Fierce Overture

Speed Demons

The Supreme Constellations Series:

Protector of the Realm

Rebel's Quest

Warrior's Valor

Pirate's Fortune

Change Horizons: Three Novellas

Visit us at www.boldstrokesbooks.com

CHANGE HORIZONS

THREE NOVELLAS

by

Gun Brooke

2013

CHANGE HORIZONS

ISBN 13: 978-1-60282-881-0

This Trade Paperback Original Is Published By
Bold Strokes Books, Inc.
P.O. Box 249
Valley Falls, NY 12185

First Edition: June 2013

Credits
Editors: Shelley Thrasher and Stacia Seaman
Production Design: Stacia Seaman
Cover Art by Gun Brooke
Cover Design by Sheri (graphicartist2020@hotmail.com)

Acknowledgments

Writing these novellas was something new for me—at least doing it like this, planned, prepared, and so on. I learned a lot while sticking to the slightly shorter format for each story, but it was tremendous fun. I loved revisiting old friends from the Supreme Constellations universe—and introducing some new ones.

Thank you Len Barot, aka Radclyffe, for your continued faith in me. I am so glad to belong to the BSB family. It's my professional home.

Dr. Shelley Thrasher, my wonderful editor, you are my rock. You are also a very good friend and I'm proud to be the writer you were first assigned to at BSB. We work very well together, and you know my writing better than anyone.

Stacia—Eagle Eyes—you are a miraculously meticulous copy editor who spots what Shelley and I missed despite a gazillion read-throughs. Your talent is nothing short of amazing.

Sheri, graphic artist—as always a pleasure to work with you. You're gracious with your praise regarding my artwork, and I love how you put it all together and make it look sharp.

Connie, Lori, Cindy, Sandy, Toni, and all the others working with and for BSB—and my colleagues as well, of course, I'm so happy and thankful for the work you do to help, promote, and support us writers.

My first readers, Laura, USA; Maggie, Sweden; and Sam, South Africa— thank you for all the hours you dedicate to reading and commenting. It's been rewarding, informative, helpful, and fun. The fact that you're all among my very best friends in the world is humbling.

No matter what anyone thinks, as solitary as writing can be, no one lives in a vacuum. I would starve and be miserable without Elon. I have the constant support from Malin, Henrik, Pentti, the grandkids, Ove and Monica, and even my dogs. Another constant source of love and friendship is Joanne, with whom I just celebrated 12-12-12-12.

I have the most amazing readers and followers. I want to acknowledge the readers, the MirAndy community, my faithful Advent Calendar readers, and anyone who has expressed how much reading my books and other BSB books has meant to them. Authors write to express themselves and be read—and you, the readers, make every hour of hard work that goes into writing our books totally worth it.

For Elon.
For giving me what I value most.
For 32 more years—at least.
And…for all the breakfasts.

Contents

Supreme Constellations: Oracle's Destiny   1

Supreme Constellations: The Queen and the Captain   85

Exodus: The Dawning   165

Glossary   219

Supreme Constellations
Oracle's Destiny

CHAPTER ONE

O h, for stars and skies, it had to be *her*." Chief Medical Officer Gemma Meyer groaned at the sight of the tall Gantharian woman striding toward her.

Dr. Ciel O'Diarda, Gantharian druid and herbal healer, moved with self-assured grace. Her black-white-silver striped hair was tied back in a low, tight braid, and startlingly blue eyes emphasized her chiseled face. All Gantharians were blue-blooded in the truest sense of the word. Their "red" blood cells were in fact the color of sapphire, which made Ciel's skin tone faintly blue, as well as her lips.

Gemma couldn't help but compare this woman to her other Gantharian friends, especially Kellen O'Dal, Protector of the Realm. Kellen had invited her to Gantharat and was grateful to have her help restore and update Gantharat's health-care system now that the Onotharian occupation had ended. But Ciel O'Diarda had not been coy about her disdain for Supreme Constellation medicine. Gemma found this attitude infuriating since the SC had just made Gantharat a free world again. On top of that, Gemma finally had a chance to visit some of the places where her plans had been implemented, and her Gantharian guide had to be Ciel. Wonderful.

"Dr. Meyer." Ciel pursed her lips and bowed slightly. "The convoy is ready."

"*Dr.* O'Diarda," Gemma replied. Ciel clenched her jaws. Good, Gemma thought. Her scornful emphasis of her title had hit home. "What a surprise." She wished Kellen had chosen someone else. To begin with, a real doctor would've been nice.

"I'm sure you're as…astonished as I was when Protector O'Dal contacted me."

"Astonished doesn't even begin to describe it." Gemma hoisted her sling-bag and walked up to the closest hovercraft. An SC soldier stood by the door leading into the passenger section.

"I'm Dr. Gemma Meyer. Which vehicle am I supposed to ride in?"

"In the second one together with Dr. O'Diarda, ma'am." The soldier saluted. "We're hauling your equipment into the cargo-craft and expect to head out in an hour."

"Fantastic. Thank you, Sergeant." Placing her hands on her hips, Gemma slowly turned to Ciel. "Looks like we're going to muddle through this together."

"I heard." Ciel's expression was stoic, but she looked like she wanted to sigh just as deeply. "According to our route, we should reach Paustenja by nightfall. We'll set up camp—"

"I know. I know. We're roughing it. I may have been a space rat most of my professional life, but I can still read an itinerary and retain the information."

"Roughing it." Ciel snorted, her eyes turning into slits of contempt. "Our definitions of what constitutes rough might differ. Staying in environmentally controlled habitats is hardly rough."

"You're right." Gemma made her voice sugary and her smile cold. "The habitats are not all that bad. That said, I can tell you haven't been to my office in the former Onotharian bunker next to the exercise fields."

"Nor do I ever intend to set foot where they conducted interrogations and conjured up all sorts of ways to torment my people."

"Interrogations?" Gemma pressed her lips together at the thought of her offices having been the place of such atrocities. "In Bunker Twelve?"

"In all of them." Ciel sneered. "Ah, please, Doctor, don't tell me you didn't know?"

Swallowing, Gemma forced the images of what had gone on in Bunker 12 and others from her mind. "Actually, no. I didn't." She turned and entered the hovercraft. When Gemma arrived on Gantharat, she'd thrown herself into the medical issues that needed her attention around the clock. Some of her peers went through a more thorough orientation, but Gemma saw the urgent need for her particular expertise. The first two weeks she had joined the trauma surgeons, and during the following two weeks, she monitored the work of some internal-medicine physicians. Long before her introduction was over, Gemma knew she would have to remain on Gantharat much longer than the six months originally in her orders.

The hovercraft she and Ciel now boarded was divided into two small quarters. It was clearly one of the bigger vehicles, as it was luxurious by Gantharian standards. Gemma put her bag on the bunk in one of the spaces and sat down. She would have to wrap her head around the fact that the one person she clearly detested would be her guide. The fact that Ciel seemed to walk around with even bigger personal issues than Gemma would make for an interesting, putting it diplomatically, journey.

Another voice called out. "Ma'am? Commander Meyer? We made good time getting ready. If you are all set, we can move out within ten minutes."

"Excellent. Find Dr. O'Diarda and let's be on our way." She poked her head out. "Is my communication panel online?"

"Yes, ma'am." The young SC soldier stood at attention, her eyes covered by sunshades. "You'll have audio and video in the more densely populated areas and, later, audio only."

"Very good, Corporal." Gemma nodded and ducked back into her quarters. She sat on the stool by the narrow desk and let the equipment scan her retina. "Chief Medical Officer Gemma Meyer to Admiral Rae Jacelon."

A low hum echoed through the hovercraft and then a throaty, clipped voice answered. "Dr. Meyer. How are you doing, Commander?" The admiral's pale features appeared on the screen. Blue-gray eyes and fiery red hair emphasized the commanding presence she projected. Gemma had known and served with the admiral for the last fifteen years and respected her highly. The fact that Rae Jacelon had married Kellen O'Dal and become an esteemed protector as well only added to her legend.

"I'm fine, thank you, Admiral. We're heading out in a few minutes and I expect to reach the first small city, Rihoa, by noon tomorrow. We're building a set of clinics in the residential areas, and I need to check up on the progress of the staff's education. They're the first to use the advanced module."

"Yes, that's quite exciting." The admiral smiled. "I saw a summary of the initial reports."

"Thank you, Admiral. I'm carefully optimistic, but—" Gemma stopped herself. "Speaking of this mission, any particular reason why I need an entire SC unit? I could travel faster if I had just a shuttle and a handful of soldiers."

"No. Part of your mission takes you to areas where shuttles can't navigate, let alone land. The radiation is harmless for humanoids and wildlife, but any high-altitude technology is useless there. The hovercraft are outfitted with protection."

"What about the sensitive medical instruments the SC is donating?" Gemma asked, alarmed.

"They're stored in protective containers. The Gantharians have been most informative and helpful. Dr. O'Diarda knows this vast area like the back of her hand. She'll be able to guide you and offer advice." Rae tilted her head. "Something tells me you're not entirely pleased regarding that."

"I'm hesitant. Dr. O'Diarda isn't a physician. We don't speak the same language, professionally. She's some sort of shaman and herbal expert. How can she know what I need to prioritize?"

"You'll find that Dr. O'Diarda knows more than most Gantharians. She's a druid and, yes, an expert on medicinal plants. This made it possible for her to keep people alive during the occupation."

"All very admirable and something I normally would find interesting, but she—"

"You're stuck with her, Gemma. When I asked the former leader of the resistance, Andreia M'Aldovar, whom to send with you, Ciel O'Diarda was the obvious choice. I even made Kellen double-check, but she claimed she didn't have to. Even she had heard of Dr. O'Diarda while she was in the resistance."

"All right." When Rae had made up her mind and issued an order, that was it. "I'll give her the benefit of the doubt. Again."

"I know you two butted heads over planning during your last encounter. Try to ignore that and learn from her as much as you teach others. That's the best advice I can give you."

"Will do my best." Gemma felt more like thudding her forehead against the screen. "Please, tell Kellen I said hello. Being a protector dealing with an interim government can't be easy. I hope you get to see her once in a while."

"Once in a while," Rae said, and nodded wistfully. "We know it'll calm down little by little. At least we're both planet-side and under the same roof."

The hovercraft began to hum louder. "We're moving out. I should let you go, Rae. I'll connect to the base in twenty-four hours and deliver my report."

"Remain safe. Jacelon out." The SC logo appeared as Rae disconnected.

Gemma had moved to sit on the bed when she heard a knock on her door. "Enter."

The door hissed open and revealed Ciel. Leaning against the door frame, ankles crossed and arms folded, she looked at Gemma and smiled faintly. "Getting comfortable?"

"Yes. I checked in with Jacelon. Next report tomorrow this time." She was oddly uncomfortable and thought it might be because Ciel's devastatingly blue eyes rarely blinked as she gazed at her.

"You hungry? There's a small kitchenette in the back with a table for four. I brought fresh vegetables and some food I prepared to last a few weeks. I can't stand the synthetic stuff."

"At least one thing we agree on." Gemma pursed her lips. "Yes. Thank you. I'm quite hungry. Can I help?"

"I'm sure you can, but right now it's not necessary. I thought I'd heat some g'benka soup. I have bread to go with it."

Things might be looking up. Fresh food and real bread? Gemma navigated a narrow bulkhead and found the kitchenette more spacious than she'd thought. Granted, Ciel was at least ten centimeters taller and, um, curvier than she was. Gemma's cheeks warmed at the too-personal observation. This was so unlike her. Her shoulders tensed into the usual square shape as she sat down on one of the stools at the small counter. Squinting, she followed Ciel's easily flowing movements as she prepared their food.

❖

Ciel didn't believe in certainties. In her experience, the only inevitabilities in life were that she would die one day and that life in general was unpredictable. Now she would have to add a third to this very short list. She was sure, beyond any doubt, that she'd never met a woman like Gemma Meyer. The woman was clearly a brilliant doctor, but she was annoying, disdainful, opinionated, and had obviously worked relentlessly without much rest ever since she reached Gantharat.

"Here you go." She placed the steaming-hot mug of soup in front of Gemma and watched her grab it with pale fingers. Her hands seemed frail, too slender and elegant to belong to an esteemed trauma surgeon from the Supreme Constellation. She knew, of course, that Gemma was also a commander in the SC fleet, which was a testament to how looks could deceive. No doubt the good doctor was as lethal as she was able to heal. Ciel's thoughts visited her own past, but as quick as a Mirisian butterfly, they skipped ahead to present time. No good ever came from dwelling on those years.

"Soup all right?" Ciel sipped from her own mug and sat down.

"It's amazing, actually." Gemma sounded surprised. "I can't even describe the taste other than it's…delicious."

"I'm glad you think so. It's also very healthy. The main ingredient is a root that only grows in the wild. So far it has foiled any attempt by farmers to grow it, for hundreds of years."

"Really?" Gemma looked into her bowl as if the root were readily visible. "Sort of like a farmer's holy grail, then."

"Holy grail? I suppose." Ciel wasn't familiar with the expression but thought she understood the meaning. "The legend says that whoever tames this root will obtain eternal bliss."

"Sounds like a dream for many poor farmers. Can it be synthesized?"

"I don't know." Ciel shrugged. "I've never heard of anyone trying. I doubt you'd get the same healing qualities if you did. There are more to things than molecular structures."

"I don't entirely agree, but I can understand, in this case at least, what you mean." Gemma finished the contents of her mug. "I don't think it'd taste the same way if you dissolved powder in hot water. The taste and the fibers are probably part of its qualities."

Ciel stared at Gemma, wondering if this was the same woman who had practically flogged her in front of some student physicians at

Ganath's largest hospital. Ciel didn't visit the capital very often, and she remembered vividly how much she'd regretted going that particular time, a month ago.

"Don't look at me like I sprouted another head," Gemma said irritably. "I may be a stickler for traditional medicine and science, but even I know that a lot of it has roots in the knowledge of herbs and plants."

"I wish you could've mentioned that to the students when we met last time."

"We were discussing post-surgery routines. Hardly enigmatic roots or teaching history." Gemma pressed her lips together, the tension around her eyes back now.

Ciel wanted to pinch herself for disrupting Gemma's reasonable mood. They would be traveling for hours at a time in the hovercraft, just the two of them. Someone had to act mature and make sure this frustrating woman could do her job unhindered.

"I shouldn't have brought it up," Ciel said, shaking her head. "We don't see eye to eye on this and we never will. I don't want to keep arguing while we're on this mission."

Gemma studied her through narrow slits. It was amazing how stunning she was. Ciel was used to being suspicious of anyone who wasn't blue-blooded like herself. She realized that a lot of Onotharians still lived on Gantharat, and most of them had lived there before the Onotharian Empire had occupied her home world. These Onotharians had either joined the occupants or remained loyal to Gantharat, but either way, it was hard to tell the difference just by looking at them. Watching Gemma now, who wasn't blue-blooded or as warm-colored as the Onotharians, Ciel didn't know how to respond.

Gemma wasn't very tall and was quite slender, her skin transparent and pale. The only thing about her that looked Onotharian was the dark-brown, slightly tousled hair that reached her earlobes. Long and slender, her neck rose from the collar of her coverall uniform, which hid the rest of her very effectively. Ciel wasn't sure why she paid such attention to detail when it came to Gemma. It had been the same the last time they met. Remembering how Gemma had lectured her in front of everybody, Ciel found herself reflecting more about how Gemma must have lost weight in the last month rather than how incensed she had been that time.

Now Gemma placed her mug in the recycler and pushed her hands into her pockets. "I have work to do. See you later."

"Yes. Oh, here. You need to keep rehydrating. These hovercraft are horrible that way." Ciel opened the cool storage cabinet and pulled out a bottle. "It has some tasteless cloves in it. It's—"

"Good for me. Yes. I understand." Gemma took the bottle. "I should have asked before I had the soup, I guess, but I assume you've checked that everything you serve me is compatible with Earth human metabolism?"

"Yes." Ciel spoke through her teeth. Really. This woman was going to drive her into seclusion due to mental issues that no herbs or chants could fix. Yes, the question was warranted, she knew that, but did Gemma have to sound like she thought Ciel was a complete idiot?

"Good. Thank you." Gemma nodded curtly and walked into her quarters.

Ciel took a bottle of clove water for herself and stomped into her own space. The door shut behind her and she leaned against it, closing her eyes. She dreaded the upcoming long days of clenched teeth and fists.

CHAPTER TWO

Ciel watched with secret fascination how Gemma's command presence made her look taller and more intimidating when she stood before the tall, burly SC soldiers. The sun-heated foliage created a sweet-scented mist around them as Gemma stalked along the group of eight men and six women, her eyes squinting as she debated with the sergeant next to her.

"I refuse to enter the medical facility of Rihoa with all fourteen of them trailing me, scaring the patients and intimidating the staff. I can't do my job that way, Sergeant."

"We're in charge of your security detail. I'm under strict orders directly from the admiral to not let anything happen to you." The man, seasoned and weathered, tried to look amicable, but Ciel could tell he was ready to grab Gemma by her neck and shake some sense into her.

"I don't enjoy repeating myself. It won't work."

"Dr. Meyer," Ciel said, not about to watch this turn into a time-consuming squabble. "What if you allow two soldiers to go with us and the others to position themselves where they need to be in case something happens?"

"Perhaps." Gemma muttered under her breath. "Fine." She slung the strap of her bag over her shoulder and looked impatiently at the two closest soldiers. "You and you. Join Dr. O'Diarda and me at the clinic. Sergeant, position the rest of them where you deem necessary, as long as it's far enough away from the patients."

"Aye, Commander. Doctor." The sergeant looked displeased, but he relented and divided his team into three groups, pointing out on a handheld computer where they needed to go.

"Guess we can make our escape now," Ciel said. Gemma would probably explode if she was delayed further. She grabbed her own bag and began walking across the dusty road toward the newly built medical unit. It would become increasingly hotter throughout the day until the temperature peaked around midafternoon.

Frowning at how mindlessly the builders had destroyed far too much vegetation near the structures, she did her best to harness her outrage at the sight of the withered remnants of edible and medicinal plants. Such waste.

"What's up?" Gemma muttered.

"What do you mean, Commander?" Ciel tried to feign disinterest, not about to start arguing with Gemma in the middle of the road.

"You're radiating discontent. It's pretty obvious." Gemma glanced at her again. "And now you're even more displeased since I noticed."

Was she that transparent? Ciel took a breath. She wouldn't let this woman just walk all over her and read her mind. It would only mean trouble. "It's just…just the plants, Commander. Look." She pointed at a pile of singuisa bushes. "They're a powerful antibacterial remedy if you make tea from them."

"Ah. Yes. Shame. But we're bringing that type of medication with us. The soldiers will deliver it later."

"That's not the point." Gemma didn't understand. How could she? "We wouldn't need the synthesized SC medication if my fellow Gantharians knew how to recognize and harvest these plants. The singuisa bush is just as potent."

Gemma shook her head. "It's also a matter of things being cost-effective and practical. Harvesting from bushes takes too long, and retraining people to do that—"

"Isn't much harder, and it doesn't take longer or cost more than this circus!" Ciel gestured at Gemma and the two soldiers. "There'd be no need for bodyguards, fancy SC equipment, or—" She stopped herself before she said too much.

"Or SC physicians who try to tell you what to do?" Gemma asked sweetly, the brown in her eyes suddenly very cold and opaque.

"Your words, not mine." Ciel tried to reel her temper in.

"Sure sounded like that's what you meant to say."

"If that's what you think, I can't prove otherwise." Starting to feel utterly childish, Ciel took another deep breath. What was it about Gemma that made her act so very out of character? She drew yet another breath and used a mind-cleansing mantra to regain her inner balance. When her equilibrium was centered once again, she exhaled and managed a smile. "I apologize for allowing this to escalate," she said, and meant every word. She was here to guide and assist Gemma, not make her job impossible. Something about the tension around Gemma's eyes, and the way she squared her shoulders until she looked like she'd break at the slightest touch, implied that this woman felt the universe depended on her efforts.

"No matter. I agree with you. If a plant is useful, no matter how, people should take extra care to preserve it, if possible." Gemma gripped the shoulder strap of her bag harder and leaned forward as they walked up a steep hill. The bag looked far too heavy for her slight frame, but Ciel knew better than to offer to carry it. Gemma most likely was a lot tougher than she looked.

It didn't take Ciel long to realize that something unusual was happening at the clinic. As far as she could see on the grounds around the structure, people were sitting or lying, some tended to by the ones around them. She tried to do a rough head count, but it was impossible as there were probably others on the other side of the building.

Inside, patients waited in a long line at the reception desk, and she couldn't see where it ended. Others sat in rows in the waiting rooms, and more severe cases waited on gurneys in another area. Ciel saw an even deeper frown appear on Gemma's face. This was not good.

❖

Gemma stalked up to the reception area. The man working behind a computer console looked frazzled, more intent on entering commands than focusing on the people next in line. A young woman was holding a crying baby, tears streaming down her face.

"Please. Just listen to me. I need to see a doctor—"

The man held up his hand in a clear sign she shouldn't interrupt him.

"My child, he—"

"Deal with him. I'll look at the child," Ciel murmured behind Gemma.

Glancing behind her, she saw Ciel bend over the child and gently touch his face.

"What is she doing? Who are you people?" the man behind the computer said, now looking up in obvious exasperation. "You can't just cut in front of the line—"

"I don't intend to. My name is Dr. Gemma Meyer. Call the clinic administrator and the person medically responsible to join me here." She showed her identification on her handheld computer.

"I will do no such thing. Can't you see we have a crisis on our hands?" The Gantharian man huffed and returned his gaze to the computer screen.

"You will, and you will do it instantly if you want to keep your job. I'm the SC representative and I designed this clinic. If you don't—"

"You...did you say Meyer?" The man licked his lips repeatedly, clearly panic-stricken. "Yes. The administrator, Ms. O'Eso. The clinic chief, Dr. O'Toresho. Right this instant."

"And why's the line this long?" Gemma propped herself against the counter, watching with interest how the man's fingers flew across the commands. "Just what crisis are you referring to?"

"We're still bringing our system online. It takes a while to register the patients who came into town yesterday. They've been walking for months."

"Where from?"

"From the correction camp in Teroshem. They're on their way home."

"On foot? Where's their transport?" Gemma leaned over the desk. "How far away is Teroshem from here?"

"About two hundred kilometers, ma'am." The man was sending messages via the computer as he spoke. "The clinic administrator and the chief are on their way." He smiled carefully, looking much too young to deal with an onslaught of displaced people.

Gemma nodded curtly and returned to Ciel, who was examining the now-whimpering baby. "I don't know how much you overheard, but these people are displaced. Refugees trying to get home from some correction camp." She turned to the mother of the sick child. "Perhaps you can tell us where you come from and where you're heading."

"I speak Premoni very badly, Doctor." The woman looked worriedly at Ciel. "Druid, can you tell me what's the matter with my son?"

"Please, call me Ciel. He's dehydrated due to a bowel infection. How long have you been on the road trying to get home?"

"My name is Tammas O'Mea. I've lost track of time, Druid O'Diarda," the woman said.

"He needs liquids and vitamins. Perhaps additional nutrition." Ciel smiled at the young mother. "It's hard to be on the road with a baby."

"I have very little milk for him." The young woman whispered, half hiding her face. "The camp closed months ago, but I've been mostly on foot. I gave birth to Ilias when I'd been walking for a week. I had to rest for a few days before I could continue."

Ciel shook her head, her jaw working before she spoke. "I can't imagine walking that far with a baby after giving birth. You're strong, Tammas."

"I want to go home to my mother and father. If they're...if they're...I haven't been able to reach them via any comm system, but people say the links are down all over the planet." Tammas sobbed. "And now Ilias is sick."

"He'll be fine. We should let Dr. Meyer look him over as well, but my assessment stands. Rehydrate and give him some missing vitamins and some anti-inflammatory tea. You should have it too, as it will permeate the milk. You'll see an increase in breast milk as well." Ciel cupped the back of the little boy's head. "He has your features."

"I know. That's a blessing. He's of mixed blood."

"So his father was Onotharian?"

"Yes." Tammas blinked repeatedly. "We were married."

"Where is he now?" Gemma asked as she ran her scanner over the boy. She examined the readings and was reluctantly impressed when her instrument concurred with Ciel's diagnosis.

"I don't know. He and some of the other incarcerated Onotharians had to go into hiding when some militant people from Teroshem stormed the camp once the occupation ended. He had managed to save some money and other valuables for Ilias and me, but I don't know what happened to him."

"I'll take this information to headquarters," Gemma said, and pocketed her scanner. "They need to know about illegal militia activities."

"How much farther to your destination?" Ciel asked Tammas.

"To Emres? Maybe two more weeks. Three if the rains begin early." Tammas looked determined but also exhausted. "I'll have to wait until Ilias is better. That means the rains will have been under way for a while."

Gemma thought fast and looked around the room where at least some sixty people sat in chairs or on the floor against walls, and stood in line. So many people seeking help from a multitude of conditions while on their way to a place that used to be home.

Straightening her back, Gemma began to create a solution to the problem. This was one thing she could do something about, no matter how many were displaced. She pulled out her communicator. "Commander Meyer to SC headquarters." She repeated the page twice before a male voice responded. Relaying the details, she smiled confidently as the lieutenant at headquarters acknowledged and promised to send transportation. "I'll report back as soon as we know if we need a mobile hospital unit to deploy," Gemma said. She wanted to report the intel of rogue Gantharian militia groups but realized that would require more investigation before HQ could take any measures. She decided to record an initial report to Jacelon when she was back in her small office area aboard the hovercraft.

"Tammas," Gemma said. "I've requested transportation for you, Ilias, and everyone else in here who is in transit heading home. I'll make sure you and Ilias have a bed at the clinic until the transportation arrives."

"Oh, thank you. Thank you so much, both of you." Tammas's eyes filled with tears. "You can't possibly know how amazing that would be. I'm prepared to walk for as long as it takes, but I'm so worried about Ilias."

"He'll be fine." Gemma looked over her shoulder and saw a man and a woman approach. Guessing they were the administrator and the clinic's chief, she stood and greeted them. Glancing at her companion, she saw Ciel pat Tammas's shoulder and then walk from patient to patient, speaking with them.

"Dr. Meyer." The administrator beamed. "I'm Ms. O'Eso. We're so honored that you are blessing us with your presence, but you've caught us at an inopportune time." She smiled nervously, clearly trying to appease the visitors.

"And by that you mean the reason why you're not seeing any of these patients?"

The placating smile disappeared from O'Eso's face. "What? No. I mean, we're not quite ready yet." She didn't sound so confident anymore. Lacing her fingers tightly, she turned to her boss. "Sir?"

"Ah, yes. All in good time, Dr. Meyer," he said, looking questioningly at his administrator.

"God, this place is like a farce." Gemma pinched the bridge of her nose. "You realize that I have the protector's mandate to change anything I don't agree with, right?"

"Certainly," the chief said cordially. "We'll make the protector and the little prince proud." Spouting platitudes was evidently what this man did best.

Gemma turned to the administrator. "Now listen. Don't bother with the computers. Use pens and paper if need be, but start treating the patients. This is an order relayed through me by the protector herself. Do I make myself clear?" She clenched her fists so hard her blunt nails pressed painfully into her palms. Willing herself to relax her fingers, Gemma saw color leave the administrator's face, turning her chalky white.

"The protector? You speak for the protector personally?"

"I do."

"Sir," O'Eso said hurriedly, "we need to simplify and speed up the registration process and begin seeing patients. By decree of the protector."

"Forgo our routines?" The chief, who Gemma now knew had to be replaced as soon as possible, frowned. "I'm not sure, what if—"

Ciel joined them, her face serious. "People might be dying on your doorstep. You need to command your staff to start doing their job."

"Medical transport units are on their way, but it will take them a couple of hours." Gemma pulled her backpack off. "I suggest we start triaging. Are your wards operational?" she asked O'Eso.

"Two wards of five, Doctor."

"What about the other three?"

"They have beds, but that's about it."

"Then send in staff, anybody, to get the beds ready. I don't care if the rest of the equipment is up and running." Gemma looked around. "I see at least five senior citizens who should be lying down instead of sitting propped up here. I can't imagine how the ones outside are faring in the heat."

"I've already begun organizing the healthy individuals out there to help move the most sensitive cases into the shade. I estimate there are at least four hundred adults and twice as many children." Ciel pointed toward the entrance.

Gemma's jaws tightened. "Children. I read the reports, but it still is unfathomable that the Onotharians placed children in camps."

Ciel's eyes, like deep oceanic ice, narrowed. "A perfect way of maintaining crowd control behind the fences. Get caught doing something against the rules, the children paid the price. Very efficient. Once in a while they made an example of someone's child just to make sure we didn't forget."

We. A chilling sensation chased along Gemma's back. It certainly sounded like Ciel had firsthand knowledge of the camps. Thinking back at the dossier Jacelon had provided on Ciel, she realized that she'd merely browsed the first half before nodding off. Clearly there was something she needed to check later.

"I know you're weary of my type of medicine, but I'm going to put those chopped-down singuisa bushes to good use. These people are no doubt suffering from all kinds of infections, not to mention dehydration."

Gemma would have balked at the idea of offering some voodoo tea to patients when the perfect rehydration fluids could be administered instantly via imbulizers and short-term infuzers. But since the clinic wasn't fully operational to receive casualties, and certainly not this many, she had to grudgingly concede that it was a good compromise. "Fine." She used her communicator and summoned the marines she hadn't wanted to bring with her to the clinic. She could hear the sergeant's slight exasperation but let it slide for now.

"Bring my subspace communicator from the hovercraft. Meyer out." Gemma stepped outside where she saw Ciel and some of the refugees heading over to the uprooted singuisa bushes. She heard moans and silent crying, but also children's laughter, and the contrast somehow gave her a feeling that this was just the beginning. Normally she paid no attention to any foreboding. The thought of a woman of science such as herself even considering such nonsense made her turn on her heels and walk inside. There was work to be done and she was not about to let a druid, no matter how charismatic, influence her into adopting that way of thinking.

The shrill voice of a woman in one of the examination areas broke her out of her reverie. "No. No! Ilias!"

Gemma began to run.

CHAPTER THREE

Gemma rushed into the examination room. She barely registered Tammas sitting slumped on the floor, overcome by deep, heaving sobs. On the examination table, Ilias's little body lay pale as several medical professionals hovered around him.

"What's wrong with him? Is this my fault?" Tammas whimpered.

"What happened?" Gemma pulled out her medical scanner and ran it over the still boy. "He needs a life-support unit. His circulation is shutting down. Move, people."

"We…they've not been unpacked yet, ma'am." One of the nurses looked up, her eyes huge.

"Oh, for stars and skies," Gemma said with a growl. She pushed the closest people aside, bent over the baby, and placed her mouth over his nose and mouth, blowing in two gentle puffs of air, mindful of his tiny lungs. "Who knows how to do compressions by hand on an infant?" she barked as she began the procedure with three fingers.

"I do," a calm voice said from behind. Ciel stepped up to the table and took over the compression.

Gemma was grateful to have someone calm and collected around as the staff was running around trying to figure out where they'd stored the crates with the pediatric equipment. After a few minutes, Gemma ran her scanner again. "I have a faint pulse, but so far he's not breathing on his own."

A wail from the floor brought her attention to Tammas, who had nearly dissolved in tears. "Can someone assist the boy's mother?" Gemma said out loud. "She doesn't have to sit on the floor and she shouldn't see this." In the corner of her eyes she watched one of the male nurses pick up the crying woman from the floor and carry her out of the room.

Suddenly Ilias coughed weakly and soon he gave a faint cry, not unlike the continued wails of his mother from the other side of the wall.

"Here. We have the pediatric crates—he's breathing?" Another nurse stared at the child and then at Gemma. "That's amazing."

"Basic CPR," Gemma said, not impressed. "Don't they teach you this at nursing school on Gantharat?"

"Nursing school?" The nurse blinked. "I haven't gone to school for this. In my family we learn from the older generations. We have no special courses for nursing."

"Oh, Gods, that's insane." Gemma shook her head. "Well, come over here and I'll show you how to put the baby on the ventilator. He's breathing, but he's not strong enough to sustain it for longer periods until his blood volume and dehydration are dealt with." Gemma pulled out a brand-new pediatric ventilator and placed it around the child's chest, neck, and scalp. "I assume you weighed and measured him as part of your routine?" she asked.

"Yes. Yes, I did." The nurse looked relieved to have done something right.

Gemma showed the young woman how she should calculate the settings and punch commands into the computer console to set the ventilator to fit Ilias. She had her repeat the procedure, and to her surprise, the nurse did it flawlessly.

"Good job. Now, assign someone to monitor him the first hour. If he's stable after that, you can look in on him once every fifteen minutes."

"Yes, Doctor." The young nurse nodded and Gemma cringed at the awestruck look in her eyes. She wasn't unaccustomed to admiring looks and words from younger medical professionals since she enjoyed a certain fame within the SC border. It was still rather embarrassing, though, since placing a baby on a ventilator was something everyone learned within the first year as a medical student.

"Let's go find Tammas," Ciel said, placing a hand on the small of Gemma's back. "She needs to know we have Ilias's condition under control."

"How did you make it back so fast?" Gemma asked as they walked toward the smaller waiting area just outside. "I just saw you going off to the uprooted plants with an axe and with some of the refugees."

"I told them what I needed from the plants and put them to work." Ciel shook her head. "In this case, it makes so much difference for Ilias that we have things like ventilators. Had I seen him a few days ago, my herbs could have been enough, but he was too far gone. His lungs are inflamed, most likely."

"How did you know?" Gemma hadn't told anyone yet what her scanner had recorded.

"His pallor, his scent, and the general symptoms." Ciel sat down next to Tammas and took her hand. "Ilias is alive and we put him on a ventilator to conserve his energy. He needs fluids, perhaps some synthetic blood, and most of all rest."

"He's…he's breathing?" Tammas looked up at Gemma and then back at Ciel, crystal-clear blue tears streaming down her face. "I thought he'd died."

"It was close. He'll need supervision for a long time. Right now he needs his mother close too. We'll arrange for a cot and a chair next to his bed. You need to get checked out too eventually."

"Not necessary. I'm fine." Tammas contradicted herself by nearly falling as she stood. Gemma and Ciel supported her as they walked her back into the room. The sight of her child all but covered by SC technology was nearly too much for Tammas. "Oh, no. He looks so small, so fragile with that thing on him."

"That thing is helping him breathe and saturates his blood." Gemma patted Tammas's hand. "Now, sit here on this chair and we'll have some of the staff bring you a cot."

"I'll be here with you and your baby for now," the young nurse said reassuringly. "You can hold his hand, if you like. He will feel your presence and it will help him recover."

"I'd like that." Tammas climbed onto the tall stool next to the bed. She carefully took his hand. "Thank you," she said, without looking at them.

"You're welcome." Gemma nudged Ciel and motioned toward the corridor. "We have more work to do."

"And I'll go find where my assistants have put the bushes. They were going to start a fire outside."

"A fire?" Gemma frowned. "Whatever for?"

"A woman from town had one of the huge pots I need."

"Gods, are we back in the Stone Age? We have the hospital kitchen and a large laboratory if you need to brew something." She glared impatiently at the serenely smiling Ciel.

"No, that won't do. The amount we need for this many people requires a much bigger burner than any modern kitchen, or lab, can provide."

"You're kidding." Gemma exhaled impatiently. Did Ciel have to make everything so difficult just to prove a point? She shook her head in dismay and hurried toward the triage area. She was relieved to see the marines, all of them with medical backgrounds as well, per her request, helping the Gantharian physicians organize it.

"Dr. Meyer, ma'am." Her sergeant approached her. "We need you over here. Male, 102, dehydrated and with multiple health issues…" He continued to describe the man's condition as they walked over to a makeshift trauma and emergency center. Gemma looked over her shoulder before she began examining the emaciated man on the gurney. Ciel was over to the side, and next to her two men were erecting some sort of rack. Movement farther to the right made her mouth fall open. That had to be the biggest cast-iron pot she'd ever seen. She had to grudgingly concede that they couldn't possibly have handled that in the kitchen or the lab, simply because they wouldn't have been able to get it through the door.

Gemma turned around and gazed down at her patient. He met her eyes and spoke the language of his home world in a very faint voice.

"If you are the last person my eyes see, your beauty will be my bliss on my way to the Gods of Gantharat."

"As lovely as that compliment is, sir, I would like to think I'm able to help you feel much better." Gemma smiled reassuringly.

"You are a doctor," the man said, his voice reverent.

"Yes, I am, and we're going to take good care of you." Gemma ran her scanner over his weak body. "And our first action will be more fluids." Turning to the nurse next to her, Gemma began issuing orders.

❖

Ciel pushed the errant strands of her hair out of her face. The sun was relentless and she had worked for nine hours without interruption.

Now she was about to oversee the last brew of the day. She pushed a mug into the boiling water and scooped up a sample. Tasting it was the only way for her to judge its medicinal qualities.

"How does it taste, really?" Gemma stood at her side suddenly, looking pale and exhausted. Ciel hadn't seen her take a break either.

Ciel tasted the brew. Perfect. "Here," she said, holding out the mug to Gemma. "Careful. It's boiling hot."

Gemma carefully sipped from the opposite edge of the mug. Closing her eyes, she sighed. "Oh, that's actually very nice. Sweet, sort of."

"Yes. And you look like you need it too. It's no wonder, the way you've gone from one patient to another today."

"I've only carried out my duty like I always do. Nothing more, nothing less."

"Normally, though, you don't work in such primitive circumstances under the blazing sun. Not to mention that backup only arrived less than two hours ago. What the hell happened to delay those transports?"

"Some of the Gantharian council members in the interim government are trying to be mindful of costs. I had to get back to my headquarters twice and remind them that people would start dying in great numbers if they didn't get here soon. I finally got hold of the protector. She made sure my orders went through instantly." Gemma sipped the brew. "Mmm. I wonder what the active ingredient is. It rejuvenates almost instantly." She drank some more and then rubbed her temples. "I think we have the situation under control. Evacuation has been going on for the last two hours, and the Security Council has deployed officers to interview and document the refugees' stories."

"Stories." Ciel sounded cold. "That makes it sound as if you think they exaggerate what they've been through."

"Don't put words in my mouth." Clearly angry now, Gemma pushed the mug into Ciel's hands. "I made no such statement, nor would I ever presume so. Just because you're highly suspicious of everything I stand for—"

"I am not!" Ciel raised her voice, something she rarely did. When you'd spent the last twenty-five years working in stealth mode, you learned how to keep your voice, and your head, down. Now she was far too angry to do either. "I know how much these camp *stories* are being regarded as exaggerations. As if the atrocities never occurred, and if they did, they were exceptions."

Gemma opened her mouth but closed it again, her eyes suddenly darker and her lips softer. "Is that what you've been told? That you exaggerated?"

Ciel grew rigid, her shoulders nearly creaking as she squared them. "I didn't say that."

"You didn't have to." Gemma rubbed the back of her neck. "Listen, I used the word 'stories' as in 'their history,' not as anything they would fabricate. Do you understand?"

Ciel's heart rate began to slow and she relaxed marginally. "H'rea dea'savh, I usually handle it better than this. I apologize." She grimaced, uncomfortable. "You're right. Of course. Their history will need to be recorded and archived with their personal data. Some of them have been in different camps for more than twenty years. That's a damn long time."

"It is." Gemma motioned toward the area where their escort had set up their new camp. Since it was no longer practical to keep the hovercraft on the outskirts of the town, they, and the backup that kept arriving, had made camp on a field behind the clinic. "We need to get some sleep, don't you agree?"

Ciel wasn't ready to leave but realized that nothing would be gained from wearing herself out. She had spent so many years working herself into a pulp; it was a way of life. No more of that, she decided. "Yes. I'll just make sure this batch is poured into containers the right way. Why don't you go ahead? If you want, you can heat some of the soup for us?"

"Oh, sure. I like your soup," Gemma said, smiling cautiously. "It actually is almost as rejuvenating as that brew you just made."

"Big words coming from you," Ciel said, smiling to show she was partly teasing. "I'll be there in a little bit."

Gemma nodded and began walking toward their hovercraft.

Ciel made sure the soldiers and townspeople in charge of the brew knew how to store it, then began to make her way back to the hovercraft. Part of the path to the field wasn't very well lit, and a sudden sound to her right made her stumble. She gasped as something sharp dug into her thigh. The searing pain made her swing her handheld light source around. At first, she saw nothing out of the ordinary to explain the unexpected sound, but as she moved her arm again, a tall bird rose from the bushes and took off. Ciel half laughed, half gasped, relieved it wasn't something more sinister.

But then her thigh began to burn with an all-too-familiar searing pain. She trembled as she carefully put one foot before the other, slowly walking while tears formed in her eyes. "Oh, wonderful," she muttered. "Just great." She was in so much trouble, but hopefully she could get close enough to camp to attract someone's attention. If she fell here, out of sight of Gemma and her soldiers, and nobody found her in time, that would be the end of her.

CHAPTER FOUR

Gemma had just begun to undress to hit the cleansing tube when someone pounded on the door.

"Dr. Meyer, ma'am!" A young male voice sounded frantic. "You have to come!"

Gemma pulled her jacket back on and hurried to the door. She grabbed her medical kit on her way. Opening it, she found a young private standing there, out of breath. "What's going on?"

"It's Druid O'Diarda, ma'am. We found her on the path among the shrubbery."

"Ciel?" Gemma flinched and began running. "What…was she attacked?"

"I don't think so. She looks very ill."

Her heart pounding and experiencing a cold sense of dread, Gemma ran to where she saw several SC soldiers standing with their light sources directed to the ground. As she reached them, she saw someone on the ground. *Ciel!* She threw herself to her knees and tore open the kit to find the scanner. Running it over the motionless form that was her infuriating guide, she had her initial suspicions confirmed. Anaphylactic shock. Against what was anybody's guess. As far as Gemma was concerned, this planet had enough allergens and poisonous plants and creatures to kill half the population.

"I'm going to give her generic anti-allergenic medication, as I have no way of knowing what she's reacting to." She didn't wait for anyone to respond, but pressed the imbulizer and administered a double dosage of her most potent version of the drug. Ciel's throat could swell shut any moment, and Gemma would rather not have to intubate her in the field if she could avoid it.

She heard running footfalls and looked up for a second. One of the Gantharian physicians came up the path, gasping for breath. Grateful to have one more set of hands and eyes, she kept her scanner running across Ciel's chest. "I'm monitoring her circulation and breathing," she said curtly. "I need O2 saturation levels."

"On it." The man busied himself with his equipment. "Eighty-four percent."

"Not good enough. We need her on oxygen."

"I have a mobile unit here." Her colleague attached a small nostril clamp and turned a dial. "Nothing like your high-tech stuff, but it does the job well in the field."

"That's what counts. We need to move her. The ground is damp, and she's cold and clammy as it is." Gemma looked at the hovercraft and down toward the clinic. "Our hovercraft is well equipped, and it can be moved nearer. Private!" Raising her voice, she got the young man's attention. "Bring my vehicle as close as you can. Are you licensed to drive it?"

"Yes, ma'am." He took off running.

Gemma bent over Ciel, touching her cheek. "Ciel? Dr. O'Diarda?" There was no reaction, but that didn't mean Ciel didn't hear her. "Ciel? It's Gemma. You're going to be all right. You're having an allergic reaction to something—"

"Bush...bushes," Ciel whispered huskily. "Think they're... sientesh'ta bushes. Allergic..."

"Oh, all right." Gemma raised her gaze to the Gantharian doctor. "Does that mean anything to you?"

"Sientesh'ta bushes aren't poisonous to most people. If you've been subjected to their thorns several times, though, you can become oversensitized to them and develop an allergy. I assume the druid, being a great herbalist, has come in too close a contact with them too many times."

"I see. Any known Gantharian remedy?"

"Just what you're already doing, when it comes to traditional medicine. As for the herbal approach, I guess Druid O'Diarda can tell you when she's feeling better."

"I'll ask her." Gemma blinked at her own words. Would she really ask about herbs and magic tricks? Honestly. "Ciel, are you in pain anywhere else? Did you hit your head?"

"Don't think so." Ciel's teeth were clattering. "I fell to my knees and then on my side. Tried calling."

"Good thing the soldiers found you." Her insides trembled at the thought of Ciel dying alone in the shrubbery from an allergic shock. Trying not to analyze why she was reacting in such a physical way to the fate of a patient, she pushed Ciel's hair from her forehead and felt how cold she was. She glanced over her shoulder and saw her hovercraft begin to move. "Oh, great. Ciel, the hovercraft is meeting us, but we have to carry you a bit. Tell us if we hurt you too badly."

"All right."

The soldiers lifted Ciel gently, and only when one of them gripped her left thigh did she cry out. "Not my leg. Please."

"Let me look." Without hesitation, Gemma grabbed a twin laser blade from the belt of the closest soldier. Carefully she cut the fabric of Ciel's trousers and tore it. She had to hold back a horrified gasp at the pus-filled crater on the outside of Ciel's thigh. "I, um, I seem to have found the culprit here. We need to move, fast. Don't touch this part of her. No wonder she cried out."

They hurried as fast as they could along the dark path, a female soldier in front to light the way, Gemma and the Gantharian physician on either side of Ciel, monitoring her. In less than two minutes they'd reached the hovercraft, where the private had opened the door for them to enter.

"Use my quarters," Gemma said, and pointed. "I think they're slightly bigger."

The soldiers placed Ciel on Gemma's bed and stepped out. Gemma knelt on the floor, opening her pack. "I'm going to have to drain the pus, Ciel," she said, wondering why her stomach clenched at the thought of how much this would hurt. "I wish I dared to sedate you, but with the way your vital signs are reading, I simply can't. I can try for some local anesthetics."

"I appreciate that. It's very painful and you're not even touching it yet."

"Before we begin, I have to get you warm. Your clothes are damp."

Ciel nodded weakly. "So cold." Her face was pale and her lips even more blue-tinted than usual.

Gemma nodded at the other physician and together they pulled off

Ciel's garments. When she wore only her underwear, Gemma tucked a thermo-energy blanket all over Ciel except her thigh. After sealing her hands with surgical gloves, she placed a sterile sheet around it and ran a sterilizing wand over the surrounding skin. "There. Now we have to hurt you some, Ciel. I'll numb as much as I can."

"Thank you," Ciel said, her speech slurred.

Gemma looked up, quickly scanning Ciel's vital signs. Her values weren't optimal, but Ciel was holding her own for now. Pressing the imbulizer against Ciel's skin, Gemma numbed it by repeating the procedure six times in a circle around the ugly wound. Then she brought out a laser-scalpel and looked at her colleague, who had taken over the scanner to keep check on Ciel's vital signs. "If she dips, I need to know instantly."

"Certainly." He nodded grimly.

"Here goes. Ciel, stop me if it becomes unbearable." Holding her breath, Gemma cut into the hard center of the crater. Ciel whimpered. Pus oozed, and she snatched another wand from her surgical kit. Running it over Ciel's thigh, she watched the pus disintegrate and turn into harmless fluids, easily absorbed by the body. It took several attempts with the wand before the swelling was reduced and the pus drained. She had to stop twice when the opening became too hot and the pain too great for Ciel. Once the wound was clean, Gemma used a derma-fuser to close it. She would have to keep checking it the first couple of days, since she might have missed some pus, but she was pleased with how it looked. "That was one evil bush out there."

"Yes. I wasn't aware of it growing so close to the clinic," her Gantharian colleague said. "I'll make sure it's removed."

"Pick the flowers first," Ciel whispered. "Pick them, then boil them in cooking oil until they melt. Use the salve on burns, scars, and insect bites."

"How ironic." Gemma shook her head. "I'm going to get you some of that soup of yours. Then I want you to sleep, preferably for twelve hours at least. I'll set an INI to help your body recover."

"INI?" Ciel frowned.

"Intravenous Nutritional Infusion."

Gemma turned to her Gantharian colleague. "I'm Dr. Gemma—"

"Meyer," he said, smiling politely. "Your reputation precedes you, Dr. Meyer. My name is Tenner O'Sialla."

"Not sure if that's a good or a bad thing." Gemma smiled wryly. "Thank you for your help, Dr. O'Sialla. I couldn't have worked as well without your assistance."

"It was my honor to assist the renowned Dr. Meyer of the Supreme Constellations."

Gemma flinched. Renowned? "Um. Thank you. I'm not sure how to respond to that. I'm hardly famous."

"Ah, but you are. Possessing medical skills beyond anyone else on Gantharat, a close friend to our protectors, and having treated them and our prince—how could you not be famous on our planet? You have helped bring us freedom."

"It's true," Ciel murmured from the bed.

"And I need to go heat some soup for you, Ciel. See you tomorrow at the clinic, Dr. O'Sialla."

She bid him farewell and hurried to the kitchenette. Famous? Hardly. Hurrying, she heated a mug of soup for Ciel. She was going to have to sleep in the recliner next to the bed and set her alarm to check on Ciel continuously.

As she returned to her quarters, she helped Ciel sit up and eat her soup. Still weak and drowsy, Ciel leaned against her shoulder. Before she realized it, Gemma found herself stroking up and down Ciel's arm. "There. Better?"

"Soup is always a safe bet." Ciel smiled faintly. "Thank you. I probably owe you the use of my left leg. I can't thank you enough."

"No need to thank me. I did my job, like you would've done for me." Gemma squirmed inwardly. "Let me start the INI, and then you can go to sleep."

Ciel looked embarrassed. "I think I need the facilities first."

"The fac—oh, the restroom. Naturally. Let me help you."

Ciel's eyes darkened. "I don't require help in the bathroom."

"I didn't mean that. I just think you need to lean on me while you move over there. It's not far, but if you fall you might tear the new skin."

"Then let's go." Ciel carefully stood with Gemma's help. "What I wouldn't give for a shower. And I mean an old-fashioned aqua shower."

"Tomorrow you can use the cleansing tube. That won't hurt the healing process."

"All right." Ciel made it to the bathroom and Gemma waited outside, finally acknowledging how exhausted she was. The entire day, starting with the baby, Ilias, and then Ciel's ordeal, was clearly getting to her.

"I'm done." Ciel's voice came through the door. "I guess I need more help than I realize."

"Oh, for stars and skies. Don't move." Afraid that Ciel would reinjure herself, Gemma slid the door open. As she wrapped her arm around Ciel's waist, she felt the other woman cling to her, trembling. "There we go. Just a few steps."

"I feel faint." Ciel gasped for breath.

"We're almost there." Gemma struggled to lower Ciel onto the bed without actually dropping her. Finally Ciel was settled against the pillows and covered with the warming blanket. "Better?"

"Much." But Ciel looked uneasy.

"What are you thinking?" Gemma knelt next to the bed. Her touch wasn't that of a detached trauma surgeon, and she didn't understand why it was so gentle. She only knew that Ciel's allergic shock had truly frightened her.

"You…I'm sorry you have to deal with this," Ciel motioned at her leg, "when I was supposed to guide you, help *you*." She pressed her lips together. "I just hate not being able to contribute, to be…" She gestured angrily with her hands with exhausted movements.

"Listen," Gemma said, capturing Ciel's hands. "If it were me who had a severe allergic reaction to that bush, or any other thing on Gantharat, and my life was in the balance, wouldn't you have cared for me? Healed me? Whichever way possible?"

Ciel blinked. "Of course. It's what I do. It's what I've always been doing." Her marbled white-black-silver hair spread over the pillow around her head like a halo. "Oh."

"Yes. Exactly." Gemma smiled. "This can happen to anyone, and I'm just so glad I was here to help you stay alive and preferably not lose your leg, or any muscle tissue, in the process."

"You're very generous and kind. I…honestly, I didn't expect that." Ciel looked down at their joined hands. "You have to take my bed and get a good night's rest."

"No. I'm sleeping in the recliner." Gemma set her jaw, expecting Ciel to object.

Instead, Ciel looked relieved. "Thank you. They're comfortable if you push them all the way back."

"I'll be fine. Trust me. I've slept in much worse positions, and in much less luxurious surroundings."

"I can only imagine. You have to tell me one day, maybe...we can compare." Ciel yawned. "I apologize."

"No need. Go to sleep. I'll probably wake you up a few times when I check your leg and vitals status. Just remember it's me and don't swing without checking, all right?"

Ciel smiled faintly. "I'll keep that in mind."

Gemma walked over to the bathroom and took care of her usual evening ablutions. Looking in the mirror, she was startled to see her brown eyes glimmering a low-burning amber. How could that be when she was so fatigued she could have slept standing up in the cleansing tube? Shaking her head, she cleaned her teeth and pulled on some soft retrospun pajamas. Then she grabbed another thermo-energy blanket and curled up in the recliner. She realized she needed a pillow and reached out for one that Ciel wasn't using.

Suddenly Ciel's hand shot forward and grabbed her wrist. "Not swinging, just checking," she murmured, her voice husky.

"Just need a pillow."

"Here." Ciel held one out to her.

"Thanks. Go to sleep now."

"You too."

Gemma listened to Ciel's breathing even out. Only when she was convinced Ciel was sleeping soundly did she relax against the pillow. The skin on her wrist tingled and Gemma had no clue what that meant. She was going to have to keep an eye on Ciel O'Diarda in more ways than one and try to figure it out.

CHAPTER FIVE

Ciel stood on slightly wobbly legs, relieved to feel only a slight discomfort in her leg. Gemma's chair was empty and the blanket folded neatly on top of the pillow. Military precision, of course. She listened for clues as to where Gemma might be and heard faint sounds from the bathroom. Desperately needing what the SC staff called the cleansing tube, she went over to her quarters and gathered a clean set of underwear and a coverall. She missed her usual airy, flowing kaftan and pants but conceded that, while working with the SC military, a generic sort of coverall was more practical. She stood out less that way, something she'd become an expert at over the years.

"Ciel?" Gemma's voice came from her quarters. "You all right?"

"I'm fine. Just getting ready to, eh, shower."

"Can I take a look at your leg before you do?" Gemma asked from the doorway.

"No need," Ciel muttered. "I'll check it out and, if I need to, I'll take care of it using the correct herbs."

"Herbs." Gemma pursed her lips. "You had such a bad reaction last night. Life-threatening. I'm not sure herbs will cut it."

"Herbs kept people alive through much worse during the last twenty-five years, and before that too." Annoyance simmered in the back of Ciel's mind at Gemma's unwavering belief in the superiority of SC medicine.

"That said—"

"That said, I'm going to shower now." Ciel hurried past Gemma, who took a step back without another word.

In the bathroom, Ciel leaned against the closed door. Exasperated, this time with herself and her temper, she groaned. "Damn." She pulled off her nightclothes and stepped into the cleaning tube. The humming sound waves made goose bumps erupt along her arms. She hated how this machine made her hair static, even if the effect didn't last. It only took sixty seconds to thoroughly cleanse her entire body. Grateful when the cycle ended, Ciel exited the narrow space and pulled on everything but the coverall that was still in her room, as she needed to apply her herbal paste and dress the affected area on her leg.

Gemma had returned to her quarters as Ciel crossed the corridor to enter hers. She thought of how she'd just talked to the woman who had saved her life last night. Her personal issues had more to do with her attitude than the fact that Gemma believed in her own profession and education. Placing her head in her hands, Ciel sighed. She sometimes spoke before she had time to edit herself, but she knew when she'd been in the wrong. She pulled on the coverall and walked over to Gemma's quarters. Knocking on the door, she chewed on the inside of her cheek.

"Enter." The door opened. Gemma was at her desk, her computer showing the SC crest, but her subspace conversation was clearly over. "Yes?" Her expression didn't reveal her mood.

"I apologize. I shouldn't have spoken to you like that. You saved my life yesterday and it was wrong of me to dismiss your efforts, as well as your way of practicing medicine." Ciel tugged at her sleeves, putting weight on her uninjured leg.

"Apology accepted. In all fairness, I'm guilty of the same suspicion." Gemma smiled faintly. "We'd both do well to remember we're working toward the same goal, albeit through different approaches."

Suddenly enthusiastic, and a lot happier that Gemma didn't hold a grudge, Ciel motioned toward the bed. "May I sit down?"

"Oh. Sorry. Of course, your poor leg."

"I'm all right, just a bit sore. Honestly. I'll let you take a look at it later in case I need more of the anti-allergen medication." Ciel sank down gratefully. "I was thinking, and this I'm sure is why the protector sent me along as your guide, that we need to find common ground for our respective treatments. Where mine fail, yours might be successful and vice versa."

Gemma pulled one leg up, hooking her arms around it. The pose made her seem so much younger. The Earth human was very beautiful in an understated way. Her triangular face, with large, hooded brown eyes, delicate nose and lips, was almost pagan, like the figures from the mountain sagas Ciel's grandmother used to read to her when she was a child. Gemma's hair, reaching her earlobes and with short bangs, was almost the same golden-brown color as her eyes.

"What?" Gemma tilted her head. "Why are you looking at me like you've just noticed me or something?"

"How old are you, Gemma?" Ciel's cheeks warmed. "I mean, you look impossibly young to hold such an important position."

"I'm thirty-eight. And you?"

"As you know, Gantharians live longer than earth humans. On average a hundred and forty years. Earth humans become about a hundred and ten. Correct?"

"Yes. And you're dodging the question."

"No, I was just trying to compare. I'm forty-four. If we take into account life expectancy, divide it by a hundred, and then remove our respective age and…what's the matter?" Ciel looked at the chuckling Gemma. She hadn't heard Gemma laugh until now, and it was a thoroughly beautiful sound. Very addictive and contagious. "What's so funny?"

"No, no. Do go on. I can't wait to hear the rest." Gemma snorted softly.

"Oh. Well, where was I? Yes, we take our respective age and divide with the percentages 1.4 and 1.1, then you're actually three years older." She looked expectantly at Gemma.

"All right. And? What's this obsession with age?"

"Oh, everybody knows that Earth humans are hung up on not having such a vast lifespan."

"We—we are?" Gemma looked nonplussed.

"That's what I've heard."

"For stars and skies, Ciel. I've never heard such nonsense. Who told you that?"

"It's common knowledge," Ciel said stubbornly. "Ever since the protector brought you to help free us from the Onotharian occupation, we've known about this. Her spouse, the revered protector-by-marriage, won't remain with us as long as the protector herself."

"Some Earth humans live to be more than a hundred and thirty.

Some Gantharians don't live to see a hundred. It's all statistics. As for the protectors, they both hold dangerous positions, so we can only hope they die of old age and not someone's plasma-pulse weapon."

"True." Ciel thought for a moment. "So, your opinion is, age is of no concern?"

"Age is many times of a definite concern, especially when it comes to medicine. As for personal relationships, I think it might play a part, but it doesn't make much difference in the end."

"I suppose, having lived incarcerated for so long, each day of survival became a victory." Ciel had spoken without thinking again.

"You were in a work camp the entire duration of the occupation?"

"Yes…and no." Ciel studied her nails. "I was officially in a camp called Gremer Esta. It means Second Star. A few of my colleagues and I found a way to slip outside to gather the herbs and find the crystals and metal ores we needed to work. I sometimes think the Onotharians knew about our nightly excursions, but they turned a blind eye since we prevented outbreaks of contagious illness. As long as they had us to care for the sick and wounded, they didn't have to bother with it."

"Are you saying you had a way out, an escape, and you voluntarily remained to care for your people?" Gemma paled.

"Yes." She looked carefully at Gemma. "Sometimes when we left to gather herbs, we would dress one of the young mothers up as a druid and then help her escape through the resistance network. The Onotharians didn't seem to actually count us. The camp was close to a wooded area and surrounded by hills. They had a security grid, like a force field, erected around the camp, and the only way for us to sneak out was to dig out the floor in one of the latrines. Everything was very low-tech inside the camp, which was immensely different to how the Onotharians were equipped." Ciel folded her arms, gripping her elbows. "I hated it. I loved the people I was there with, but I hated being imprisoned more than anything."

"I won't even presume to say I understand what you went through. I really have no idea what it would be like to spend twenty-five years of my youth in a camp." Gemma's voice was filled with empathy, but she didn't gush, something Ciel was grateful for.

"It's left me suspicious and scarred. I become defensive really fast and I'm protective of my people…to a fault."

"That's natural." Gemma rose from the chair and took a seat next to Ciel. "I knew, when I signed on for this mission, that you'd been incarcerated at some point. I'm not sure why I wasn't informed of the exact details, but I assume the protector and her spouse both agreed that I'd need to find out about your past on my own."

"Your guess is as good as mine." Ciel shrugged. "I truly am sorry for acting so ungrateful—"

"You apologized. We both did. Don't worry. I've been known to step on a few toes too. As you say, I'm fairly young for my position, which doesn't always sit well with my peers or those climbing the career ladder just beneath me. I've developed a cynical side, and I can be sarcastic when it really isn't called for." Gemma smiled self-deprecatingly. "Trust me. I can go toe to toe with you on all these *issues.*"

Ciel returned the smile, for the first time sensing they'd be able to find some sort of common ground. Sitting so close to Gemma she noticed, not for the first time, her scent. Something sweet and airy, like the loc'tialdo flower just before their buds burst open, when warmed by the sun. She wanted to ask, but Gemma hadn't shown any sign that she'd accept personal questions like that.

The humming sound from the outer door chime made them flinch.

"Oh, well, time to get back to work," Gemma said with a wry grin. "Let's hope the hospital administrator has seen the light and stepped up her game."

What light? Ciel had no idea what this analogy meant, nor the one about stepping up games. "Can you tell me this again, in Premoni?"

"I just did." Gemma frowned, probably as she really had spoken in the intergalactic language of Premoni.

Ciel rose to open the door. "Sure. Your words were in Premoni, but the sentences just didn't make sense to me."

"Oh, that." Gemma accompanied her to the door. "It meant the administrator needs to focus and keep sharp to solve the situation. There's only so much we can do for the people waiting to be seen. The clinic personnel need to implement their routines sooner rather than next week."

"Agreed." Ciel opened the door. Outside stood the very person they'd talked about.

"Good morning, Doctors," Ms. O'Eso said, holding on tight to the strap of her shoulder bag. "Glad to see you up and looking so well, Druid O'Diarda." She all but curtsied before them. "We were just seeing how the routines are starting to work, and we plan to implement the last of them this afternoon. That's why we need your assistance. There's no way we can assemble a trauma team to deal with the new situation." She tugged at the strap, her hands white-knuckled.

"What new situation?"

"It came in via our analogue transmitter. Seventy-five or so refugees are stuck in the Siengash Mountains, behind the Sien Dela Pass. They're in the valley behind the pass, and some of them are suffering from a bad infection, as far as our physicians and the SC medical staff can estimate."

"We need to take them supplies and medication, and evacuate the ones that can't wait." Gemma turned around. "I'll contact SC headquarters and the protectors. Ciel, can you make sure we take what we need, including yours and of the SC's resources?" Turning back to the administrator, Gemma narrowed her eyes and the jumpy administrator immediately seemed to focus. "Do we have any idea what kind of outbreak we're dealing with?"

"According to our only reports, the patients have skin and respiratory problems."

"Stars and skies. That could include just about anything." Gemma ran a hand through her hair. "All right, let's get going. I'm going to let the highest-ranking physician from the SC backup unit remain here to monitor the refugees that are already here. The rest of us will convoy to, what was it called? The Sien Dela Pass?"

"Yes." Ciel placed a hand on Gemma's shoulder, stopping her from walking back to her communication center in her quarters. "You just need to know one thing. We'll be able to go by hovercraft most of the way, but the last thirty or so kilometers, we'll have to walk and carry what equipment we can manage. No hovering is possible in the Siengash Mountains, due to the metal ores found in the bedrock. I just wanted you to know this before you contacted SC headquarters."

"Walk. Of course." Gemma pinched the bridge of her nose. "Your herbs will really have to prove themselves, since they're easy to carry. We'll take all the portable and lightweight medical equipment we can carry. Is the terrain rough or can we pull carts on wheels?"

"It'll be difficult. Once we can establish the exact coordinates and pinpoint the needs, you can have the SC drop more equipment and food from the air. If they maintain the minimum altitude above the mountains, they can do that."

"Good. I'll arrange it. Let's go, people." Gemma squeezed Ciel's upper arm and walked into her quarters.

"She's rather intimidating," Ms. O'Eso said in a muted voice. "She frightens me."

"Dr. Meyer is quite formidable," Ciel said, not about to have anyone else criticize the woman she was slowly getting to know. "I suggest you head back and call a staff meeting in," she checked her chronometer, "about half an hour."

"Yes, Druid," the administrator said quickly. "We'll be in the large conference room. Do I notify the SC medical staff as well?"

"I believe Dr. Meyer will take care of that. Unless you hear otherwise, gather your own staff first."

Ms. O'Eso left, half running back to the clinic. Ciel knew she would need more of that potent SC pain medication if she was going to hike to the Sien Dela Pass. It was beautiful scenery, true wilderness, but also rough, unforgiving territory. She took a deep breath. This would be the ultimate test of how well she and Gemma could work together. She also sensed that it would show her the nature of her attraction to the prickly physician.

CHAPTER SIX

Gemma decided their hovercraft needed to take point and they should both ride up front with Sergeant Tacrosty, who was in charge of maneuvering the hovercraft and his crew. As the ranking military officer, she felt the burden of command settle on her as a second, slightly too-tight skin. Used to it after having been on the fast track ever since the academy, Gemma had taken the middle seat between the sergeant and Ciel. Behind them, four more hovercraft joined them as they traveled at maximum speed toward the Siengash Mountains.

Checking her chronometer, Gemma realized they were less than half an hour from their landing site, from where they'd be traveling on foot. She was wary of trekking along difficult paths planet-side, as she'd lived aboard space stations or space ships for the last twenty years. She was in great physical shape because working out was not only mandatory, but the only way to stay alive when you lived like she did, but running on treadmills or around hangar decks was hardly the same as stumbling around in nature, especially alien nature.

"Not far now, Commander," Sgt. Tacrosty said.

"You familiar with the navigational instruments of this vehicle?" Gemma asked Ciel. "It would be helpful to have you verify that we're where we're supposed to be when we set down."

"Not really, but from what I can tell, the chart seems pretty self-explanatory. The map system looks familiar."

"It should be, ma'am," Tacrosty said, punching in controls that took them to a comfortable altitude. "We've worked with your cartographers to upgrade the computer."

"Impressive." Ciel ran her finger down the screen. The map scrolled and changed colors as it showed the topography. "Nice!"

"And that's still just the two-dimensional hardware. Over by Corporal Lund's station, you can get all that as a holographic image—"

"Thank you, Sergeant," Gemma said. "I'm sure you'll get the chance to demonstrate these toys to Dr. O'Diarda later." She smiled faintly at Ciel, who looked stunning in the light of the early-morning sun. It wasn't difficult to understand that Tacrosty was doing his best to impress Ciel. Her dark-blue eyes reflected the sky in front of them, and the many layers of her hair seemed to emphasize her otherworldly beauty.

"I look forward to it, Sergeant. You'll have to be patient with me, as I'm not...technologically proficient." Ciel shrugged self-deprecatingly.

"No problem, ma'am."

Ciel turned her eyes back to Gemma. "As for landing at the correct coordinates, I can assure you it won't be hard for me to tell. Once you've seen the Siengash Mountains, you'll never forget them. The topography is unique, and their beauty will do the rest."

"In other words, as dangerous as they're stunning. I might as well confess that the last time I hiked in the mountains on Earth, I was twelve. I hated it."

"Why?" Ciel turned in her chair, looking curious.

"I was a tech-bore already then. I wanted to stay home and play with my interactive lab that my father gave me. My mother insisted I needed fresh air and took me to a famous area on Earth called the Pyrenees. Mountains and more mountains. I had enough fresh air to last me a lifetime."

Ciel tossed her head back and laughed. "If you hated it that much, no wonder you settled for outer space."

Gemma shook her head at Ciel's mirth, but inwardly she confessed that it was a beautiful, unabashed sound that was quite contagious.

"Commander? Major Vesmonc, operating the craft behind us, reports noticing a disturbance from the ground. We need to increase our altitude the last twenty minutes, or our instruments might become compromised," Cpl. Lund said from behind. "I recommend climbing another thousand feet."

"Thank you, Corporal. Climb a thousand, Sergeant." Gemma double-checked her harness. These large hovercraft had inertial dampeners but didn't match those of a spaceship. If the instruments were off when they went in for landing, she didn't want to be tossed headfirst against the helm. "Buckle up, people," she ordered them, keeping an eye on the instruments and glimpsing Ciel tighten her harness as well.

The friendly conversation was now over and Gemma knew they were all sensitive to any unfamiliar movement of the vehicle. Fifteen minutes later, Tacrosty punched in new commands. "Corporal Lund, open a communication channel to the other vehicles," he said through his teeth. "This isn't going to be pretty."

"Go ahead, sir." Lund echoed his sergeant's tone of voice.

"Sergeant Tacrosty to SC vehicles in convoy. We're going to reach our landing area in less than three minutes and have to set down in rapid-mode." He reached under the helm and folded up what looked like a mesh glove. "Use the Virtual Digits. This will give you more control since you can't trust what you see on the gauges. Make sure everybody is strapped in before you commence setting down. Land-pattern, a six-edged star. Good luck. Tacrosty out."

Gemma knew she'd been given the best of the best for this mission, but she was still impressed with how Tacrosty handled what had to be a first for all the hovercraft pilots. Landing in the pattern of a star would keep them from dropping down on top of each other.

"All right. This it, Dr. O'Diarda?" Sgt. Tacrosty asked, pushing his hand into the Virtual Digit glove.

"This is it. We're in position." Ciel gripped her armrests.

"Brace for impact. We're going in for rapid-mode landing." Tacrosty's jaws tightened as he clenched his gloved fist and began moving it in a well-measured pattern.

Gemma was certain they were plunging to their death as the hovercraft fell like a rock toward the wilderness beneath them. She curled her fingers around her harness and held on with what could only be described as a death grip. This was another reason for loving space travel. No rapid-mode toward alien bedrock.

"H'rea dea'savh!" Ciel cursed in Gantharian next to her.

Just as the ground came into sight through the front windows, Tacrosty raised his fist and opened it. The vehicle set down hard but remained intact and they were alive.

"What a ride!" Tacrosty turned to face her and smiled. "We're safely down, ma'am, and so are two of the others. Three more to go. We can't exit until they all land."

"I think my kidneys ended up in my mouth, but that was a stellar job of getting us here alive, Sergeant." Gemma unbuckled her harness and glanced at the others. The eight marines looked unfazed, but Ciel was pale. She didn't want to single Ciel out by drawing attention to the fact that she looked like she might faint any moment, but she needed to check on her. Stepping closer, Gemma pointed at something arbitrary outside the window and checked Ciel's pulse at the same time. "Those your stunning mountains? They're quite beautiful."

"Thank you. Yes." Sounding a little drowsy, Ciel tipped her head back, looking up at Gemma. "I'll be fine," she whispered. "My leg hurt when we landed. Or should I say, fell out of the sky."

"Let me know if you need me to check on it," Gemma murmured. Ciel's color was returning slowly. "Just sit here while the other vehicles fall, and then we'll get some of that infamous fresh air. It'll do you good."

"You too." Ciel smiled. "We don't have much time to reach the pass, as the refugees might be deteriorating."

"I know. We'll be on our way soon."

"All the vehicles are down in one piece. No damage or casualties, ma'am," Cpl. Lund said.

"Very well. Let's go outside and start pulling our gear together." Gemma knew they'd have to carry everything, as the terrain was too rough to even pull anything along on carts. Her backpack was loaded to the brim with medical equipment and portable laboratory. She knew Ciel had packed her own backpack, even bigger than Gemma's, and four more of the marines' with the herbs she felt they might need. The rest of the marines carried technology, medical and otherwise, blankets, inflatable tents, and cubicle dwellings.

Outside, the air was indeed so crisp Gemma felt she ought to be able to scratch it with her nails. She inhaled deeply, and suddenly the headache that had simmered in the back of her head was less painful. Perhaps there was something to this whole fresh-air concept after all. She could definitely see it had a positive effect on Ciel. She ran up and down the ramp to the cargo area at the back of the hovercraft, then hurried into their quarters, bringing out mugs and a pot of what now was a familiar scent, the soup, for everyone.

"Have some of this before we start walking," she said, and began handing out mugs. "This is new territory to all of you and you'll need your strength."

The marines looked into their mugs as if they thought it was poison. Gemma sighed. "Come on. Be brave and have a sip. It's very good. If I love this herbal concoction, I can promise you, it has to be good."

Tacrosty smiled sheepishly at Ciel and drank some of it. Looking surprised, he downed the rest quickly. "That wasn't just good, that was delicious."

The other marines clearly took his word for it, and soon they'd hoisted their backpacks and all they could carry in their hands. Major Vesmonc planned to stay behind with four of his marines to guard the vehicles and also serve as communications liaison between the ones going forward and SC headquarters, in case their communicators began acting weird.

As Gemma took up the lead with Ciel next to her and Sgt. Tacrosty on her other side, she hoped they weren't too late.

CHAPTER SEVEN

The sun was directly above the convoy, not providing much shade anywhere. Used to the outdoors, Ciel drenched a large piece of cloth in a brook and sprinkled some dried petals from tisslas, a night flower with cooling qualities. She used it on burns, mainly, but also as a way to cool someone with persistent fever. After she wrapped the cloth around her head, the tissla swelled together with the water and the process cooled her scalp, which in turn had a similar effect on the rest of her body. She glanced over at Gemma, who was fiddling with her uniform cap. She turned it inside out and pressed a sensor.

"Makes it cool." Gemma put the cap back on. "Thank the stars."

It was rather amusing that they were achieving the same results with completely different methods. Ciel smiled. "As long as it works. How long will that keep you cool before it runs out of power?"

"It's solar operated, so it'll work as long as the sun's up." Gemma grinned only to curse under her breath when her foot caught on a root sticking up from the ground. They were walking along a very narrow path, barely allowing two people to walk side by side.

"Careful. You don't want to fall into any shrubbery next to the path," Ciel said. "They look harmless enough, but as an Earth human, you don't know which plants you might have an adverse reaction to."

"Wonderful." Gemma glared at the offending foliage. "One more of those roots and I might fall into a bush and swell up like an old-fashioned balloon."

"Balloon?"

"People used to inflate plastic bags of some sort several hundred years ago on Earth. Usually on happy occasions as birthdays—"

"Birthdays?" Ciel marveled. "You mean, when a baby was born?"

"Yes, then, and on the anniversary of their births, weddings, and holidays."

"You celebrated birthdays every year?" This was an interesting custom. "Sounds…excessive."

"We still do. Your birthday is considered your special day." Gemma shook her head. "I haven't really adhered to that custom since I left my home to join the Academy. I usually end up forgetting about it."

Ciel tried to imagine what might go on at these celebrations. She assumed that food was a big part of it, as with any celebration on Gantharat. Even in the camp, the fun-loving and amicable Gantharians made sure to find something to celebrate. Unknown to the Onotharian guards, they loved most to celebrate helping someone escape.

"Where did you go?" Gemma looked quizzically at Ciel as they were forced to walk one at a time past a protruding part of the bedrock.

"Back in time," Ciel said honestly. "Celebrations are a big part of the Gantharian traditions. Even in the camp we prepared feasts, though they were pretty meager."

"Good for morale that you managed some semblance of normalcy when nothing about it was normal."

Amazed at how intuitive Gemma was, that she understood without Ciel having to elaborate, she extended a hand to help Gemma up a steep part of the path. "Yes, you're right. It especially did the children good. The camp council was divided into two parts when it came to what they valued most. I always thought it was just as important to not breed hate, no matter how I sometimes detested the occupants. But plenty of others believed that indoctrinating the young ones at an early age to become fighters was more important. My comrades and I called them the militia, and we were often at odds with the leaders of that group." Ciel was taken aback at how easy it was to share this with Gemma. "I maintained that keeping such traditions as Spring Feast and Fall Glory alive was just as important as covert missions."

Gemma smiled. "Though I'm of a military mind-set, I still happen to agree with you. I mean, life was going on while you were in the camp. The children wouldn't get a second chance at childhood, and as you say, not breeding hate is what will help lay the foundation to how well Gantharat succeeds in regaining its independence."

"Yes, absolutely." Ciel rounded a large protrusion in the bedrock, then stopped, gazing across what used to be a slowly moving river. Now it was forcing its way between boulders and tall trees, as if determined to bring them along. "Damn."

"And we have to cross without any dependable hover-packs." Gemma turned to Sgt. Tacrosty. "Suggestions, Sergeant?"

"Old-school, Commander." He looked serious. "Fire a filament-arrow into a strong-looking tree. Find our best swimmer to take a rope over, tethered to the filament. Have them secure the rope. Then we go over, two at a time, to not put too much strain on the rope as the water's too wild to risk it."

"Sounds like a plan, but I can't say I look forward to going into the water. Seems cold." She glanced at Ciel. "Guess we'll be lining up for that soup of yours to warm us afterward."

"No problem. I have enough base to make more." Ciel had no idea what a filament-arrow was, but she agreed with Gemma. Going into the wild water, no matter the temperature, wasn't tempting.

"All our bags are sealed shut, so our gear should be fine." Tacrosty removed his bag and pulled a plasma-pulse rifle from his back. "I'm a good marksman when it comes to shooting projectiles, but Corporal Lund is a competitive swimmer."

"Give Lund the chance to volunteer. If he doesn't, I'll do it. I'm a good swimmer, but I'm used to swimming in pools on space stations or at resorts when on shore leave."

Tacrosty approached his subordinates and soon Cpl. Lund came over and acknowledged that he'd be swimming. In the meantime, Tacrosty had removed the nozzle of his rifle and attached a strange-looking device consisting of a cylinder-shaped nozzle with a flat, circular protrusion underneath. He walked to the riverbank and planted his feet firmly on the ground. "How about the third from the right, next to that rock, ma'am?" He pointed across the water.

"Good choice. Denser than the older trees," Ciel said.

"You heard the expert on anything that grows." Gemma motioned for the sergeant to take the shot.

Tacrosty raised the rifle, took aim with his feet slightly apart, and pressed the sensor to fire. Faster than the humanoid eye could detect, something pierced the air and then Tacrosty smiled broadly. "Dead center of the trunk, ma'am!"

"Excellent. Secure the filament on this end."

Ciel walked over to Tacrosty and examined the thin wire. Barely thicker than sewing thread, it ran across the river and was clearly attached to the tree. "This will be impossible to hold on to. Won't it cut into Lund's fingers?" She frowned as she let her fingertips strum it like a string-operated musical instrument.

"Oh, he won't be holding on to this with his bare hands, if he holds on at all. We'll attach his harness to this, and also, his gloves are reinforced to handle the friction against the filament."

"Ah, I see." That made sense. Ciel watched Tacrosty secure the filament around a tall boulder. He used another instrument to measure the tautness.

Gemma motioned for Ciel to follow her. "While Lund gets ready to swim, let's make sure our bags are sealed and the technology protected against the water."

"Why do you carry technology with you when you know the readings won't be reliable?" Ciel examined her bags, letting her fingers run along the fastening to ensure there were no gaps.

"Oh, I didn't tell you. These instruments have a built-in protection from any interference. Smaller items are easier to protect than huge ones like hovercraft."

"I see." Ciel looked down at herself. "I assume we should remove some of our clothes so we can swim more easily."

"Yes, absolutely. Better keep on something with long sleeves and that covers your legs. We don't know what's under the water. Less risk of scrapes and cuts that way."

"Not to mention the mini-leeches."

Gemma stopped short. "The what?"

"This part of the mainland sometimes suffers from an infestation of mini-leeches in the water."

"And what exactly are they? I mean, what do they *do*?" Gemma looked positively nauseous.

"They're usually harmless, but it's not fun to find yourself covered with them. If too many get on you, and you don't get rid of them instantly, they can make you anemic."

"Oh, for stars and skies. I wish I'd never asked."

Ciel had to laugh. The expression of disgust on Gemma's face was rather endearing in a strange sort of way. "Don't worry. I don't think it'll be a big problem in such rapid waters, and we'll inspect each other once we're on the other side. We should inform the troops to do the same."

"Absolutely." Gemma glanced toward the water. "Corporal Lund's going in. Come on."

❖

Gemma stood at the bank of the river with her arms crossed over her chest. Not taking her eyes off the bobbing head of the young corporal, she spoke with a low voice that her longtime colleagues would recognize well.

"Keep the rope taut but don't pull, Sergeant."

"I've got it, ma'am."

"How are his vital signs?"

A younger female private checked the monitor on her sleeve. "So far, it's like he's taking a walk in the park, Commander."

"Good. Temperature?"

"Lund's core temperature is 36.2 Celsius. Water temperature is 16."

"In other words, damn cold."

Suddenly Lund's head disappeared. Gemma dropped her arms and took a step forward. "Sergeant?"

"He's good, ma'am." Tacrosty glanced at the private's monitor. "There. There he is. He's up."

Breathing evenly out of sheer willpower, Gemma watched the dark head slowly move toward the opposite bank. It had begun to rain, which in a way indicated that everything was being as difficult as possible. "Is everyone ready to help Lund by tightening the rope on this end?"

"Yes, Commander." Tacrosty nodded. "As soon as he's out of the water, he can connect the communicator. We didn't want to risk it in the water, even if it's supposed to tolerate being submerged."

Gemma turned to Ciel. "Sergeant Tacrosty will be the first to go over. You will accompany him—"

"I'd rather go with you." Ciel's eyes took on the steely blue-black nuance that was so familiar by now.

"No. You—"

"Please."

Gemma stared. Ciel never pleaded. Whatever reason she had to prefer to swim with Gemma, it had to be compelling for her to beg. "Very well." She cleared her voice. "Sergeant. You will go first with Private…" She read the nametag quickly. "Vollenby. Once you're over, start a few fires. That way we'll save our portable heat units for the patients." The fine drizzling rain chilled the air, and the previous heat that had bothered everyone was gone. "Better make them large enough that the rain won't drown them out."

"Yes, Commander. On it." Tacrosty had already undressed into the long-sleeved SC fleet-issued undergarment, as had Private Vollenby.

"Lund to Meyer. I'm safely on the other side, ma'am."

Gemma turned her eyes back to the corporal, smiling now as he waved at them. "I see you, Corporal. Secure the rope and let us know when it's safe to tighten it from here." She hoped that the rope would run just above the waterline, within reach but easy to spot and not obscured by the torrent water.

Soon the rope was attached at both ends—taut enough to support the swimmers, but hopefully not so tight it risked breaking its moorings. Tacrosty and Vollenby had tied their backpacks at their highest position on their backs and now entered the water, beginning to swim with long strokes. Tethered to the rope by a short wire that slid along it as they swam, they made their way steadily with a few meters between them. Impatience gripped her. It would take them the better part of the day to get everyone across the river safely.

"You all set?" Ciel asked from behind.

Turning, she saw that Ciel had removed her coverall and was stowing it in her large backpack. It barely fit among the herbs and other things she'd packed.

"Don't frown. Many of the herbs have lots of air in their containers to help preserve them. That'll act as a floating device in itself." Ciel pulled the backpack on and hooked it onto her harness. She adjusted the shoulder straps and then leaned against a tree to take the weight off.

"Almost." Gemma watched the two in the water reach the bank on the other side, greeted by Lund, who met them with firewood cradled in his arms. "I'll get ready while two more of the privates go over."

Two young men jumped in and began swimming, one of them

unable to keep from uttering a curse. "Freezing," he groaned as he began to swim.

"Wonderful," Gemma muttered, and began removing her coverall. She wore the same undergarment as the other SC soldiers; the only difference was the color, as commissioned officers wore black. She tucked her discarded clothes and boots into her backpack, grateful that they were made of a material that could be thoroughly compressed.

When the previous pair reached safety, Gemma took a deep breath as she connected her harness to the rope. She waded into the water, and only her rigorous SC training over the years kept her from gasping. She hated cold water and the way it made all her nerve endings contract in disgust.

"H'rea dea'savh," Ciel muttered behind her. "We better start swimming, and fast. I don't want anyone to think I'm a weakling whose teeth start clattering as soon as she walks into the water."

"I agree." Gemma drew a deep breath and began swimming along the rope.

The current gripped her immediately. Though it tore and tugged at her, she forged ahead, swimming with sure strokes. Her instinct told her to hammer away at the water to get to the other side as fast as possible, but that would be foolish. Long strokes, long and slow, she told herself, long strokes to make it over at a steady pace. The water pulled at her backpack. This made her worry for Ciel, who had a much larger pack. "Ciel?"

"Yes?" Ciel sounded remarkably calm behind her.

"You all right?"

"Yes. Keep swimming. Your pace helps me."

"Good." Gemma had to stop shouting as water gushed into her mouth.

Estimating that they had covered a third of the distance, Gemma dared to glance behind her. The water was becoming nearly impossible to struggle against. Was she really in such bad shape? Ciel looked like she found it hard to maneuver with the large backpack tipping her sideways.

"The current's getting worse," Ciel gasped.

"I think so too." Gemma coughed as water gushed over her face. "Just keep going. Drag yourself along the rope if you need to."

"I…my arms are giving out, Gemma." Ciel suddenly disappeared under the surface.

Gemma stared at the loop securing Ciel to the rope. "Ciel!" She backed up, tugging at the loop. Suddenly Ciel's head was above the water again.

"H'rea—"

"Dea'savh. I know." Gemma was relieved that Ciel was well enough to curse in Gantharian. "Hold on to the rope. Got a good grip?"

Ciel nodded.

"Good. Use your other hand and hold on to my harness. I can't pull us both along, but use your legs and kick. That way we'll swim together and use our bulk to fight the water."

"All right." Ciel looked pale and her blue-toned lips were dark blue from the cold.

"Remember, you have to help me."

"Understood."

Gemma clenched her teeth and began swimming. She felt a push from behind, propelling her through the water. This was working. Every time Gemma kicked her feet and used her arms to make strong and steady strokes, she could tell Ciel used her legs to help push them forward.

Just as they were a little more than halfway across the river, something hit Gemma's right leg mid-thigh. Numbness rather than pain made it impossible to move it at first.

"What's wrong?" Ciel gasped behind her. "I felt something. A thud."

"My leg. Something…hit my leg."

"Keep using the other one and your arm. We're heading toward calmer water."

Gemma struggled to comply, but the numbness was changing into an overwhelming dull ache, making it harder. Still, Ciel had to have dug deep for extra energy as she kicked them ahead. Gemma gasped for air and did her best. She counted silently the strokes, thinking, *just ten more, just ten more after that.* Her throat ached from the spray of the water. The only upside to its high level of salt was that it made it marginally easier to stay afloat.

"Look. Just a little longer," Ciel said. "Don't give up on me, Gemma."

"Never." Appalled at how badly her teeth chattered, Gemma shoved her arms through the water, feeling the taste of blood in her mouth. She didn't even want to think about having to do this again when going back to the hovercraft.

Suddenly other arms wrapped around her. A deep voice told her she was safe. "Tacrosty?"

"For stars and skies, ma'am, we were worried about you." The seasoned young man sounded upset as he dragged her up onto the riverbank. "The water seems to be calming down again, at least to the level where it was when Vollenby and I went over. Not sure what happened when you and Dr. O'Diarda were crossing. It just went crazy."

"Crazy describes it well," Gemma said, her vocal cords hurting. "I need water."

"Of course. Here you go, ma'am." A bottle was pressed to her lips and she forced herself to drink slowly. "Ciel?" she managed after a while.

"Here." A hand landed on Gemma's shoulder. "Now we need to see what happened to your leg. We also need to get warm. It's still raining."

"We're putting up smaller habitats over by the clearing. I started a few of the portable heaters. The fires aren't quite cutting it." Tacrosty simply removed Gemma's backpack and carried her, despite her objections.

"I can walk."

"I'm sure you can, but I can't risk you damaging yourself any more. We need your expertise once we reach the displaced individuals. Besides, Dr. O'Diarda is shooting daggers at me with her eyes, so I know what's best for me. You're not walking yet."

Gemma tried to look over at Ciel, but she was behind Tacrosty. "Scared of her, are you, Sergeant?" she muttered.

"If you'd seen how she glared at me before I lifted you, you'd know why, ma'am." He smiled sheepishly. "Here we are. This is your habitat. Yours and Dr. O'Diarda's." He placed Gemma on a small cot. "I'll be down by the bank overseeing and helping the troops."

Gemma stopped him. Looking up into his kind eyes, she placed a hand on his arm. "Thank you."

"Get tended to, Commander." Looking a little flustered he nodded at them both and left the small habitat.

Glancing around them, Gemma saw this wasn't the very smallest of the habitats. It had room for two inflatable cots as well as storage for their gear. When they reached the people in need, it would also be able to house the portable laboratory equipment.

"Commander? Dr. O'Diarda? Here's your gear." Vollenby and a male private placed their backpacks just inside the opening.

"Thank you." Ciel nodded briefly and closed the opening after they left. "Now we have to get out of the wet clothes and look at your leg." Ciel pushed off her dripping undergarments. Pale and trembling she stood there dressed only in a semi-transparent camisole and briefs. She shivered as she glanced at Gemma. "Your turn."

CHAPTER EIGHT

Ciel was colder than she could remember ever being. Her teeth had even stopped clattering as her jaw felt rigid and so tight that she found speaking difficult. Looking down at the more slender Gemma, she knew she had to be even worse off.

"I need to quickly check you for leeches and look at your leg. Here, this blanket is one of those fancy thermo things, right?" Ciel began pulling off Gemma's undergarments. "Let's get this one off and then you can wrap the blanket around you."

"Thank you." Gemma tried to cooperate, but it was clear that she was in no condition to. "It hurts to be this cold," she whispered huskily.

"Yes, it does." Ciel refused to give in to the shivers. "This one too. The less wet stuff you have on your skin, the better." She took off Gemma's camisole. "You're not supposed to be the blue one." Her attempt at joking made Gemma smile tremulously.

"True. I do look a little better in pink."

"We'll have you pink in no time." Ciel's heart nearly broke at the sight of the formidable commander looking so small and fatigued. "You'll be back bossing us around and saving lives before you know it."

The ghostly smile made Ciel push to work faster at Gemma's clothes. Once she'd pulled off everything, she ran her hands all over the chilled skin. "You seem to be leech-free." She pulled the thermo blanket around Gemma and pressed a sensor. She found she could use different settings, one actually named Hypothermia Therapy. Pressing the sensor, she could tell that the heat was instantaneous. "Ah. Nice."

"Oh, stars, yes." Gemma closed her eyes briefly.

"Now the leg." Ciel tugged her backpack close. "You haven't broken the skin, but the pulsations in your right foot aren't as palpable as in your left. I think you have compartment syndrome in your right thigh."

"Damn." Gemma looked at her leg. "I should be able to open the fascia with a derma fuser using the opposite setting. That doesn't help with the accumulated blood, though."

"What would you do if it was my leg?" Ciel carefully felt the bruised and swollen thigh.

"I'd sedate you, use a laser-scalpel, and open it up to drain. Old and proven method."

"Old and proven sounds good. Any of your medical staff present that can perform such surgery?"

"They're internalists mainly. You would do just as good a job." She tilted her head, looking exhausted. "Please, Ciel. I trust you."

"Can we do it with local anesthesia?"

"It won't be fun, but yes. I think we can."

"I'll get set up. I have some herbs that will make it endurable for you."

Gemma raised an eyebrow. "Really?"

"Don't give me that look. They're not narcotics." Ciel shook her head. "Honestly, Gemma. You'd think I was a bujjadin."

"I don't think that. What's a bujjadin?"

"A person marketing illegal substances."

"Ah. No, then. I definitely don't think that."

Ciel had used their banter to prepare herself. "I need to wear something warmer than this so I don't tremble and sever an artery." She pushed off her wet underwear and looked hesitantly at Gemma. "Are you feeling all right enough to check me for leeches?"

"Sure." Gemma made a twirling movement with a finger before she took another tight grip of the thermo blanket. "Spin."

Turning under Gemma's scrutiny, Ciel was relieved when Gemma shook her head.

"I don't see any."

"Good." Ciel donned a set of comfortable undergarments. She then pulled out a few small bags of herbs, which she put in a bowl and ground to a fine powder with a small pestle. She mixed it with water and gave the mug to Gemma. "Drink it slowly. If you gulp it, it can make you nauseous."

Gemma complied, sipping the herbal drink slowly. Soon her facial muscles relaxed and she tipped her head back. "Oh. This is a nice buzz."

"It's temporary. Once your system is saturated, you'll feel a certain numbness, but you'll be less dizzy and…just calm and soothed."

"Calm and soothed. Sounds nice."

Ciel smiled at Gemma's blissful expression. "I bet it does." She could understand the high that came with the sudden absence of pain. She opened Gemma's backpack and looked for the small case she had seen that contained the derma fuser and bone knitter. Frowning at the alien markings on the cases, she grabbed one that looked like it was of the right size.

"Yes. That's it. But don't grab the bone knitter by mistake. That might irreparably damage my veins."

"I do know the difference between the instruments." Ciel pursed her lips. "Now, it's the setting that I'll need your help with."

"No problem. The laser-scalpels…in a blue container with red markings. See them?"

"I do." Ciel glanced into Gemma's pack and pulled out the case.

"They'll hum alive when you grip them. They're self-sterilizing, so you can just go ahead and use them."

"Very well." The method was actually the same, even if the tools were as different from Ciel's low-tech instruments as it was possible. She gently prodded the hard mass on Gemma's leg. "Will I need to wash your skin?"

"No. The laser-scalpel takes care of any contamination. Just do it." Her lips pale now, Gemma closed her eyes.

"I trust the derma fuser will help fix any potential mistakes?" Ciel's attempt at another joke fell flat to the ground. "All right. Here we go." She grabbed a scalpel that indeed did hum into working order once she held it correctly. Gently, she pressed the tip against Gemma's skin. The blade took on a higher tone and pierced the skin. Making the incision about two centimeters, she stopped to check Gemma's expression.

"Go on." Gemma looked pale but composed.

Ciel carefully cut through the tissue until a dark, shiny bulging surface came into view. Cutting into it, she was prepared to mop up any blood, but she was unprepared for how dramatic dark-red blood would seem to her. Gemma relaxed marginally as she relieved the pressure against the muscular tissue, though, which reassured her she'd done the right thing.

"Now, make sure the clots are out. Use regular water that you've placed in the portable sterilizer. That one there, strapped to the side of my bag. Then…the derma fuser."

"All right." Ciel took a bottle of water and placed it in a small cylindrical container. It opened on its own after about ten seconds. She flushed the incision four times before she was convinced it was clean of clots. "What setting for the derma fuser?"

"Lowest for the muscle fascia. Middle setting for the subcutaneous layers, and then…" Gemma slumped sideways.

"Gemma!" Ciel pressed her fingertips to Gemma's neck. A rapid, slightly weak pulse fluttered beneath her touch. "Just hold on. Almost done." Working as fast as she could, Ciel closed the fascia and then the layers above it. She ran the derma fuser at the highest setting at the top and made sure Gemma wouldn't get an unnecessary scar. When she was done, she took what she usually considered a ridiculous item from Gemma's backpack, the cleansing wand, and ran it over both of them. This was not just to feel clean, as great as that was, but also to ensure that no tiny leeches hid so deep in folds and orifices that they were impossible to spot at a glance. It was a nice side effect of these wands that they killed parasitic life forms that size and smaller, unless they were well inside the person. It also had the ability to dry hair, which in this case was crucial for Gemma to get warm faster.

Once she'd cleaned both of them, Ciel grabbed another thermo-blanket and wrapped it around Gemma, then lowered her onto one of the cots. She was shivering so badly herself now, she knew they needed the shared body heat. Careful not to push Gemma off the cot, Ciel slid in next to her. It was bliss to be under the blankets. Gemma was still cold, but not as bad as when they came out of the water. Ciel tried to disregard the fact that Gemma was naked against her, which of course was futile. She just didn't have the heart to haul Gemma up into sitting position and remove the warm blankets to dress her in sleepwear. Gemma needed rest. They both did.

Gemma murmured and tried to move.

"Shh. Lie still or we'll both fall off this thing. We need to stay warm. Just relax. Once we're warm again, I'll make more soup for us."

"Soup. Yes." Gemma reached back and grabbed Ciel's left arm and tugged it around her. "Better."

Ciel held her breath for a moment. She had lost count of how many people she'd helped save one way or another, but one thing she did know. Nobody had gotten to her like Gemma had, and nobody had certainly made her lose her breath in a life-and-death situation by their mere presence. "Just rest," she whispered, and held Gemma closer. Ciel inhaled the sweet scene that had to be all Gemma, as the wand neutralized anything with perfume or other scents.

It had been years since she'd been in the same bed as someone else, let alone held them like this. *And it never felt like this anyway.* Feeling protective, and her whole body humming from the closeness of the beautiful, sometimes infuriating, woman in her arms, Ciel knew she was in big trouble. This mission would end in a week or two, and Gemma would move on with her next assignment. Why this felt like the ultimate loss after everything Ciel had been through the last twenty-five years, she had no idea. Or maybe she did, and that was why she was torn between never wanting to let go and backing off instantly.

As keeping Gemma warm and safe was her top priority right now, she'd stay here. Even if it ended up breaking her heart, nothing would stop her from holding Gemma tight and reveling in the fact that she had stopped shivering.

❖

Gemma sat up on the side of the cot, the blanket getting stuck in something and falling off her shoulders. Rubbing her arms to ward off the cool air in the habitat, she realized she was naked.

"What the—?"

"You were out cold. You needed to sleep." Ciel's husky voice behind her made Gemma turn around so fast she nearly toppled off the cot. "Careful," Ciel said, and took hold of Gemma's arm, steadying her.

"Thanks. Um. Yeah. Oh, the surgery." Gemma managed to get one of the blankets around herself and then examined her leg. There was a faint line on her thigh, but that was it. She felt no more than a vague tenderness, which was a relief. "What time is it?"

"Very early morning. We don't have to get up yet. If you sleep one more hour, you'll be doing much better once we break camp. We're only two hours from the pass."

"I should really…oh, all right. If you're going to look at me like that," Gemma said grumpily. "Stars and skies, has anyone ever said that you take too much advantage of those blue eyes of yours?" Realizing what she'd just said, Gemma knew she was blushing. She lay down hastily, her back still against Ciel. To her amazement, Ciel wrapped her arm around her waist.

"Just so you won't kill yourself now that I had to use SC technology to fix you. Do you have any idea how hard that was?"

"Using the technology or the procedure?"

"Both." Ciel cleared her throat. "I was afraid of inadvertently damaging your leg. I didn't want to give you a scar either."

"Gods of Gantharat, you're not telling me you worried about a scar?" Gemma was agitated now and managed to turn around with Ciel's help. "A scar?"

"You've got such soft, perfect skin. A scar would be…wrong."

"I have plenty of scars." Gemma tried to see what was behind the opaque blue in Ciel's eyes.

"That may be, but I haven't caused them. I may sound silly, but I don't want to…hurt you."

"Ciel?" Gemma's heart was thundering so fast now that she was feeling it hit her ribs from inside. "What do you mean?"

"Your well-being matters." Ciel shifted, tucking Gemma in under her chin. "Go back to sleep. We both need to."

Gemma knew this would be impossible as thoughts tumbled in her mind. Why was her well-being important to Ciel? And why did this thought create an emotional as well as a physical response to such a degree that Gemma felt sweat break on her forehead and at the small of her back? She snuck an arm around Ciel's waist, telling herself she needed the support on the small cot. In fact, it was a lovely feeling to hold on to the soft, curvaceous body next to her. Ciel really was stunning. Feminine, but tough and strong at the same time. *So not my type.* Gemma had to fight not to snort in self-deprecating mirth. Type?

She had no type. When would she have had time to find anyone during the last decade, let alone look for a *type*?

Startled at how well their very different body types fit together on the narrow cot, she closed her eyes, thinking she would just rest for fifteen minutes. She should have known she'd fall asleep within five.

Chapter Nine

They broke camp at sunrise and Gemma was amazed at how quickly she'd recovered from the ordeal in the water. Perhaps it was the combination of SC technology and Ciel's famous soup? An unexpected inner voice suggested that the mere presence of Ciel and the way she'd cared for her throughout the night had something to do with her regaining her strength so quickly. Gemma smiled to herself, which was surprising in itself. Normally such thoughts brought out a sarcastic retort, but not now.

"The pass is coming up around that bend, Gemma." Ciel broke into her reverie and pointed to where the path disappeared farther ahead. "We should come across the refugees soon."

"All right." Gemma tapped the sensor to her communicator attached to her lapel. "Meyer to Tacrosty. We'll reach our destination within minutes. How are things at the rear?"

"Just fine, ma'am. We're ready."

"Good. Meyer out." Gemma adjusted her backpack as they kept moving forward. "You're all prepared, I assume?" She glanced at Ciel.

"Yes. Ready to triage as soon as we get there."

Gemma nodded, pleased that Ciel sounded focused and ready. The marine privates would set up camp with their habitats and also the larger habitat that would host the worst cases.

"Oh, Gods of Gantharat." Ciel gasped and nearly stumbled. "This…oh, Gemma, look."

Gemma just stared. The intel had not been accurate. The refugees were scattered around the pass, in groups of different sizes. The report had stated there would be about seventy-five of them. Gemma did a quick estimate. She saw at least two hundred. "Oh, damn." She tapped her communicator again and called Tacrosty to join her at the front.

As he made his way forward, the closest refugees had spotted them and looked startled. A small child cried out and ran toward a reclined man wrapped in blankets. Gemma recognized the Gantharian word for "father." Clearly they'd spooked the child.

"For stars and skies, ma'am. There are hundreds of them."

"I can see that, Sergeant. This changes things. Let headquarters know instantly. They'll have to at least triple their supply drops. We need three times as many blankets and lightweight habitats."

"On it, Commander. I just hope the damn interference from the bedrock doesn't mess with my signal. I'll have to double back to a better spot if it does."

"Do what you need to do, just keep me apprised, all right?" Gemma gazed around them. "Over there looks like a good place to set up camp. I understand Private Vollenby is in charge of logistics when it comes to the habitats."

"I am, ma'am," Vollenby stated from behind. "Why don't you let me take that backpack from you while you triage? I'll put it in your habitat once we have them up and secured."

"Good thinking." Gemma pulled her emergency triage pack from the larger backpack. Motioning for the medically trained to approach her, she spoke grimly. "We will still work like we planned, according to the alpha-grid scenario. But now each part of the grid is three times as big, with more potential patients in each. Any questions?"

Nobody spoke up.

"If you come upon cases that need surgical attention or where life is clearly hanging in the balance, break the grid and bring them to the first habitat that Vollenby puts up. Notify me immediately."

A mumbled chorus of "yes, ma'am" met her and she nodded shortly. "All right, let's move out, people."

Gemma walked along the perimeter, noting that the four marines in charge of security were carrying out their assignment with well-practiced efficiency.

The first people in her grid, a mother and her three teenage children, sat huddled under blankets. Gemma introduced herself in Premoni, which the oldest child spoke fluently.

"Mother has not been able to keep anything down in more than three days, Doctor," the thin girl said. She wore her hair in two long white-blond braids, and her clothes hung on her slight frame. "My little brother is doing a little better, but mother is so weak she can hardly talk."

"Let me check her out, please." Gemma ran her medical scanner along the woman, who was shivering among the tattered blankets. Dehydration seemed to be the biggest problem at the moment. "Tell your mother I'm going to inject her with a rehydration agent that will hold her over until supplies get here."

The young girl spoke to her mother in Gantharian before Gemma pushed the imbulizer to her neck. The affected woman flinched as the medication hissed through her skin.

"It should take effect in minutes. I'm leaving this note for the next medical staff that checks on you, in case it's not me." Gemma didn't say that she was likely to forget the details about each patient, even if she was the one taking care of the little family next time.

After fifteen consultations, she began to see a pattern. Meeting with Ciel for a few minutes, she voiced her concern. "This isn't a mere stomach infection."

"What makes you think that?" Ciel looked around. "The symptoms fit."

"Yes, but when I scan them, I see no parasites, no signs of a virus or any bacteria."

Ciel frowned. "Maybe the SC scanners don't know how to pick up indigenous Gantharian germs?"

"That could well be true, but they don't even pick up any unknown germs." Gemma ran her fingers through her hair. "They should've detected something by now. Let me finish the rest of my grid and we'll regroup and compare notes."

"All right." Ciel turned to leave, but hesitated. "Several people told me about a smaller group hiding among the line of caves over there." She pointed due west. "Some called them traitors. Others seemed genuinely concerned about them."

Gemma looked toward the cave openings. "You and I can check that out once we complete triaging our grids."

Ciel nodded. "Fine. Back to work."

Gemma kept collecting information and treating dehydrated

patients, and soon the families were all a blur as they all manifested the same symptoms. The last patients in her part of the grid turned out to be four unsupervised children. A young boy spoke some Premoni, but he was so ill he could only whisper. Gemma asked him his name, how long they'd been ill, when they ate and drank last, and if they were in any pain.

"I'm Naqq," the boy said weakly. "These are my friends. We... we're sick, Doctor."

"I can see that," Gemma said kindly. She ran her scanner and then stared at the readings, hardly able to fathom what she saw. "Naqq, I'm going to help you feel better." She explained about the imbulizer, but still the youngest child, a little boy, maybe four years old, started sobbing, a terrible dry, heaving sound. Knowing this meant the child was so severely dehydrated that he had no tears, Gemma merely scooped him up. "Can the rest of you walk a little bit?"

The way the children helped each other as Gemma carried the trembling child toward the camp made her swallow unexpected tears. She felt a hand hold on to her harness, and she slowed her steps to not lose any of the older children.

❖

Ciel pocketed the scanner and walked to meet Gemma and the others. She hadn't come upon any deathly ill patients in her part of the grid, but she had seen from a distance how some of the others had moved people on stretchers. When she saw Gemma carrying a small bundle, followed by what had to be young children, she started running.

"Here. Let me." Catching up with Gemma, Ciel reached for the small child.

Gemma handed her burden over and then ran her scanner again. "Damn. He's hardly breathing. We have to hurry!"

Ciel didn't wait. She rushed along the narrow path, dodging branches and bushes as she ran. The little body wrapped in a blanket was so still, she feared they were too late. The first habitat was ready to receive patients and Ciel hurried inside, placing the child on the closest examination table. She peeled back the blanket just as Gemma practically fell through the door.

"Set an IV, push neutral fluids," Gemma barked at a nurse. "If I'm right, he's going to need something for the pain. Something that doesn't overwhelm his system."

"Something from nature," Ciel said, and pounced on her backpack sitting next to Gemma's inside the door. "I have an extract that can be mixed with IV fluids. It's mild and very close to the endorphins the humanoid body makes."

Gemma frowned for a second, but then nodded decisively. "Very well. Get it ready."

"Why do you think he's in pain? I mean, *this* kind of pain?" Ciel asked as she prepared the solution. "Nobody else has spoken of any bad pain in my part of the grid."

"If my suspicions are correct, it's just a matter of time. The child is worse off, thus with more advanced symptoms." Gemma's eyes were darkened by what looked like total fury. That wasn't good.

"Run a full workup on this child. The others too," Gemma said, and pointed at the other three children that sat in the corner.

Ciel guessed they were too weak to remain standing. Another nurse helped them sit on an examination table and began carrying out Gemma's orders.

"Ciel, you may as well prepare this concoction of yours for the other three too. They'll be as bad off as this little guy soon."

She had often seen Gemma annoyed and irritated, but never this furious. Her lips a fine line and her dark eyes burning with a fire dangerous for the target of her wrath, Gemma still handled the children patients with tender hands and spoke to them in a voice like a soft caress.

Once the four young ones were settled together on two cots, which worked well since they were clinging to each other, Ciel pulled Gemma aside. "Tell me."

"They…at first I was uncertain, thinking it was just my suspicious mind that was seeing ghosts. Then I found the kids and remembered how many times I've been right over the years." Gemma leaned against a stack of crates, running a hand over her face as if wiping something foul from her skin. "They've been gradually poisoned. I think they all have."

Ciel's mouth fell open for a few moments. "Poisoned? H'rea

dea'savh…" Her voice only a whisper, she wondered why she was so shocked. The Onotharians had committed such atrocities that poisoning prisoners was hardly surprising.

"And these are *children*." Gemma's chin trembled, but then she clenched her jaws.

"Children who grow up to become resistance fighters." Ciel spoke hollowly. "It makes sense. In some horrible, inhumane way, it makes sense."

"Given that the leaders of Onotharat are callous, greedy monsters, I guess so." Gemma touched Ciel's arm briefly. "I'm sorry. These are your people."

"Yes, they are." A sudden sound from outside, a large thud, followed by more, made her flinch. "What was that?"

"I'm hoping it's the supplies. Let's hope they got the correct coordinates so they don't kill anyone. I swear those flyboys and girls sometimes…" Gemma rushed outside with Ciel right behind. "Oh, good."

The field to the west of the camp now became the target area for the high-altitude drops. The parcels landed with soft thuds after silk parachutes opened up, saving the contents from being crushed. Tacrosty stood just outside the perimeter, speaking into his communicator. Ciel heard him ask the person at the other end to repeat several times.

"Guess the interference isn't making communication very easy."

Tacrosty waved to them, indicating it was safe to approach. "That's the last of the first shipment, Commander. We'll gather it and start handing out supplies to the refugees."

"Good. Dr. O'Diarda and I will take two of your marine medics and head to the caves. We don't know how many are over there hiding, but two should be enough. While I'm away, you're in charge."

"Yes, ma'am." Tacrosty frowned. "Only two marines? I—"

"Two is enough. Thank you. I'll just report over to the medical staff and then we'll head out."

CHAPTER TEN

The sun shone through the clouds, making the air unbearably humid as they made their way to the caves. Seen from the camp, it didn't look that far, but with the difficult terrain and winding paths, it still took them more than an hour to get there.

Ciel adjusted her backpack and kept an eye on Gemma, whose limp became increasingly obvious. Gemma had to be in pain, but she respected that she didn't offer any explanation or complain.

"Ma'am," the marine who had taken point said quietly. "Movement up ahead. Two o'clock." He raised his weapon and, looking back, Ciel saw the other marine do the same.

Gemma raised her binoculars and gazed up at the dark openings in the bedrock. "I count four humanoids moving around on the outside. They are walking very slowly. Wobbling. I'd say they're showing symptoms of illness or severe fatigue."

"Let's make sure, Dr. Meyer," the first marine said. "There's probably a very good reason for these people to stay secluded."

Ciel agreed with the marine, but she doubted that anything or anyone among the people in the caves was of danger to Gemma and her rescue team.

"Let's move in with caution, but we need to hurry. If these people are as bad off as some of the ones over by the pass, they need help now."

The marines nodded solemnly in unison, and they all kept hiking toward the caves. Ciel made sure she walked close to Gemma, as she kept stumbling over the roots and rocks in her way.

"Your leg's bothering you," Ciel said in a low voice, making sure their security detail didn't overhear.

"I'm fine."

"Don't even try. I'm not visually impaired. You're stumbling, you're limping, and you make strange faces."

"I do not. And besides, I'm not the one who needs attention." Gemma looked annoyed. The small crease in her skin between her eyes grew deeper.

"No, you're not. Not yet. I want you to chew on a few leaves as we approach the cave dwellers." Ciel pulled out the herbs she'd picked while passing them, immediately recognizing their anti-inflammatory qualities. "I've rolled them into packs. Chew them until they liquefy in your mouth. Spit those out and chew one more. I have more for later if you need them."

Gemma glowered at the small green bundles in Ciel's hand. "You're not joking, are you?" Eyeing the first little roll suspiciously, she then popped it into her mouth and began chewing as they hurried to keep up with the marines. "At least it tastes all right."

Ciel merely smiled, knowing full well that these particular leaves were tasty.

A female voice called out in Gantharian. "Soldiers. Go back, go back!"

"Ciel!" Gemma pulled at her. "Tell them we're here to help."

"Listen to me. I'm Ciel O'Diarda, druid and Gantharian. My comrades here are from the Supreme Constellation. We're here to help you. So are the SC soldiers. The weapons are only for our protection, so unless you attack us, you have nothing to fear."

"Collaborator!" The woman, a very young, dark-skinned girl, stood before the others, her arms full of firewood. "We have sick people here. We're in no shape to fight anyone. Just leave us alone!"

"We can't do that." Ciel forced herself to sound calm and reassuring. "Please, let us closer. We have reason to believe that you've been poisoned while in the hands of the Onotharians."

"Why would you think that? And why would the Onotharians poison us? We're of their blood. We're Onotharians too."

Gemma had clearly been able to follow the gist of the conversation. "All the more reason, if they were incarcerated for being Gantharians at heart."

Ciel repeated what Gemma had just said. "We mean you no harm."

"Let us help you." Gemma spoke Gantharian with a thick accent, but it wasn't hard to understand her. "Listen. One of my friends is Boyoda, a code name for the resistance leader who now also is known as Andreia M'Aldovar. You might know that she's Onotharian by birth also."

The young woman dropped the wood and began to stagger sideways. Ciel didn't think. She simply hurried forward and caught the girl in her arms before she hit the uneven ground. "Gemma!"

"I'm here. Let me scan her." Ciel held on to the emaciated woman as Gemma ran the scanner all over her body.

"She's dehydrated, her fever is more than 40 degrees Celsius, and she's jaundiced."

"Her liver is impaired."

"That'd be my estimate also."

"*Raviciera!*" A pale woman, equally thin, stumbled out of the closest cave. "Get away from her." She sank to her knees in spite of the sharp rocks. "What did you do to my child?"

"The Onotharians running the camp poisoned all of you over a period of time. Gantharian and Onotharian prisoners alike. We have medication, food, and shelter set up down at the pass. How many of you are here in the caves, and can you walk?"

The woman gazed back and forth between Ciel and Gemma. "You…you're not here to take us back?"

"Not at all," Gemma said. "We're here to assist with the medical emergency and to help you reach your home."

"Oh." The woman still looked hesitant, but at least she wasn't trembling in full-blown panic anymore. "I'm Pomaera. This is my daughter, Raviciera."

"I think the shock of seeing our soldiers was simply too much for her," Gemma said, sounding reassuring. "She fainted. I'll infuse her with a stimulant with enough of a boost to keep her ambulatory during the time it takes us to go back down to the pass. So, how many of you are up here?"

"Sixteen. We're all Onotharian by birth, but they define us as naturalized Gantharians. This is our home planet. We were all born and raised here."

"Anyone too ill to stand?"

"Perhaps old Jemo. Everyone else...they're sick, but not to such a degree that they can't move. I warn you, it'll be slow."

"Slow is fine as long as we get you down to the shelters. We have portable habitats, which will be much more comfortable for you than these caves."

Pomaera blinked rapidly and wiped her suddenly misty eyes on her sleeve. Raviciera looked up at her mother, clearly reassured that these strangers might not be bad news after all.

The cave closest to them was inhabited mainly by younger people, most of them looking weak rather than ill. Ciel helped Gemma administer a filter-drug that would help them fight off the poison fed to them over time. Ciel also provided them with different strengthening herbal solutions.

The marines constructed a stretcher made of two young trees interwoven with long leaves. They placed the fragile old man on it after Gemma and Ciel both had tended to him. Appalled at his oozing wounds and the state the thin man was in, Ciel asked if any of the refugees were strong enough to help with the stretcher.

A tall man limped forward. His left arm was in a sling, but he grabbed hold of one of the young trees and stood there, proud, if a bit shaky.

"Thank you." Ciel grabbed the tree opposite the man. "What's your name?"

"Camol." He chewed his lower lip for a moment and then spoke with a tremulous voice. "I don't suppose you've come across more refugees from Teroshem? A large group left together a few weeks ago."

"Yes. We did. They came through Rihoa while we happened to be there to evaluate the clinic. It became a very different humanitarian effort instead."

Camol walked a few paces in silence, his face pensive and so pale, his lips and earlobes looked amber in the setting sunlight. "I know you must've seen a lot of people during the last few days, but I have to ask anyway. You didn't happen to come across a young pregnant woman. Gantharian. Her name is Tammas?"

Ciel looked up hastily. Gemma was walking right behind them, supporting an elderly woman who looked almost as bad off as the poor man on the stretcher. "Tammas? Tammas O'Mea of Emres?"

Camol gasped, nearly losing his grip on the stretcher. "She's all right? Oh, please tell me she's all right."

"Last I saw Tammas and Ilias, her little boy, he was doing much better. They were being airlifted to—"

"Little boy?" Camol looked like his knees were giving in. Furious at herself for speaking without thinking first, Ciel called out for the marines to stop.

"She had the baby? I've been in this godforsaken place so long, I've lost track of the days...weeks." Camol ran his uninjured hand over his face. "A boy. A son. And she named him Ilias, after my father." He sobbed quietly and wiped at his tears. Then it was as if he became aware of his surroundings. "A boy? A son." He gripped the stretcher harder and seemed energized. "Tammas," he murmured. "Ilias."

"What's up?" Gemma peered down at the man on the stretcher.

"Meet Tammas's husband and Ilias's father, Camol." Ciel smiled through tears. "How's that for amazing?"

Gemma looked over at Camol and smiled. "Glad we found you. She was very concerned." Then her eyes returned to Ciel. "And you're such a softie." She wiped an errant tear from Ciel's eyelashes with her thumb. "That said, we need to get going. You all set?"

"Yes, Doctor," Camol said, now looking as if was ready to carry the old man entirely on his own.

Ciel held her firm grasp of the stretcher. In her mind she could still hear the tenderness in Gemma's voice as she called her a softie. Her feet moved automatically as they made their way back to the pass. So far they'd carried out their assignment with good results, but they still had a lot left to accomplish. They had to establish what poison was used and figure out how to evacuate the patients since they couldn't cross the river like the trained soldiers had. Ciel certainly wasn't looking forward to another swim in the cold, rapidly moving water.

Gemma stood outside the large habitat where the patients worst affected by the poison and exposure to the wilderness were cared for.

She had worked nonstop since they returned from the caves, and so had Ciel and the other physicians. Several of the elderly had almost had kidney failure, but dialysis and herbal remedies that Gemma knew nothing about seemed to work instantly. Ciel had tried to explain about her dried roots, but all Gemma really cared to know about at this point was results.

"Gemma?" Ciel showed up next to her and pushed a mug into her hands. Its mouthwatering smell was familiar. Of course. The miracle soup. "One of the marine privates is starting a campfire over there." She pointed further to the southern side of the camp. "Since we don't have habitats for everybody, we've moved them closer and set up a new perimeter." Ciel made a funny face. "See, I'm even getting good at this military-speak."

"Sounds like a good idea. The closer they are, the better access if we need to assist them."

"How are we going to get them out of here?" Ciel gestured around them, indicating the refugees.

"High-altitude airlift. All of them."

"Oh. Us too?"

Gemma smiled over the rim of the mug. "You're really not keen on going back into that river, are you?"

"Gods of Gantharat. No!" Ciel shuddered. "Are you? You were the one hurt, not me."

"But you hated the cold water more than I did."

"True."

Gemma sipped her soup and, unless she was imagining things, she was feeling calm and reassured, and more at ease than she'd been in... months. This woman. This damn soup. Ciel. Not thinking about work or any other repercussions, she gently cupped Ciel's cheek. "You're such an amazing woman. So strong, so beautiful."

Closing her eyes for a moment, Ciel then opened them slowly and gazed down at her. She slid a hand up along Gemma's arm and held her hand against her face. "I don't know what makes you say this, since I feel I can't compare even remotely to you."

"You must be joking." Gemma smiled now, seeing the warmth in Ciel's eyes reflected toward her as the distant campfire reflected in them. "You're not the vain type, nor am I, but the way you carry yourself, how you deal with horrible situations...I'm in awe of you."

"Gemma. Am I reading too much into what you're saying? If I am, please tell me now." Ciel pressed her lips into Gemma's palm. "I know the place and the situation aren't ideal, but I've learned the hard way that if I wait for the right time, most likely I'll lose my chance forever."

Gemma's heart thundered, struggled against her ribs like a caged animal. Ciel's eyes spoke of passion, desire, even, and—more? "What do you want to say?" Afraid to ask, but even more afraid to lose her own opportunities to find something more than work in store for her down the road, Gemma held her breath.

"I need to know if you can see yourself caring more for me than an appreciated colleague. Do you find me attractive and worthwhile enough to keep seeing me after we get back to the capital?"

Gemma dropped the mug, and what was left in it splashed on top of her boots. "Ciel." She lifted her free hand and pushed it into Ciel's hair, under her braid. To her amazement, Ciel was trembling and it dawned on her that Ciel was perhaps even more nervous or apprehensive than she was. And still so brave, speaking first of deeper feelings, and in the midst of a mission at that. "I can see that." Gemma whispered against Ciel's jawline, suddenly standing close together. "I can see us spending a lot of time together. Exploring Gantharat…and each other." Her bold words, so unlike her and yet so deeply honest, made Ciel visibly shiver.

"I want to show you the area I come from. I don't have any relatives left after the occupation, but the scenery is beautiful." Ciel wrapped her arms hard around Gemma. "As for exploring each other, I don't want to sound pushy or presumptuous, but I'm not sure I can wait until we're back in the capital." Looking a little afraid, Ciel kissed Gemma's lips gently.

Suddenly so greedy, aching so very badly for the woman whose life she'd saved, only to have Ciel save her right back, Gemma parted her lips and deepened the kiss. She wasn't even sure this was how Gantharians kissed, but judging from how she'd accidentally observed Kellen and Rae kiss, she had enough confidence to caress Ciel's tongue with her own.

Ciel's response, which consisted of her lifting Gemma up to straddle her hips and then carry her to their small habitat behind the mobile infirmary, showed Gemma beyond a doubt what the deep kiss did to her.

Inside the habitat, Ciel paused, putting Gemma down, but held her close. "This sure would seem like I was indeed presumptuous. My carrying you off like this." She rubbed her neck, one arm still around Gemma's waist. "Just stop me if this is too much, too soon."

"Not too much. Too soon?" Gemma tilted her head, caressing Ciel's face with the back of her curled fingers. "I don't think so. We're mature women. We have a demanding job, both of us, that can take us away on dangerous assignments from one moment to the next. I think we would be smart to grab happiness with both hands when it comes our way." Gemma rose on her toes and kissed Ciel again. "I want you."

"Gemma, oh, damn..." Ciel buried her face in Gemma's hair. "I've tried to keep a professional distance, but being around you, and you're such a passionate woman, no matter what you're doing, it...it rubs off. I was so set on clenching my teeth and just getting along as best I could with the high-and-mighty SC physician—"

"And another thing I love about you is how you pay the best compliments." Gemma smiled.

"Hush." Ciel shook her head. "And there you were. Angry a lot. Passionate even more. And always with the patient as your main concern. Then your coworkers. Only after that did you put yourself. Last. Always last."

"So was that one of the reasons you started feeding me the magic soup?"

"Yes. I made it my business to look after you, as you weren't too good about doing that."

"You're my protector, you mean?"

Ciel pushed her hand under Gemma's tunic. Her coverall was off her shoulders already, and she'd used the sleeves to tie the upper part around her hips while working in the main habitat. "So soft. Like silk."

Gemma moaned at the gentle touch, only to find herself echoed by Ciel. "I want your touch. I can't wait." Gemma was certain now her needs would be met and reciprocated. Ciel's eyes burned with an ice-blue flame, and when she pushed her hands into Ciel's coverall, she could feel the same heat radiating off her.

"Tell me what you want. I'll do anything you ask for." Ciel gasped. "Anything."

Gemma nudged Ciel until she sat down on one of the cots. "You have to be really quiet, Ciel. These habitats have horrible insulation when it comes to sound. Can you be? Quiet?" She pushed the coverall off Ciel's shoulders. Beneath it, Ciel wore a gray tank top. It had to go.

"I can be very quiet. I survived because of it."

Gemma vowed that she would make it clear to Ciel that she wanted to hear everything about her years in the prison camp, if Ciel was ready to share her history with her. Right now, what Ciel wanted was obvious. Gemma straddled Ciel's legs again, kissing her lips and down her neck, and fondling her breasts. She promised herself that she'd take her time during her next opportunity, but now she knew, from how she felt and from how hungry Ciel seemed for her touch, that it was time.

Pushing her hand into Ciel's coverall, she cupped her and slid gentle fingers in between slick folds. "Oh, Gods of Gantharat," Gemma said, moaning at the damp heat that met her there. Now that they finally had the situation with the refugees under control, Gemma was so overwhelmed by her desire for this woman.

"Gemma...I have to..." She felt Ciel yank her own clothes down far enough to return the feverish touch. Soon, agile fingers played with her, not even bothering to tease.

"Yes, like that. Like that." Her movements became uneven, jerky, as she balanced on the edge of pleasure but just out of reach. Gemma sobbed in frustration. So like her to get too worked up.

"Shh. Don't worry. I have you," Ciel whispered. "You're so stunning, so hot against me. The release will be so sweet. Just trust me, henshes."

The Gantharian term of endearment was familiar, but Gemma had never thought anyone would ever say it to her. Especially not this amazing woman. "Henshes," she said quietly, just under her breath. *Darling.*

"You are."

The two words, uttered so without pretense or hesitation, made Gemma throw her head back and bite her tongue to keep from moaning too loudly as she climaxed in one long shudder after another.

"Oh, Gemma." Ciel's voice broke.

She nearly fell off Ciel's lap backward, but righted herself and focused on what gave her lover pleasure. *Lover.*

It seemed as if Ciel had barely managed to hold off her own orgasm since she convulsed within seconds after Gemma pushed her fingers inside her. Out of breath, Gemma could still appreciate the utter beauty before her as Ciel gave a muted cry and pressed her legs together around her hand.

"Ciel," Gemma murmured. "It's actually a real word on Earth. One of the lesser-spoken languages in our time, but still around."

"What does it mean?" Ciel tipped them sideways so they could lie down together.

"It's a French word that means 'heaven.'" Gemma nuzzled Ciel's neck, reveling in the damp, wonderful-smelling skin. "So appropriate."

"How so?" Ciel pulled the blanket over them.

"When you want to describe something truly and amazingly wonderful on Earth, you say it's heavenly. Like our expression, 'stars and skies.'"

"Oh." Ciel hid her face in Gemma's hair again. "Thank you."

"You're welcome." She hoped Ciel was all right. "Something wrong?"

"Absolutely nothing." Ciel moved and kissed Gemma's lips gently. "Just a little…taken aback. It's been a long time since I allowed… closeness."

"Same here." Her words seemed to relax Ciel. "Let's push these coveralls off. Um. And the boots?"

Ciel laughed, a low, contagious chuckle that made Gemma join in.

"I can't believe I didn't even let you take your boots off," Gemma said, moaning as her cheeks warmed.

"You know? I take that as a true compliment. You clearly find me very alluring." Ciel smiled broadly, which transformed her serene face into a whole different kind of beauty.

"I do. I'm falling in love with you, Ciel. So no wonder I find you alluring."

"That makes me very happy. I'm falling for you too. I've never heard it put quite like that, but it's true nonetheless. I've fallen many times during this mission, in a manner of speaking, and the biggest fall I took for you."

"Well spoken." Gemma helped Ciel by pushing off her boots and clothes. Being naked under the blankets with the tall blue-blooded woman she'd come to love very deeply reignited her passion. As she set out to explore every part of Ciel that brought her lover pleasure, Gemma knew no matter how long her assignment was meant to be, thanks to Ciel, Gantharat now felt like it could be her home.

EPILOGUE

Camol couldn't let go of his wife. Tammas in turn couldn't stop crying. Between them on the bed lay little Ilias, now a healthy, somewhat plumper baby, asleep and blissfully unaware of the drama.

"I will come back later," Ciel said, not wanting to intrude on the couple's reunion.

"No. Stay, please." Tammas extended a hand. "I need to ask you about Camol's arm, because he will downplay it if I ask him. I also want to know about the rescue. The nurses told me that large space vessels hoisted you up with…with ropes!" Her eyes were huge as she looked between Camol and Ciel.

"They did," Camol said. "Somehow they managed to get some signal up despite the interference from the bedrock, and soon long, thick ropes with the biggest cages you ever saw appeared."

"Cages?" Tammas looked shocked.

"Not cages," Ciel said, sending Camol an admonishing look. "Actually a sort of reinforced habitat with beds and medical equipment inside. Some of them had rows of chairs with belts. We were able to hoist twenty patients at a time with those."

"It sounds amazing. Thank the Gods for the Supreme Constellation for bringing such technology."

"Yes, some of the people from our camp would have died from the poison if—"

"Poison?" Tammas sat up straight so fast, the baby began to stir. "What poison?"

"Camol, you and I will have to discuss proper bedside manners,"

Gemma said from the doorway. Her look was serious as she entered and Ciel's heart twitched painfully. Now what?

"What is he talking about, Dr. Meyer?" Tammas's chin trembled and she clung to Camol with one hand and settled her baby by patting his bottom with the other.

"It turned out that the Onotharians were slowly administering a poisonous substance in some of the camps. It seems that most of the poison was given to Onotharians who wouldn't join in the fight on their side, so your husband received rather a lot. However, the Onotharian biological makeup made them less receptive unless they were old or weakened by illness and so on. Camol is a strong young man. After we started treating everyone in our care with dialysis for their kidneys and several liver-cleansing substances provided by Dr. O'Diarda, we realized that the effect of the poison was reversible for the most part."

"What does that mean?" Tammas asked.

"It means Camol will live a productive, healthy life with you and your son."

"But?" Tammas asked.

"I told you. She's as stubborn as she's strong." Camol smiled faintly.

"I think this type of poison can have other long-term effects. I wouldn't recommend that you have any more children. Your DNA can be compromised when it comes to reproduction." Gemma clenched her hands behind her back. Ciel could see from how the skin tightened around Gemma's eyes how hard she found delivering such news to a young couple.

"Oh! Oh." Tammas hid her face against Camol's chest. Then she took a deep breath and looked at them with huge eyes. "We have Ilias. We will simply love him all the more."

Ciel swallowed at the bravery of the young woman who had been incarcerated for most of her life, as had Camol. She watched Gemma exchange a few reassuring words with the pair before leaving them to enjoy their reunion.

"You didn't tell them everything, did you?" Ciel placed a gentle hand at Gemma's lower back.

"I just couldn't." Gemma stopped and faced her. "Soon they'll start asking questions about Ilias, but as I don't have any definite answer yet, I didn't think it necessary to bring it up."

"And when they start asking if the poison could be transferred to the baby via her milk?" Ciel's stomach clenched at the thought.

"By then hopefully we'll know. We'll also have to consider what the poison might have caused in utero."

Ciel knew that they had to factor in the risk that the poison could have traveled over to the fetus during the pregnancy.

"Look who's here." Gemma tugged at her sleeve.

Over by the nursing central stood Protector Kellen O'Dal and her spouse, Admiral Rae Jacelon. Surrounded by staff and patients, they smiled and talked briefly with everyone.

Ciel had met the protector on several occasions, but she'd never encountered the admiral. To Ciel's surprise, the protector and the admiral both embraced Gemma. Obviously the woman she'd come to love was a personal friend of the people who were closest to Prince Armeo.

"And you know Ciel, right?" Gemma said, interrupting her reverie.

"I do. Dr. O'Diarda was a well-known name and the source of much admiration during the dark years." Kellen took Ciel's hands between both of hers. "Many people owe you their lives, Druid."

"Thank you, Protector, but they don't owe me anything except to live long and happily."

"I'm glad to finally meet the woman who first made Gemma foam at the mouth, only to then have her fall head over heels."

Gemma groaned and glared at the admiral. "Thank you, Rae."

"It's my honor, Admiral...Protector?" Ciel hesitated.

"I prefer 'Admiral.'" Rae grinned at her wife.

"Not sure what that saying about the heels means," Kellen said, frowning slightly. "I don't think I've ever seen you in gala dress and high heels, Druid."

"Oh, but that would be a sight," Gemma said, clearly now in on some secret joke. Ciel looked at her lover and honestly didn't mind being the source of the teasing, as she loved the new spark in Gemma's eyes. Whereas fatigue and exhaustion had recently weighed on Gemma, since they'd returned to the capital, Gemma seemed light and exuberant even though she'd worked night and day.

"We're being awful people," Rae said, shaking her head. "I fully intend to kidnap you right here. My people tell me they have everything under control when it comes to the refugees and their health situation. No doubt something new will show up soon, but for now, you're on leave and you're staying in the new wing at the palace." She winked at Gemma. "That's an order, Commander."

"Aye, ma'am." Gemma glanced at Ciel. "Sound good to you?"

Ciel waited until the protector and her spouse were a few steps ahead of them. "More than good." She took Gemma's hand in hers. "It sounds heavenly."

Supreme Constellations
The Queen and the Captain

CHAPTER ONE

It's time to board the *Koenigin,* Your Majesty." A young man stood respectfully at a safe distance from EiLeen, where she sat on the long couch beneath a window. She turned her head slowly, trying to not bite the man's head off for using her old title. Being Queen EiLeen of Imidestria was a closed chapter in her life, but the public seemed determined to not let her move on.

She had never sought to inherit a title, but when her brother, the former King Reidder, had died in a hunting expedition on Imidestria's second moon twenty years ago, EiLeen was next in line to the throne. Having no choice, she tried to fulfill her duties but also determined to work toward a more modern system. Imidestria had long sought to join the Supreme Constellations Unification of Planets, but certain requirements had to be met, and not having a feudal system was one of them. Four years ago, EiLeen had signed the documents stating that Imidestria was now a democracy, governed by a planetary leader and their sectional administrators, all elected every five years.

Never before had EiLeen felt so liberated, so free to do what she wanted and not have to be accountable for every second of her life. She had a mind for business, which had stood her well even as a queen, and it had taken her two years to double her already immense wealth. Now her latest business endeavor was to board the *Koenigin* en route to Gantharat, the planet the Supreme Constellation forces had helped liberate from the oppressive Onotharian Empire.

EiLeen stood and walked briskly down the gate to where the vessel was moored. The *Koenigin,* a luxury cruiser, catered to the wealthy.

Usually, she traveled on her own space yacht, but the situation with space pirates made such a voyage beyond SC borders dangerous. Hunt-and-assault fighter craft escorted the *Koenigin* whenever she went on these longer cruises.

As she stepped through the opening leading into the lobby, the captain and her senior crew greeted her.

"Welcome aboard the *Koenigin*, Madame Maxio. I'm Captain Dana Rhoridan and this is my next in command, Tory L'Ley. My crew and I will do our utmost to make this journey pleasant for you." The tall ice-blond woman stood at attention before EiLeen, and though it was a relief that the captain hadn't used her obsolete title, she had the distinct impression that Captain Rhoridan wasn't too thrilled at her presence.

"Thank you. I wish to be shown to my quarters immediately." She was exhausted after sitting through endless business meetings, and, though she hated to admit it, she felt every single one of her fifty-one years.

"Certainly, madame. Commander L'Ley will escort you. We'll be on our way as soon as the rest of the passengers have boarded."

EiLeen nodded curtly and followed the commander to her quarters. Behind them trailed several crew members and her personal assistant, Mock, hauling her hover luggage. Located on deck two, the quarters consisted of three bedrooms, en suite luxurious bathrooms, several rooms for entertaining, and an office with state-of-the-art computer and communication technology. She dismissed the commander at the door and allowed only Mock inside to unpack her baggage.

Mock had been her court attendee and footman ever since she was a mere princess. He was the closest thing to a father figure that she'd had, as her brother, the former king, had been a notorious rogue. King Reidder had hunted, chased both women and men for pleasure, and enjoyed his status as sovereign without much though for his nation's well-being. Taking over the reins had been hard on the young EiLeen. She'd been ruthless out of necessity while reconstructing the way Imidestria ought to be governed if it was to ever become a democracy.

"When you're done, Mock, do get some rest. We've been on our feet for two days straight. That's how I feel, at least." EiLeen removed her gloves and coat. Glancing longingly at the en suite, she knew she had more work to complete before she could indulge in a long, hot aqua-bath.

❖

Dana Rhoridan removed her gold-collared captain's jacket and tossed it onto a chair inside the door to her ready room. She virtually growled as she slumped back into her chair, frustrated with the new assignment. Flipping her computer screen open, she noticed another message from Fleet Admiral Ewan Jacelon. Yes, it was flattering for the highest-ranking officer in the fleet to contact her, but this mission was utter crap.

Dana had gotten used to working undercover during the last five years. She actually enjoyed being among mostly civilian spaceship personnel and had made some lifelong friends as their captain. Only two of her crewmembers knew of her military rank as captain: her first officer, Commander L'Ley, and the head chef, Paymé Soth. Paymé was a security officer in the SC fleet, and L'Ley held the same rank in the Marine Corps and had been undercover for almost a decade.

"And now we're babysitting a damn celebrity. A party princess. Oh no, *excuse* me, a *queen*." Dana pursed her lips as she drummed her fingers against the alu-carb desk. "Let's see what Jacelon wants." Dana opened the voice message, thinking it couldn't be a good thing, really, to hear from the fleet admiral himself.

"Captain Rhoridan, I trust by now that you've rendezvoused with EiLeen Maxio and have made sure she is installed in your presidential quarters." The white-haired handsome man who commanded the fleet and had faced down space pirates and the Onotharian Empire, and whose only daughter held one of the most powerful positions in the military as well as being a citizen of Gantharat, smiled politely. "I know you are under the impression that you're merely delivering her like an expensive, high-profile package to Corma, but that is only half the truth. You will go via the Corma home world first, but then you need to take Ms. Maxio to the small cluster of planets between the SC and Gantharat. This is where we helped heal and train the surviving resistance members we rescued from the Onotharian asteroid prisons. Ms. Maxio has urgent business at Revos Prime and I've made a personal promise to her that we'll take her there, swiftly and safely. I look forward to updates via security subspace communication channels." Ewan Jacelon nodded curtly. "Safe journey, Captain. Jacelon out."

Why the hell would EiLeen Maxio go to a planet inhabited only by rehabilitation staff, patients, and training camps for soldiers struggling to regain their strength to get back to reenlist? No doubt whatever endeavor the glamor-loving woman was up to involved money. The ex-queen must've pulled every string she'd ever collected to make someone like Jacelon dance to her tune. It still didn't make sense, and Dana knew better than to jump to conclusions too swiftly. Something was just completely annoying about this woman—her way of dismissing people like they were nothing but space dust clinging to her survival suit. Dana hadn't met EiLeen personally, but she'd of course read about her and seen her on transmissions when she was still the sole sovereign on Imidestria.

"And that's another weird piece of the puzzle. Why would such an attention-seeking celebrity give up practically owning an entire planet?" Dana murmured as she rose to prepare herself for the evening's dinner. Tradition dictated that Dana, as captain of the cruise ship, dine every evening with the VIPs. She undressed and stepped into the cleansing tube in the small en suite of her ready room. Just as she stepped out again, it dawned on her that EiLeen would most likely be at the table tonight. *Wonderful.*

An hour later, Dana went by the bridge to check on the unreliable space vortices they would pass later in the evening. The dust-filled maelstroms endangered ships unless the crew paid attention to the readings, as they moved without warning. If they managed to surprise a ship, its structural integrity could become compromised with micro fractures or even a full hull breach. So far, the vortices had stayed beyond the Bramanian asteroid belt, which meant Dana had no chance of having her dinner on the bridge instead.

She strode into the restaurant, its grandeur never ceasing to amaze her. Tall, old-fashioned brass columns supported the ten-meter ceiling. Vast viewports displayed the beauty of space on one side and a large stage at the far wall. The entertainment that commenced after dessert had been served was something new and fantastic every evening.

The table was impressively set as usual. As captain, Dana was expected to greet the VIPs chosen to accompany her, another duty she found rather silly, but she carried it out with the same diligence as she did everything else. Being the fourth generation in her family to captain a starship, Dana knew her reputation for being by-the-book and a stickler for rules and regulations preceded her.

Soon the dinner guests trickled in and Dana donned her best smile, shaking hands with dignitaries and celebrities as they took their seats. It hadn't escaped her attention that the seat to her right held a name-cube with the Imidestrian royal insignia. Just as she started to get her hopes up that EiLeen Maxio would not show, a faint murmur traveled among the five hundred and some passengers. Dana looked over toward the entrance and couldn't stop a gasp.

EiLeen Maxio might have abdicated, but the woman framed by the door opening radiated regality where she stood, scanning the room. Meeting Dana's eyes, EiLeen walked with obvious confidence between the tables toward her.

"Madame Maxio, welcome." Dana took EiLeen's hand to greet her like she'd done with the other eighteen guests at her table.

"Thank you, Captain." The proud stance and slight disdainful tone of EiLeen's voice grated on Dana's nerves.

Still holding EiLeen's hand in hers, Dana felt an utterly out-of-character spark ignite in the back of her mind. Not sure where the impulse originated, she raised EiLeen's hand to her lips and kissed the impossibly soft skin. She then let go of it and pulled the chair out. "I believe this is your seat."

EiLeen's violet eyes with their unique star-shaped pupils narrowed as she examined Dana's appearance. Dana refused to be intimidated by the former queen and sat down. Unfolding her napkin, she placed it on her lap as she nodded to the waiters to begin. As soon as they had served the first course, Dana raised her glass, as was her duty, and toasted the guests. "May your stay aboard the *Koenigin* be relaxing, pleasurable, and safe."

"Safe?" A woman two seats to Dana's left frowned. "Surely that is a given? I've heard about pirates, but isn't that a thing of the past, Captain?"

"Hush, darling," her husband said. "This ship has its own security detail. Like a small army." He smiled reassuringly. "Do you think Queen EiLeen would travel with this ship if it wasn't safe?"

Dana chewed on a Cormanian asparagus as she listened to the conversation. She wasn't surprised that the other guests knew who

EiLeen Maxio was. The reputation of her extravagant way of life and the many juicy details of her private life no doubt fascinated the public.

"Just call me EiLeen." The sonorous voice of the former queen made the man color faintly. "It's been years since I abdicated."

"Eh. Yes, of course, Your M—EiLeen."

Dana smiled inwardly at the man's discomfort. EiLeen had a way of shrinking the person she homed in on. Her eyes were like lasers, piercing right through the layers of garments and skin if you let them. Dana would make sure EiLeen knew this method didn't work on the captain of this ship.

"Tell me, Captain, how long have you commanded the *Koenigin*?" Another guest farther down the table, a young man sitting next to his parents, asked the question. He was handsome with his long, wavy hair in a ponytail. Dana estimated he was at least twelve years her junior.

"Four years." Dana smiled politely.

"You're very young to hold such a position," the young man's father said. He raised his eyebrow as if to imply that he found her *too* young.

"I started early." Dana was used to these types of questions. She kept her polite smile, but inwardly she sighed at the repetitiveness of this part of her job.

"Most civilian starship captains started in the military," an older woman to Dana's left said, her voice kind. "Was that the case for you as well, Captain?"

"Yes, it was." Dana forced herself not to shift uncomfortably. Sooner or later this topic appeared, and she was already preparing for the almost unavoidable follow-up question.

"Well, I don't blame you for getting out, with the war effort and everything," the first young man said, wrinkling his nose. "I mean, I'm all for letting the hardened soldiers deal with that." He pointedly elbowed his dad, who clearly agreed with him, judging from how he pursed his lips and nodded.

"We can thank the stars that not everyone reasons in the same spineless manner as you," EiLeen said, and put her utensils down. "If all people regarded the universe like that, empires with a knack for oppression would soon take over every planet in our sector."

"What—who do you—you cannot sit there and call my son spineless!" The young man's father looked like he was about to choke.

He stared at EiLeen, and Dana surmised that only her previous title kept him from demanding her thrown overboard for being insolent toward his offspring.

"I think I just did." EiLeen smiled maliciously. "Fortunately we live in a sector of space where we're allowed to have our opinion and not be jailed for voicing it. You see your son as the heir to your personal empire of…what is it you produce, Mr. Ta'Yans? Oh, now I remember. Among other things, you've built your wealth on plasma-pulse cassettes, haven't you? I imagine the war effort has increased your wealth tenfold." She wiped her mouth on the napkin and looked over at the approaching line of waiters. She turned to Dana, her eyes glittering. "Oh, look, how timely. The main course is here."

Dana wasn't sure whether to applaud EiLeen for putting the men in their place or smack her for being deliberately rude and not caring that she was. Was this what being a former queen did to you? As queen of Imidestria, EiLeen hadn't had absolute power, but damn close to it. The political experts had speculated about her reasons for abdicating, but so far, they were a closely held secret. Dana slowly shook her head at her, wanting her to know she wasn't entirely pleased with her display. To her surprise, EiLeen pressed her lips together and chuckled quietly while the waiters served the main course.

The rest of the meal passed without incident, but Dana was still relieved when the staff lowered the light and the entertainment began. Sitting to EiLeen's left, she moved her chair so she wouldn't hinder the other woman from seeing the stage. This brought them closer together and suddenly she was engulfed in EiLeen's scent. Discreet, but distinctive, the sweet and warm perfume, mixed with something dark and spicy, wrapped around her. A woman began a gentle Imidestrian song, her voice following the enticing scent, helping it to reach yet another of her senses. She turned her head just enough to look at EiLeen, who seemed to be listening intently to the song. Such a proud profile, completely regal with high cheekbones, a delicately bent nose, and a tall forehead. EiLeen's gray hair was combed back in stylish waves and she wore makeup that enhanced her beautiful features with a soft shimmer.

"Yes, Captain?" EiLeen suddenly murmured without turning her head. "Something I can do for you?"

Furious at being caught staring, Dana felt a blush creep up her neck and cheeks. "Just making sure I wasn't in your way, Madame Maxio."

"Please. EiLeen." A faint curl of EiLeen's lips made it clear that she wasn't buying Dana's explanation. "And I can see just fine."

Dana cursed herself inwardly and kept her eyes on the performers for the duration of the show.

CHAPTER TWO

The captain was an enigma and EiLeen was uncomfortable with things, or people, she couldn't fully figure out. Looking indeed far too young for her rank, Dana Rhoridan must have doctored her past. EiLeen sat on the bed in her quarters, computer on her lap, and searched the vast files she had access to, yet she could find only the basic information regarding the *Koenigin*'s captain. Thirty-four years old, Earth-born human, brought up by an aunt and uncle after being orphaned at age eight, graduated from college at age sixteen while living on the Alpha VII space station, and granted early entry to the SC Fleet Academy the same year.

EiLeen studied the formal cadet picture of a very young, fresh-faced Dana glowing with obvious pride. No doubt being accepted to the academy was her dream, but something else was present in those gray eyes that narrowed so easily while displaying contempt. EiLeen pulled up more official pictures of the *Koenigin*'s captain. In every single one, the woman looked impeccable. She kept her blond hair in a neat, low bun, her uniform without flaws, and the same guarded expression in her eyes.

A sudden thought made EiLeen use her top security-clearance codes, which included a rather intrusive retina scan, to access Supreme Constellations data. Surely she would find more on Dana Rhoridan in the top-secret files? She entered the search parameters and waited while the computer browsed the vast assortment of documents.

A strange beep and orange-colored screen informed her that, regrettably, all information regarding Dana Rhoridan was sealed. EiLeen stared, highly annoyed. Her security clearance equaled that of

Marco Thorosac, the SC's elected leader, and still she couldn't access these files. Infuriating! She pushed the computer aside and rose from the bed. Her legs felt jittery and her entire soul seemed to be restless. Not bothering to call on her discreet security detail that was always present, albeit quite invisible to most other people, she threw a golden-lace wrap around her shoulders and left her quarters.

The promenade was nearly void of people at this late hour. The ones awake were dancing or gambling in the vast rooms dedicated to this purpose, but even if she'd been known to gamble once in a while, it held no allure for her tonight. She had too much on her mind regarding her ongoing project and the purpose of this trip.

EiLeen followed the promenade on its outer track where she could enjoy the spectacular view of space whirling by. They were traveling at high velocity yet still within the limits that made it possible to enjoy the stunning colors of distant stars. EiLeen thought of Imidestria, her home world, which she'd governed for decades before her work behind the political scene came to fruition. The day she officially abdicated was the first day she'd been able to breathe freely after her brother died. The new planetary leader and sectional administrators, elected in the very first free election at such a level on Imidestria, had replaced her office, she had stepped down, and the next phase of her life had begun. She had no idea how the rumors of her being a luxury-loving, self-centered, manipulative bitch had started, but since these ideas about her seemed firmly cemented in people's minds, they worked as a great smoke screen.

"Madame Maxio? Is something wrong? Can I help you?" A low, soft voice spoke politely next to EiLeen, breaking into her thoughts.

EiLeen forced herself not to flinch, but turned toward Captain Rhoridan with what she hoped was a courteous smile. "Captain. Why would something be wrong? I'm merely taking an evening stroll. Much like yourself?"

Dana placed her hands on her back and shrugged. "This is part of my routine, to make one last round before bedtime. I learned that a long time ago."

"Can't be all that long, as you're not that old." EiLeen started walking again.

"Does your security detail know of you playing hooky like this?"

"Excuse me? Playing what?" EiLeen frowned as she tried to decipher the foreign word.

"Playing hooky? Stealing away without your guards?"

"My guards?" Scandalized at what that sounded like, EiLeen squared her shoulders and lengthened her stride. "You make me sound ready for an asteroid asylum."

"I wouldn't go that far," Dana said calmly. "And you're dodging the question."

"I had no idea I was accountable to a luxury-liner captain." EiLeen knew from the darkening of Dana's eyes that she'd struck just the right amount of haughtiness in her tone.

"You're correct. I'm the captain. That means I'm in charge aboard the *Koenigin* no matter the rank of her passengers. My first duty is passenger safety. You know you still have enemies, even if you've abdicated, madame. You shouldn't walk alone anywhere."

"So, not even abdicating and handing over the absolute power gave me my freedom back?" Surprised at how she allowed her bitterness to show, EiLeen stopped walking, resorting to anger. "I can certainly do without presumptuous individuals hell-bent on telling me how to live my life."

Dana blinked. "I…I apologize, madame. I had no such intention. I was merely concerned for your safety." Meeting EiLeen's anger with softness, Dana placed a hand on her arm. "May I escort you to your quarters?"

The anger seeped out and left EiLeen not exactly deflated, but tired and pensive. "By all means, if you must."

❖

Dana nodded politely and walked in silence next to EiLeen. She was slightly taller than the maddening woman, but the way EiLeen marched along the promenade forced her to lengthen her stride.

Dressed in a soft off-white suit and a golden throw made of some intricate lace, EiLeen definitely looked regal. Dana remembered seeing the abdication ceremony on her media screen in her captain's quarters. EiLeen had stood there, completely alone, but so rigid and determined despite the teary-eyed Imidestrians outside the palace area;

it was obvious this woman meant every word when she handed over her political power as well as her office.

They were just about to turn a corner to reach the corridor that contained the ship's elevators leading up to the presidential suites when the *Koenigin* lurched underneath them.

"What the—" Dana steadied herself against the railing along the wall and grabbed EiLeen's upper arm. "Hold on!" When she saw EiLeen clutch at the railing, Dana yanked her communicator from her lapel. "Captain Rhoridan to the bridge. Report."

"We're under attack, Captain," her next in command said hurriedly. "Two unidentified vessels on our port bow."

"Damages?"

"So far they are firing disruptive charges right next to the stabilizers. No actual hits. No casualties reported. Yet."

"I'm on my way. Red alert." The klaxons began their blaring sound through the corridors. "You heard that. I need to get to the bridge. I suggest you return—"

EiLeen shook her head. "No. I'm going with you."

"You're a passenger—"

"I'm going with you." EiLeen's eyes narrowed and it was clear she didn't intend to give in.

"Very well. Can you climb in those shoes? We can't use the elevators." Dana sighed inwardly as she reached the ladder leading up to the bridge. She began climbing and only allowed herself to glance down to make sure EiLeen wasn't falling to her death or something equally disastrous while climbing dressed in shoes with four-inch heels.

Opening the hatch leading onto the back of the bridge, Dana entered and, extending a hand to EiLeen, she helped her through the narrow, low entry.

"Captain on the bridge," an ensign called out smartly.

"Where are they now?" Dana moved to her chair, which her next-in-command, Tory L'Ley, vacated smoothly.

"Holding their position. They haven't fired a round in twenty seconds." Tory had barely finished speaking before another wave hit the *Koenigin*. Dana whipped her head around, looking for EiLeen, who was standing just behind her with a steady grip on the bar running behind the command chairs.

"Open communication channels," Dana said. "Unidentified vessels. This is Captain Dana Rhoridan of the cruise ship *Koenigin*. We are a civilian ship and not out to cause trouble for anyone. Cease firing or we will be forced to defend ourselves." Dana waited a few moments. "Unidentified—"

"You cannot match our firepower," a gruff voice growled over the sound system. "You have scanned us and seen what we're capable of."

"At first glance you might think you have the upper hand, yes," Dana said calmly. "You obviously do not have access to the upgraded specs of my vessel or you wouldn't be so bold."

"You? A damn pleasure ship? I think not." The man huffed and then the *Koenigin* reeled again.

"Commander L'Ley. Demonstrate to our buddy out there what he's missing. Just graze him."

"Aye, Captain. Firing."

Dana kept her eyes on the view screen and saw how a small green light traveled with startling speed toward the closest ship. A gush of dying sparkles appeared where the missile hit. "Now, that's what I'm talking about. Rhoridan to unidentified vessel. Next time I'll take out your weapons array, and if there is a third time, your propulsion system."

"What the hell was that?" the man on the ship yelled. Behind him Dana heard his klaxons nearly drowning out his voice. "Scan me again, Rhoridan. I have antimatter missiles targeting your ship dead center on your port side. That's where your guests are sleeping like babies and partying the night away, right?" He chuckled.

Dread ran down Dana's spine before she harnessed it and channeled it into the intense fury she was infamous for. "Close transmissions. Target the weapons array and the propulsion system on both ships. Do not miss."

"On it, Captain." L'Ley punched in commands, and soon eight green lights pierced the space between the *Koenigin* and the two ships. "Brace for impact."

Dana stood and pushed EiLeen into her chair. She pressed the sensor that strapped the clearly surprised woman into the command chair. Grabbing the bar behind the backrest, Dana followed her XO's advice.

The *Koenigin* rose like a bucking horse when the wave of the blasts reached them. "Speed one! Back us up. Keep weapons locked on them. Damage report."

"Minor injuries being reported from the infirmary, Captain. Inertial dampeners went offline briefly at the first blast, and apparently the first-class dining room is a mess."

"Then we're lucky if that's all." Dana rounded the command chair. "You all right?"

"I'm fine." EiLeen moved her hand as if to open the harness, but Dana stopped her by placing a hand on top of hers.

"Stay there. I'll have one thing less to worry about if you're safe in that chair," Dana murmured, leaning down. "I suggest you let your people know you're safe."

"I already have." EiLeen motioned to the screen where the immobilized strange vessels sat motionless. "We need to find out what they want."

"What's more," Dana said, and walked over to her operations officer's station, "we need to find out why this was way too easy. Why would they not disable us all at once, get what they came for, and then take off? Why give us time to retaliate and disable them when—"

"Intruder alert! Intruder alert!" The computerized voice over the communication system answered her questions in part.

"Report. And silence the damn klaxons so I can hear myself *think*." Dana turned back to the center of the bridge and watched her crew work their stations.

"Hull breaches on lower maintenance deck two. Unidentified individuals on board," the ensign at ops said.

"Assemble security team and intercept them. We can't allow them to reach the passenger decks. Can you tell how many?"

"Negative, Captain. Sensors indicate more than a dozen."

Dana squinted and sucked her lower lip in between her teeth as she processed the events to date.

"Captain! Several vessels decloaking on both sides of us. Ten smaller assault craft and two larger destroyers."

"What the hell's going on?" Dana turned and regarded EiLeen. "Battle stations. Ship-wide alert. All hands, this is the captain. Intruders are present on the lower decks and hostile ships are surrounding us. Secure the passengers and take your duty stations." Her crew was well trained when it came to security measures. Space pirates were always a concern, and while the war had raged between the Supreme Constellations and the Onotharian Empire, they had been prepared for all kinds of attacks.

"Lt. Freya, put as much space as possible between us and them while we sort this mess out."

"I can try, Captain, but their assault craft will gain on us soon enough," her trusted helmsman said. He punched in commands and the *Koenigin* shot forward between some of the small craft, its propulsion system sending them hurling to the side.

"I want to know why our shields failed to keep the intruders out." Dana was furious. Not long ago, during the war, space pirates had boarded the *Koenigin* and nearly hurled her and her bridge crew into open space. Her ship had spent several months in a Guild Nation space dock undergoing repairs and now *this*. A sudden thought hit her and she turned to EiLeen, who patiently sat in the captain's seat, observing everything.

"This happens within hours of collecting you. They attack within SC space, before our own assault craft and security detail escort us."

"You're probably correct." EiLeen was actually a little pale. "They could possibly be after me. Like you, I didn't foresee our own space as dangerous. In retrospect, I realize that assumption was naïve of both Admiral Jacelon and me."

"You're going to tell me all about what's going on once we've put enough distance between us and these...whoever they are."

"Shots fired on deck eleven, Captain!" the ensign at ops reported, her eyes huge. "Plasma-pulse fired on both sides. Commander Callah reports two of her officers injured and one of the intruders is dead. Eight of the intruders managed to reach the ladder system on that deck."

"So, they're willing to die for whatever they're after." Dana placed her hands on her hips.

"Am I wrong to assume the *Koenigin* is equipped with smaller star shuttles for emergencies?" EiLeen stood and approached Dana. "I cannot stay onboard and risk the lives of the passengers. If I leave, I will draw their attention and you can alert SC Command."

Dana stared at the calm woman who clearly had lost her mind. "You're not going anywhere. We're already transmitting to—"

"Apologies, Captain, but we're not transmitting anything to anyone." The ops ensign's red face spoke of even worse trouble.

"Whatever these people are doing, it's scrambling our long-distance sensors and communications. Putting distance between us and those in pursuit doesn't matter. They evidently brought the scrambler onboard with them."

"All the more reason for me to leave, Captain. Give me a shuttle and I'll draw them away."

"As heroic as that sounds—"

A sudden blast made the *Koenigin* rock under their feet. Inertial dampeners went offline for a few moments, sending EiLeen crashing into Dana, who managed to stabilize them. Holding on to EiLeen, Dana felt her tremble, but something told her that adrenaline from fury rather than fear had caused it.

"Now what?" Dana snarled the words, frustrated at how intruders were once again handling her ship.

"The intruders are attaching explosives, and if they keep that up, they'll cause a major hull breach on the passenger decks. Their path is taking them directly to the bridge."

"Damn it. If they have that type of explosives, not even our safety doors will keep them out." Dana thought quickly. EiLeen's idea had some merit, but no way would she allow any of her passengers to put themselves in danger alone, least of all a former queen who was connected among the SC leadership.

She rushed over to the tall cabinet that held the bridge's stock and pulled out a plasma-pulse rifle and a few sidearms. Then she filled a backpack with as many ammunition pods as she could carry. "Commander L'Ley, I hereby put you in command of the *Koenigin* and leave the welfare of her crew and passengers in your capable hands. Madame Maxio, you're with me. We're going to have to make it down to the shuttle deck and make sure they see us leave. Once we're far enough away, L'Ley, your duty is to take out the intruders and alert SC Command. Make sure Admiral Ewan Jacelon hears of this and that they send backup. Do not engage the enemy on your own. The passengers' safety takes precedence."

"Aye, Captain." L'Ley pressed her lips together. "Just…the two of you in a shuttle—"

"They've been upgraded at the Guild Nation dock. These fools might not realize that." Dana glanced at EiLeen. "You won't be able to bring anything from your quarters. We need to move fast."

"I have what I need and, what's more, what I think they're after, right here." She extended a hand. "I'm quite able to handle a sidearm, Dana."

Dana hesitated only for a moment and then handed one of them over, knowing this was the safest way since they would have each other's back from now on, at least until help reached them. "Set to stun."

"Of course. Very humane." EiLeen checked her weapon expertly.

"Let's go. Sail with the stars to protect you, Commander L'Ley."

Her next-in-command shook her head in obvious dismay. "And you, Captain."

CHAPTER THREE

EiLeen wished she had worn something a little more practical as they once again climbed through one ladder tunnel after another. Her suit was comfortable enough, but even though the *Koenigin* crew kept the cruise ship immaculate, she was starting to look worn and disheveled. If that wasn't bad enough, her suit had no pockets, which meant she had to tuck the sidearm Dana had provided her inside her waistband. She kept feeling for it as she struggled to keep up with Dana.

"This is where we change tunnels. Level twelve. Only eight more to go to reach shuttle deck," Dana whispered. She poked her head out into the corridor. "Damn."

"What's wrong?" EiLeen pressed closer, peering over Dana's shoulder. "Source of divinity, what's happened?"

"Someone fired their weapon in here. Those are burns from plasma-pulse weapons." Dana pointed at the scorch marks on the walls and the floor. "Only one good thing, no sight of bodies or blood."

"Unless it'd been their bodies," EiLeen said calmly. She pulled her weapon and checked the setting. "Sure we should keep them at a stun setting?"

"Yes. I can't say I have any warm feelings for anyone boarding my ship, but I'd rather keep them alive to question them."

"I see." EiLeen watched Dana duck into the corridor and followed her, staying close to the damaged wall. "At least the passengers are staying clear of these people."

"So far, yes." Dana stopped at a junction and peered around the corner. She pulled her head back quickly and pressed closer to the wall. "Damn. Two individuals in black coveralls twenty meters down that way. We need to get across to reach the last tunnel. How's your accuracy?"

"I'm a good shot." EiLeen wasn't bragging. Her chief of security had trained her for years to become proficient with several types of weapons.

"We only get one chance or they'll alert the others, and we have no way of knowing how close they are." Dana gripped her sidearm with both hands. "I'll aim for the one to the left. You take the one to the right."

"By all means." EiLeen double-checked her weapon and nodded.

Not making a sound, Dana stepped out into the intersecting corridor with EiLeen only a fraction of a second behind her. They aimed and fired as one, and the two people dressed in black fell silently to the floor.

"Should we check on them?" EiLeen raised her gun to her shoulder.

"No. No time. Come on!" Dana tugged at her arm, and they rushed to the tunnel and began descending again.

EiLeen wasn't prone to mind ghosts, but this time she fully expected voices to yell into the tunnel and fire at them as they hurried down the steps. Her legs were beginning to tremble from the repetitive movement, but she forced herself to keep going. She wasn't used to this type of physical exercise, even though she took pride in keeping fit and in good shape. It was hardly a surprise that Dana barely broke a sweat despite everything.

"Almost there, madame."

"For all divinity, call...me...EiLeen!" Growling the word and hating to sound so out of breath, EiLeen gasped as she nearly lost her grip of the ladder. Her foot missed the next step and she was trembling too much to regain her footing.

"EiLeen!" Dana suddenly gripped her calf, steering her foot to the next step. "Don't let go. Can you feel the step? There?" She kept her hand firmly where it was.

"Yes, yes. I'm fine." Clutching at the ladder, EiLeen continued her descent. Dana's hand seemed to be what she needed to stabilize the tremors. Was she having an onset of nerves in her middle years? Ridiculous. Nerves? If she was infamous for anything, it was for inducing bad cases of nerves, not suffering from them.

"We're here. Let me check the corridor. Something tells me they're not stupid enough to leave our shuttle deck unsupervised."

Unwilling to be left alone in the suffocating tunnel, EiLeen shook her head. "I'm going with you."

Dana looked hesitant for a moment but then nodded. "Actually, I'd rather have you where I can protect you. Good point, Ma—EiLeen." She smiled mirthlessly and motioned for EiLeen to once again move in behind her. "Stay close."

That last order wasn't hard to follow. Only a few centimeters shorter than Dana, Eileen not only felt safe with the fierce captain, but for the first time she didn't become entirely volatile when someone else took command. Well, Dana did know her own vessel best and was officially in charge.

"I hear…something." Dana leaned back, whispering. "Who or whatever it is, it's getting closer. It sounds…off."

EiLeen listened hard. Yes, something sounded off, all right. An eerie sound as if something slithered along the corridor made the small hairs on her arms and legs stand up. The flickering light in the corridor from the now-muted red-alert klaxons didn't help.

"On three?" EiLeen suggested, half-joking, half-frustrated.

"Yes. We can't stay here. They'll find us sooner or later." Dana raised her weapon and nodded grimly. "One, two, three!"

Dana going high, EiLeen low, they did a quick glance outside. At first EiLeen didn't see anything, but then she lowered her gaze and the sight of the woman on the deck made her gasp.

"Ensign Saghall." Dana hurried over to the young woman who was crawling along the bulkhead, clutching her leg. Behind her a trail of blood told the sad story of her nearly severed limb. "Keep a lookout for the intruders, EiLeen." Dana fell to her knees next to the chalk-white, perspiring ensign.

EiLeen kept an eye on the corridor, but the only movement came from the ensign, who seemed determined to continue along the corridor floor. Not about to stand idly by when she was needed, she knelt next to Dana, not caring that her trousers now absorbed a fair amount of blood as well. "Ensign, stop, please." She placed gentle hands on the young woman's shoulders as Dana removed the ensign's belt to place around the bleeding leg. "Your captain is helping you. My name is EiLeen and you're safe with us. No, Ensign, please. You have to remain still. You're hurting yourself."

"Got to alert…the captain…intruders…" Ensign Saghall's words were hardly intelligible because blood trickled between her lips at every syllable.

"I'm here, Saghall. See? Here." Dana pulled the belt tight and the bleeding woman whimpered. She leaned over Saghall. "I'm here and you've done very well getting this far. Did they surprise you in the shuttle bay?"

"No. Deck two, Capt—" Saghall shuddered.

"She got here from deck two?" EiLeen looked over at Dana, who pressed her lips into a tight line.

"Elevator," Saghall said, then closed her eyes and slumped to the floor.

"Damn. I can't just leave her here. I have to risk alerting the medical staff." Dana ran a hand over her face before she grabbed her communicator. "Rhoridan to the infirmary. Casualty, Saghall, ensign, on deck four. Immediate evacuation required. Life-and-death situation."

"Aye, Captain, Lieutenant Irah here. We're close already but have to move with caution." The calm male voice over the comm channel spoke solemnly.

"Use caution, but hurry. Ensign Saghall is in a bad way."

"There in two minutes, ma'am."

EiLeen had kept her fingertips on Saghall's neck and was growing rapidly concerned. "She's weak. Very weak, Dana."

"They'll be here. We should move on to the shuttle bay area, but…" Dana paled. "I can't."

"Neither can I, so just take a deep breath, Captain." EiLeen spoke Dana's title with a gentle, teasing tone, wanting to reassure her. Another out-of-character action. How odd.

"I think I hear the med staff. Watch Saghall." Dana raised her weapon and directed it toward the elevators. "Guess they would have to use the elevators to move fast enough."

The door opened farther down the corridor and a security detail moved out first, looking relieved at finding their captain and their wounded crewmate.

A tall, burly man hurried over to them and took charge. "Damn it, Saghall, what have I told you about doing stuff like this?"

"Sorry?" Saghall looked up. "Captain?"

"Here, Ensign." Dana bent over the woman. "Yes?"

"Just…watch out. Strange weapons. Unknown. Weird-looking…"

"Understood, Ensign. Now let Dr. Irah take care of you. I expect to see you well on the road to recovery when I return."

"Yes, Captain." Saghall closed her eyes again.

"And we have to hurry." Dana stood and extended a hand to EiLeen, who studiously ignored it and jumped to her feet as well. She wasn't old enough that she needed help getting up yet.

"We better hurry. They might have picked up on you alerting the infirmary." EiLeen raised her hands, palms forward. "I know. It had to be done."

"Let's go. Be careful, Irah."

"And you, Captain." The doctor nodded grimly before focusing on his patient.

EiLeen was relieved that the door to the shuttle bay was only a short distance away. When it closed behind them, Dana punched in a command and spoke rapidly. "Computer. Place a security seal on this door. Senior staff access only." A long beep confirmed her command. "Good. That will delay them if they try to enter while we're still here."

Following Dana, EiLeen found herself standing next to what had to be the smallest shuttle known to SC space. "Are we going in that?"

"No arguing. Trust me." Dana opened the back hatch and motioned for EiLeen to get in. The interior appeared marginally larger than the exterior, but it would still be a cramped space for two people. Especially when one of them was used to her own suite while traveling.

"Strap in," Dana said, continuing her terse orders. "We have to be really, really quick if we're going to get the head start we require."

EiLeen knew it was fruitless to argue and strapped herself into the co-pilot seat. As soon as she heard Dana click her harness closed, the shuttle was hovering and the wide doors opening just enough to let them through. Stars lit up the interior with a cool light that made Dana's hair look like the Imidestrian silver brooks.

"So, they need to see us leaving but not have time to react too fast and gain on us." Dana spoke in a muttering voice. She punched in more commands and then leaned back and briefly closed her eyes as they shot through the opening. "Imagine that only a few hours ago, my main concern was that you had insulted a man at the captain's table."

"He had it coming." EiLeen looked in dismay at the state of her clothes. "For all divinity, please tell me this dinghy has computers strong enough to replicate?"

"Yes. It may be small, my *Queen*, but it's more fully outfitted than any of your own ships, small or big."

Grinding her teeth at the deliberate use of her former, and so loathed, title, EiLeen unfastened her harness and stood. "Then I will clean up and change. I may be running for my life and trying to save the *Koenigin* passengers, but I see no reason to look like a space pirate's third harlot."

"For stars and skies! Has anyone ever told you how annoyingly shallow you can act?" Dana flung her hands in the air.

"Several people have. And frequently." EiLeen smirked and entered the miniscule restroom. Gazing at her reflection, she made a face. Yes, a vain, shallow, and luxury-loving bitch. She had cultivated this image for years, yet it stung when the bitter words fell from Dana's lips.

Only when she had recycled her torn and sullied clothes and stood in the cleansing tube, did she realize how Dana had worded her accusation. "...how annoyingly shallow you can *act*?" Not be. *Act*. There was a difference. Could it be that Dana realized she was acting, that there was more to the former queen she seemed to loathe so much than the fancy clothes and taste for luxury?

CHAPTER FOUR

Dana double-checked the long-range sensors and saw that the decloaked ships that had surrounded her beloved *Koenigin* now were in pursuit, but at a reasonably safe distance. She overviewed the autopilot settings before she finally relaxed. Rubbing the back of her neck, she moaned.

"You should clean up. It's remarkable what it does to revive the spirits." EiLeen's voice from behind her made Dana jump.

Turning around, she took in the vision of the woman she had to protect until she could deliver her to Admiral Jacelon. Dressed in a light-gray coverall, EiLeen still managed to look poised and elegant. Her short hair lay in stylish waves around her face and she stood as if on display on some podium. Such dignity had to come naturally to her after being the leader and constantly in the public eye for so many years.

"Sounds wonderful, but I can't leave the helm. They're in pursuit." She hoped she didn't come off as too acerbic.

"I do know how to read sensors and pilot a shuttle," EiLeen said, sounding bored. "It will take you only a few minutes."

"You know how to pilot a star shuttle?" Dana knew she sounded disbelieving, but the idea that any royalty piloted anything was too much.

"Yes." EiLeen offered no explanations but sounded confident.

"Please." She stood and offered EiLeen her place. "It's not that I think you're exaggerating, but perhaps I should make sure you—"

"Sensors are there. Our guests are far enough away to not cause too much worry." EiLeen let her fingertips grace the console. "We're traveling at optimal speed for a shuttle of this type, and you've set the weapons array on standby to be brought online within seconds, should we need it. You can leave."

Dana had opened her mouth to tell EiLeen just where she could tuck her superior attitude, when she saw a faint sparkle of amusement in her eyes. Suddenly hard-pressed not to burst into undignified giggles, Dana nodded curtly. "Fine. I'll only be a minute." She squeezed by EiLeen, involuntarily inhaling the typical scent of cleansing agent and something that had to be EiLeen's own. The dark, faintly woodsy fragrance fit her well, and the stars only knew where she had kept it. Did the woman carry perfume oils in her pockets?

Efficient as usual, Dana tore off her clothes, entered the cleansing tube, and felt the hum of the sonar waves run through her body and rid her of the sweat and grime that crawling around the inner parts of the *Koenigin* had bestowed upon her. She grudgingly had to concede that EiLeen was right; it did feel better, much better, to be clean. About to replicate a new uniform, she thought better of it and chose the same gray coverall that EiLeen wore. It was softer and wasn't as tight or confining as her uniform. Realizing that the hairclip she used to put her hair up in its usual low bun was broken, she replicated elastic and created a simple ponytail. Not about to admit any form of vanity on her part, Dana was secretly proud of her long, blond hair and reluctant to cut it even when it was a chore to maintain.

She returned to the small bridge and stood watching EiLeen. How infuriating she was, and how utterly beautiful. EiLeen was studying the helm console with complete focus, her brow marred with a few wrinkles as she concentrated.

"What's our status?" She let EiLeen remain in the pilot's seat and took the navigation officer's seat right next to it.

"Same distance to the pursuers. All systems are functioning. Nothing new."

"Then we have some time before we decide where to set down and get you to safety."

"And apprehend these...these thugs." EiLeen turned darkened eyes to Dana. "They've shown nothing but callous determination. An SC asteroid prison seems too lenient."

"That's what we have to offer. We can't disregard the directives of our legislators."

"I know. I merely keep seeing that young woman, Ensign Saghall, dragging herself along the corridor soaked in her own blood. I'm sure these fools could not care less about her and potentially ruining her life. If she survives that type of blood loss."

"The *Koenigin*'s medical staff is highly skilled to deal with trauma. If they got her there in time, they'll save her." Dana realized she was trying to convince herself as much as EiLeen. "I know seeing such wounds in real life can be hard."

"I've seen my share of wounds, but it's gut-wrenching to realize these criminals were after me and are hurting innocents in the process. I sincerely hope they left your ship alone once they realized I'd escaped."

That was Dana's fear as well. "I might be able to reach the ship via subspace communications." She turned to the console and punched in a few commands. "Shuttle One to the *Koenigin*. Come in." Waiting for a moment, she repeated the process. "*Koenigin*, this is Shuttle One. Do you read?"

"—*nigin*. L'Ley here, Captain. Secure channel implemented."

"Excellent. Status report."

"Sweeping the ship for hostiles as we speak, Captain. From what internal sensors suggest, they all took off after you. Are you all right, ma'am?"

"We're fine. Staying well ahead of the enemy. What about Ensign Saghall?"

"I regret to inform you that Ensign Saghall didn't make it. She'd lost too much blood. I'm sorry, Captain."

Dana heard a muffled gasp behind her and turned around. EiLeen was pale now, her breathing erratic. "I'm sorry to hear this, Commander. Ensign Saghall will be missed. Very much so." Dana swallowed hard. "So young…"

"Yes. She was. I have taken steps to notify next of kin and prepare for the return of her remains. What a complete and horrible mess. This is a cruise ship, for stars and skies." L'Ley's distraught tone came through, even though she clearly tried to stay collected.

"Agreed. I'll try to contact you every hour on the hour. In the meantime I expect you to return to our closest emergency port. As soon as you can safely do so, file a subspace report to SC Command." She stopped talking when EiLeen briefly touched her arm. "Yes? You have something to add, Madame Maxio?"

"Commander L'Ley. This is EiLeen Maxio. When you contact SC Command, you must give the details only to Admiral Ewan Jacelon. It's imperative that you understand this."

"Ma'am?" L'Ley's voice showed trepidation as well as confusion. "Captain?"

"Sound advice," Dana said, frowning at EiLeen. "Contact only Jacelon until we know what we're dealing with."

"But you need backup ASAP, Captain."

"We do." EiLeen interrupted, looking unperturbed. "That said, if you talk to the wrong person within the SC, you might as well be signing our death sentence. There's far more at stake than you realize, Commander. Do I make myself clear?"

"Captain?" L'Ley sounded as if she was torn between being cordial to former royalty and thinking said royalty was being a presumptuous busybody.

"For now, Commander, I second Madame Maxio's *suggestion*." Glowering at EiLeen, daring her to object to her choice of words, Dana closed the subspace communication link. She studied EiLeen, secretly amazed at how confident the woman appeared. Here she was, being pursued by ruthless people who clearly didn't care who they hurt to get to her, and she wasn't above issuing orders as if she were still the reigning queen of Imidestria. "Now, tell me how you can presume to give my next-in-command orders."

"I know about the positions that your Commander L'Ley and one of your chefs hold within the SC Fleet. You're not just a cruise-ship captain, as admirable as that can be, but you hold the same rank within the fleet." EiLeen tilted her head, her narrowing eyes studying Dana closely. "Same goes for L'Ley and the chef."

"Why would you dream up something like that?"

"Because as an intelligence operative, I have top security clearance." Leaning back in the pilot's seat, EiLeen smiled enigmatically. "And before you call me delusional, I'd suggest you check in with Jacelon at the first opportunity to corroborate this. He's the one who...hmm, drafted me." She chuckled. "I wasn't all that hard to persuade, as I was beyond bored with doing nothing after my abdication. When Jacelon pointed out how the SC could benefit from using me and my network of powerful friends, I agreed to go through the training. That's one of the reasons we need to return to Revos Prime."

"God. You're a spook?" Dana slumped against the backrest. "So, what is it you have, or know, that these fools chasing us are after?"

"It's not what I have. It's what I mean to hand over. I promise you, all will be revealed."

"And you're not going to tell me now?"

EiLeen shook her head, now with a cautious expression in her eyes. "I can't be careful enough. I know you're trusted, and certainly your actions speak volumes about how dependable and dedicated you are. That said, you don't have high enough clearance for me to brief you." She shrugged but didn't look very apologetic.

"This is insane. I can't understand why Jacelon would keep me in the dark. I've been undercover as a civilian captain for years. Damn!" Slapping her right armrest, she pressed her lips together to stop from saying anything that might make matters worse.

"Dana, please. This is a mission that can't fail." EiLeen's voice changed, losing its flippant tone. "Lots of people depend on its success. I ask you to trust me, and your admiral, and help me reach Revos Prime—or a vessel that can take me there. Quickly."

"I can't hand you over to just any vessel." Aghast, Dana envisioned such a scenario ending in total disaster with her as the scapegoat. "This shuttle can't travel much faster than this, which means it'll take us at least three weeks to get to Revos Prime."

"Then we need to use another type of spacecraft."

"Yes." Dana agreed. "Let me work on a plan for us to do that without the official hassle."

"Are you saying you're prepared to accept my orders?" EiLeen raised one eyebrow in a trademark example of her ever-present disdain.

"No. I accept Jacelon's orders, and that's it. If they coincide with your *suggestions*, then fine." Dana motioned for EiLeen to change seats with her. "I need to make course corrections."

"Very well, by all means." EiLeen rose to switch seats.

As they passed each other in the confined area between the chairs, Dana accidentally brushed against EiLeen's arm. Her skin erupted with goose bumps. The soft scent engulfed her, traveled along her senses, marked her. She glanced at EiLeen, wondering if she'd noticed anything. It was hard to tell as EiLeen had her superiority mask slapped on so hard, no personal expression was readily distinguishable.

Dana pulled up the star chart that showed every miniscule civilian space station. "Your idea has some merit," she said, muttering. "If we lose this shuttle and move on in another…um, acquired ship, we could go faster and make things harder for our 'friends.' By the way, who are they? Or is that beyond my security-clearance grade?"

"I honestly couldn't tell you. I know what they want, or at least I think I do." Sitting down with her usual elegant grace, EiLeen tapped her lips with her index finger. "They're well financed, well connected, or they wouldn't have half a squadron of ships at their disposal, let alone people ready to die for the task at hand. Ridding ourselves of this rowboat of a shuttle gets us to Revos Prime faster, that much is clear, but how do you propose we do that?"

"I can see only one way. Look here." She tapped the star chart. "This space station is a sordid little run-down pleasure dome where outcasts and shady characters gamble their hard-earned, or stolen, credits. What many of them have is really nice ships. That's how they stay clear of the SC patrols."

"Don't the SC patrols close down such places as this station?" EiLeen leaned in close, her hair tickling Dana's temple as she placed a hand on her armrest.

"They try, but as soon as they do, someone toggles the empty station somewhere else, and the word spreads fast among these people. It doesn't take them long to have it up and running. Sometimes rich and very bored passengers who travel with the *Koenigin* ask us to detour to one of these stations. I never do, but their requests make me aware of their location. Or last known coordinates, at least."

"So, what's your plan?" EiLeen supported herself against Dana's knee as she perused the star chart.

"Steal a ship, of course." It was a thrill to see EiLeen's eyes widen at her words. She held back a wry smile as EiLeen nodded thoughtfully, an odd look on her face. She actually appeared a little impressed.

"It'll take us about four hours to reach the station. At our current speed, that should give us about two hours, wouldn't you say, to obtain another vessel. A fast one, at that. Any idea how to go about it? I mean, nobody would leave their ship unsupervised at such a place, and there are just two of us." EiLeen's star-shaped pupils shrank as the light from the stars outside hit them.

"I think they'll perceive us, two women traveling alone, as quite harmless," Dana said. "I do have a plan, but you might not like it."

"As long as I don't have to sleep with any of them to procure a ship." EiLeen straightened and looked regally at Dana.

"I wouldn't go that far," Dana managed to say after nearly choking on EiLeen's words. "No sex for favors or coercion—that's not how I operate."

"No sex." EiLeen tilted her head again, a movement that clearly indicated that she was trying to probe Dana's mind.

As Dana hatched the plan of their heist, she briefly touched her temple. Oddly enough she still felt EiLeen's soft and silky strands caressing it. She was starting to think she was imagining things and was due for a long vacation, so she squared her shoulders and pulled at her coverall. She missed the protection of her leather-like jacket, but no garment invented or designed would protect her from attraction, welcome or not. "For my plan to work, I'll need your full cooperation, no questions asked."

This statement did not sit well with her ex-majesty. Her lips suddenly pinched, her eyes a stormy color of pale gray, and her body language rigid, EiLeen nodded slowly. "Against my better judgment and only because Admiral Jacelon praised your service record and your ability to, and I quote, 'think on your feet.' That is a weird expression, but I understand the meaning. You're very good at being undercover."

Dana's cheeks warmed at the matter-of-fact praise. She wasn't used to being the subject of a humanoid sensor sweep like this. It disconcerted her and made her nervous. The fact that EiLeen's steadfast, scrutinizing once-over left her breathless was shocking as well. Not only was it completely unprofessional to react physically to those placed in her care, but she hadn't allowed herself to feel anything of a personal nature for a long time. This woman, almost twenty years her senior, was way out of her league, socially and, according to EiLeen's description of her new duties, professionally. Still, she couldn't allow herself to be concerned about that. She needed to get them to the illegal space station before their pursuers showed up.

A lot was at stake and their lives depended on it.

CHAPTER FIVE

EiLeen walked over to the narrow alcove that held a bunk bed. Reluctantly admitting she was bone-tired, she lay down and pulled a blanket over herself. The propulsion system had a soothing effect as it hummed and reverberated throughout the hull. She closed her eyes and immediately saw the vision of the blond beauty that was her captain. Dana Rhoridan infuriated her at times, but her undisputed courage and allure were as mind-blowing as they were unexpected.

EiLeen admired Dana's fierce nature, but she didn't welcome the attraction she experienced. She had no time for such complications in her life at this point. She had so many obligations—perhaps even more than when she was queen. That was another refreshing aspect of Dana—she didn't bow and scrape or try to bask in the royal glory like so many others did. Instead, Dana seemed to question and challenge her every chance she got, which of course also annoyed her.

Turning on her side, EiLeen held the blanket close to her chest. What would Dana's hair look like when not pinned up in that austere bun? Would it curl around her fingers or…? Gasping at where her train of thought was taking her, EiLeen pressed a hand to her chest as if to calm her suddenly racing heart. "Really." As she muttered into the pillow, she tried to erase the imagery of lacing her fingers through long blond tresses of hair, or even burying her face just like so.

"I set the alerts on high sensitivity so we can both rest for a few hours." Dana's voice made EiLeen jump. "I don't know about you, but I'm exhausted."

"I'm fine. I can take the helm if you like."

"Not necessary. The computer will alert us if we need to correct

anything manually or if sensors detect anything remotely suspicious."
Dana climbed into the upper bunk and gave a muted moan as she settled
onto the mattress. "Stars and skies, I'm sore."

"Are you all right?" EiLeen peered up at the top bunk.

"To quote you, I'm fine. Just sore. I'm pretty sure you're feeling
it too?"

"Feeling what?"

"The tendons, the muscles, and fatigue. We need some emergency
rations. We haven't eaten since dinner."

"Tell me where they are, I'll get them." EiLeen sat up.

"No need to get up. You'll find some rations and enhanced water
in the cabinet to your right. This shuttle will sustain us for more than
two months."

"How utterly comforting." Knowing she sounded pesky and out
of sorts, EiLeen opened the cabinet and was soon munching a tasteless
ration bar. "Would it hurt anyone to spice it up a little?" she muttered
around the bite. "And make it less like paper?"

"They're nutritious but definitely not gourmet fare." Dana
chuckled and leaned over the edge of her bed. "Actually, they're not
too bad once you get used to them."

"Yes, they are. They're awful." It was impossible not to return
Dana's smile when she saw the impish look on her face. It was
refreshing to see the otherwise stern captain joke. Suddenly Dana's hair
came undone and tumbled down toward her. She drew a deep breath as
the fragrant masses of blond locks swayed right next to her. Without
thinking, she touched them reverently. "Oh. Such beauty."

"Damn. That was my last clasp. The other two broke earlier. Sorry
about that." Dana turned a pretty shade of pink. "I know. I should cut it
to a decent length. My commander tells me that all the time."

"No!" Stopping herself from gushing, EiLeen shook her head.
"That'd be a crime. You have beautiful hair."

"And this is a totally surreal conversation to have aboard a star
shuttle while hounded by thugs." Twisting her hair into a low knot,
Dana snorted. "But thank you for the compliment. I guess it's a sign of
vanity to keep it like this."

"Nothing wrong with that." EiLeen turned on her back and gazed
up at Dana. "Sometimes it's hard to remember that we're also women,
really just regular people with hopes and dreams like everybody else.

We give so much of ourselves to our nations, to the SC, and it's all about duty. I admit that at times I've felt completely drained. Depleted."

"Was that why you abdicated?"

EiLeen flinched. "No." She wanted to share the reason, but habit, perhaps more than anything else, made her remain silent.

"Sorry. None of my business, I suppose." Looking awkward, Dana disappeared from view.

"It's all right. I'm just not used to talking about it. It's not really a secret or interesting, but I didn't abdicate because being a queen exhausted me."

"You don't have to explain if you're uncomfortable." Dana's face showed up again. "Mind if I join you a bit? I'm certainly not comfortable hanging upside down."

"By all means." Her heart rate increased when Dana climbed down and even more so when Dana sat down next to her, pulling her legs up and wrapping her arms around them.

"Then share what you can…and want, please." Dana looked so young with her hair once again tumbling around her shoulders.

"Oh. All right." Hating how she dithered, which was something she *never* did otherwise, EiLeen took a breath. "I was never meant to be queen. My brother, however, was groomed from day one of his existence to be king. We even went to different types of schools, which is why he and I had a different outlook on things." She plucked at her sleeve and then pushed herself up into a half-lying position against the pillows. "I had traveled incognito for years, seen other worlds, visited Earth and Corma multiple times and observed how their societies thrived in complete democracy. I felt Imidestria's government was reactionary and old-fashioned. When I was crowned, it was as if my life was over."

"Why was that?" Her eyes darkening with sympathy, Dana placed a hand on top of EiLeen's foot.

"I enjoyed working as an ambassador of sorts. But I was a prisoner at the palace, and the only other place I saw regularly was the Manbular Nesto. That's our governmental building in Imicaloza, our capital."

"Yes, I know. I've been to Imidestria several times, but I've seen only the main sights while on leave from the *Koenigin*."

"Then you know, it's a large, not very beautiful structure, and it's even less appealing inside. Anyway, I was dreading having to be the one with the ultimate, if not complete, power. My first session at the Manbular Nesto…it was horrible. The things the local politicians and businessmen bring before their queen is astounding. I broached the idea of altering the ruling system. If Imidestria was to gain membership in the Supreme Constellations Unification of Planets, we needed modernizing. Getting rid of myself, so to speak, was the first step. I proposed a course of action that would make me obsolete, but it took much longer than I had hoped.

"Then, four years ago, the moment arrived. Finally I was ready to hand over my role to a democratic, freely elected government. I was free, or so I thought. As it turned out, SC Intelligence made me an offer that was too good to pass up. I realized that working as an undercover liaison would let me remove myself from Imidestria and not hinder progress. I could use my status as former queen of Imidestria and gain access to the inner circles on most worlds within or outside SC space." Tipping her head back, she closed her eyes. "It was in my interest, and I suppose in the SC's as well, that I cultivate my image as a luxury-loving, harmless ex-royal bitch."

"Even when it deterred potential personal relationships," Dana said softly.

EiLeen flinched and snapped her eyes open. "Yes. Quite."

"Sounds lonely." Dana seemed unaware that she was actually rubbing gently along EiLeen's lower leg.

"It can be. As you know, that's the nature of the beast, so to speak, when you work undercover."

"Yes, but I don't feel I have to act out of character every single day." Dana frowned.

"Who says it's out of character?" Laughing mirthlessly, she tried to ignore the escalating tingling where Dana's hand now merely rested against her shin.

"I've only known you for, what is it? A little more than a day? I think I've seen enough of how you conduct yourself when we've been alone together to claim that you are not that one-dimensional. I'm sure you can be—what did you call it—a luxury-loving bitch? Oh, quit glaring at me. I mean, that's hardly all you are. If you were, no way you'd give up the throne, risk your life like this." Dana suddenly stared at her roaming hand and then yanked it away. "Sorry."

"Don't be." A lump, immovable and nearly choking her, sat in her throat at Dana's words. "Believe me, not many people dare to touch me. Really haven't for many years."

"Wha—? Really?"

"You sound surprised." EiLeen chuckled at Dana's baffled expression. "Well, apart from an endless series of hand-kissing, which I detest now, apparently my level of intimidation forestalls any potential attempts. Until just now."

"I find it hard to believe that someone as lovely as you doesn't happen upon people brave enough to do more than kiss your hand." Dana tentatively shifted and placed her hand on EiLeen's ankle. "Why are you frowning? Surely you know you're attractive?"

"If I'm frowning, it's because I wonder about your motives. Why would you suddenly call me lovely, touch me, and act so interested in why I abdicated, etcetera?" EiLeen knew she was pushing Dana away like she did with everyone else, but it was how she operated, what she was used to.

"Hey, no need to be pesky. I have no other motives, or agendas, than getting us out of this mess alive. As for this," Dana said in a low voice and squeezed EiLeen's ankle lightly, "I think you know I have no reason to lie or be obtuse. We have a break right now before things get dicey again, so it's just me, responding to you. You confided in me, and if you regret it, I can't do anything about that, but I appreciate you leveling with me. Regardless of your former status I can safely say I've never met anyone quite like you. You're something of an enigma. You intrigue me."

Only her many years being scrutinized by an entire world kept EiLeen from gaping. Who but this nearly ethereal-looking young woman had ever spoken to her like this? Like she was a normal, feeling person, a woman who elicited an emotional response within another person. She shied away from asking herself which response exactly, but couldn't deny that the unexpected touch, chaste as it was, stirred new and surprising feelings.

"You expect me to believe that you're intrigued by me, not the former queen part of me or even the undercover-agent part? Just me?" The very idea was unfathomable. When had anyone ever asked about her as a humanoid being?

"That's exactly what I'm saying." Dana leaned her chin on the top of her bent knees. "We have," she checked a built-in chronometer in the bulkhead, "three hours before we reach the space station." Dana slid closer. "Unless you tell me in no uncertain terms to go back up there, I'll assume you don't mind if I…stay."

"How can you be so bold?" EiLeen's heart hammered now and made her dizzy. "You sit there, looking like this water-lily fairy goddess. If I hadn't seen you in action, I would've thought you were too fragile, too beautiful, to be anything but a model or a pampered actress. Then again, all I have to do is look into your eyes to discern your strength, your character."

"Not sure if this is all flattering, but believe me, I've been underestimated before while out of uniform." Dana shrugged. "I've set a few people straight over the years. When I was younger, I had a lot to prove, and I did, constantly, until I convinced my superiors I'd earned my promotion."

"And on a personal level?"

"What personal level?" Dana snorted and tossed her hair back with an impatient flick of her hand. "I've lived and breathed the *Koenigin* ever since I assumed command. As you surmised, only L'Ley knows my double duty, and of course my chef."

"What are you suggesting, then, since you seem reluctant to return to your bunk? I admit that you have me at a disadvantage." Cautious, she gazed at Dana, down to her hand where it still rested on her ankle, and back at her eyes.

"I don't know about you, but I have all this adrenaline coursing through me and I can't make myself relax. You just admitted you find me attractive…"

Her heart fretted like a crazed, caged animal. Was Dana really suggesting they have sex? Just like that? EiLeen had just confessed how out of practice she was when it came to physical nearness! Was this a joke on Dana's part? Was it a way of taunting an insufferable woman who needed to be put in her place? Or…or was it what it sounded like? Could she take Dana's words at face value?

CHAPTER SIX

Dana tried to decipher the expression, or rather, the several different expressions that ghosted across EiLeen's face. Trepidation, certainly, and something like fear mixed with anger struggled for dominance. Not surprisingly, anger won out.

"You are joking. Surely." EiLeen pinched her lips, her cheek flushing an annoyed red.

"Joking? No. About what, by the way?" Keeping her gaze level, Dana watched EiLeen pressing herself farther into the pillows, glowering at her.

"About this whole seduction scene. Acting as if you honestly would find a woman past her prime attractive."

"Past her...?" Gaping, Dana tried to follow EiLeen's reasoning. Could this larger-than-life woman really be that insecure? "First, you're not past your prime, as you put it. You're stunningly beautiful, not that beauty is all that matters. Second, I'm not joking. I do find you very attractive and I think we could be very good together, if you'd allow it to happen." Dana persuaded herself to continue talking even if she risked EiLeen's wrath. "I'm not a player. In fact, I'm usually rather shy when it comes to personal relationships."

"Shy?" EiLeen laughed joylessly. "If that's your being shy, I'm not sure I could handle you being confident."

"Am I wrong to think that you're something of a shy woman yourself?"

"Hardly." EiLeen closed her eyes and sighed. "Perhaps, in a way."

"There. You see. We're not that different. Age seems to be another hang-up for you."

"And it isn't for you?"

"No. Never has been."

"You sound very certain all of sudden." EiLeen shifted and moved nearer, her eyes darkening. "You sound like you think you can handle getting closer to a woman who's seen every damn planet within the SC and then some. Who's met every dignitary worth meeting and been the leader of an entire planet with its moons and asteroid belts as well."

"I have no intention of getting closer to your leadership persona, or the front you put up while shaking the hands of dignitaries. I want to just feel the genuine, authentic EiLeen, the woman who had to recede into obscurity when she inherited a throne that was never meant to be hers. That's the woman I'm interested in."

EiLeen's eyes were wide and her fists clenched and white-knuckled. "You sound like you mean it."

"I don't usually lie."

"I'm not sure you truly comprehend what you're implying." EiLeen touched Dana's cheek with unsteady fingertips. "So soft. I admit I'm wondering whether the rest of you is just as soft." Clearly startled by her own words, EiLeen closed her eyes and groaned. "I can't believe I just said that."

"Would you like to touch me?" Dana lost the last of her oxygen after her spontaneous question. She trembled where she sat, her legs tucked up against her.

EiLeen's eyes turned almost black as her star-shaped pupils swallowed what was left of her irises. "Yes," she whispered.

Balancing on her knees, Dana pulled down the coverall from her shoulders, baring her upper body. She slid up to EiLeen and just sat there, waiting to see what EiLeen would do.

"Oh, you're wicked." EiLeen shook her head. "You're like this evil sindianah, out to tempt me."

"What's a sindianah?"

"A mythical water creature said to live in the sea and occasionally claim the heart of a sailor." She cupped Dana's shoulder and skimmed her hand down her arm. "Yes. Soft. Even softer than I thought."

Dana's skin broke out in goose bumps. "As are your hands, EiLeen." She wasn't sure where her courage and conviction came from, but she ran her fingertips along her neck and traced the modest neckline. "And your skin."

"Temptress." EiLeen's eyes roamed all over Dana's naked expanse of skin.

"No. That'd be you." Dana moved in, claiming EiLeen's pale-pink lips with her own. She lingered there for a moment, unmoving. Slowly parting EiLeen's lips with the tip of her tongue, she deepened the kiss.

EiLeen moaned against Dana's mouth. "Been so long. Too long."

"I'm here now," Dana said, her voice husky. "I'm here. Let me, EiLeen. Please, let me."

"What do you want?"

"To feel we're alive. To feel you. This closeness." The words, whispered with such heat, passed her lips with each hot breath. Dana cupped EiLeen's cheeks and tilted her head, angling it perfectly for an even deeper kiss. She caressed EiLeen's tongue, her lower lip, ran the very tip of her own tongue along EiLeen's upper lip.

"We are. Alive. And close. And I don't think I can stop." EiLeen looked pained. "I don't want to. I mean, I should know better, but I need…this." She framed Dana's face with her trembling hands, combing through her hair with her fingers. "So stunning." Tugging at the tresses in her hands, she pulled Dana closer, recapturing her lips.

The kiss tore open something inside Dana, something that had clearly obstructed her breathing before. Suddenly it was easy to take deep breaths through her nose as she returned EiLeen's kisses. EiLeen in turn seemed insatiable. Her mouth, so warm and soft, her teeth sharp and nipping at her, and, oh stars, the *sounds* EiLeen made in the back of her throat. Whimpers, moans, and the sexiest way of grunting she'd ever heard, all blended into a harmonic masterpiece that drew Dana in.

"How can you smell so delicious when you've used the same cleansing unit as I did?" EiLeen spoke in a raspy, tremulous voice. "How's that even possible?"

"I don't know." Dana inhaled EiLeen's scent greedily. Somehow, the expensive perfume, or whatever it was that made her olfactory sense stand at attention, lingered. Perhaps it was not just the faint perfume, but EiLeen's own scent, that stirred these emotions in her? "All I know is that you drive all my senses crazy—scent, touch, sight…taste." As if to prove her last point, she latched on to EiLeen's lips. "So good—"

The blaring of the alarm klaxons made them jerk part. For a moment the pain of losing the connection was more than she could take. Her entire system cried out for the sensation of holding EiLeen close, but then she was on her feet, bolting for the helm with EiLeen right behind her.

"Damn, it's them. No, I take that back. It's not." She punched in commands with hands suddenly steady. Inside, her body and mind were screaming, protesting the abrupt way they'd been yanked apart.

"Who are they?"

"Same type of ships, same marking, but the computer still says these are different. They had backup? Who the hell are they if they're this well financed and equipped?"

"No messages from the SC command?" EiLeen pulled up another computer module. "Until we know who we're dealing with, we can't trust anyone who isn't at Jacelon's level. We have no way of knowing who's involved and how far this spreads."

"What the hell are you carrying that they want so dearly?" Dana glanced at EiLeen, seeing the dullness in her eyes and wondering if the way their emotions had come to a sudden full stop had caused it. For all she knew, EiLeen could have decided not have anything more to do with her. Shaking her head to rid herself of this disturbing thought, Dana focused on the readings. "They're less than twenty minutes behind us. I don't see how we can outrun them on our way to the station. And even if we did, if they follow us there, it'll be damn near impossible to escape undetected from it."

"Didn't you say the Guild Nation equipped and upgraded this shuttle? Surely they put in their famous masking features?" EiLeen scanned the console.

"Of course. It's been a while since I piloted something smaller than the *Koenigin*. I'm not sure how you know about the MAFE, but I'm glad you reminded me." Dana punched in commands. "I altered our trace emissions into in-space background noise. If they're unaware that our shuttles have this feature, we might just be able to make a run for it."

"Changing our course to see what happens." EiLeen was immediately on top of what needed to be done, and Dana drew a tiny breath of relief that the woman she was meant to protect was able and self-assured. "Turning eight degrees, starboard. Setting a detour course to the space station."

Dana couldn't take her eyes off the monitor. She stared at the readings until her eyes stung from lack of blinking. Inside her mind, the danger they found themselves in was much less important than the way EiLeen's kisses had affected her, and, stars and skies, the way Dana had returned the caresses. How could the physical bond she'd just experienced still exist so clearly even if they weren't touching and were in the midst of a life-saving operation?

Dana watched EiLeen pull up files on the monitor.

"They're still on the original trajectory, Dana." EiLeen turned and smiled, the first unabashed, full-blown smile she'd ever seen light up her features. "Some of the smaller vessels are scurrying on parallel tracks, but nobody has veered off toward us. Seems the MAFE is working according to the specs."

Dana wanted to respond with her usual professionalism. She opened her mouth to say something like "affirmative" or at least "yes, it sure looks like it," but all she could do was stare at the transformed face before her. EiLeen was a stunningly beautiful woman on any given day, but that smile, oh stars, that smile; it rendered her a certain softness that made her beauty esoteric and unforgettable.

"Dana?" The smile waned a bit and a frown showed up on EiLeen's forehead.

"Yes. Yes, that's promising. The MAFE, I mean. Not the smile. I, oh, stars." Huffing in frustration, Dana decided to stop talking.

"Smile, what smi—ah." EiLeen's smile broadened again. "I didn't know you were ever prone to babble, Captain."

"Oh, don't." Her cheeks warming, Dana wanted to groan and thud her head against the console. "Don't listen to me if I ever babble again. I'll try not to do that again. And if I do. Don't listen."

"And I would suggest that you stop panicking. What happened to the confident woman from over there on the bunk bed?" EiLeen motioned with her head.

"She...*I* was rudely interrupted." Dana huffed. "I don't know about you, but I'm still reeling. Sorry for acting so weird."

"Weird now or weird then?" EiLeen didn't elaborate and she didn't have to.

"Now." Annoyed at her loose hair, Dana twisted it into a messy bun by tying it into a knot.

"What a crime." Star-shaped pupils dilated again as EiLeen followed her every move with her eyes.

"Excuse me?"

"A crime to hide that abundance of hair."

Flustered, which was even more frustrating than the hair issue, Dana busied herself at the helm, reading the sensors again. "They're still on our original course. That doesn't make us safe, though. They possess cloaking capability. I've tried every sensor sweep available and I can't make out any traces, but they can still be there, tricking us."

"Any signs at all from alien propulsion-system waste particles?"

"None. Just space dust."

"Any chance of sampling the space dust and running a few tests? Does the shuttle keep a LABKIT?"

Dana snorted. "Don't tell me you hold a degree in chemistry too?" She wouldn't be surprised.

"No. I minored in physics at the Imidestrian Royal University." Looking entirely serious, EiLeen laced her fingers and leaned back in her chair.

Not sure if EiLeen's deadpan expression hid another way of ribbing her, Dana shook her head. "I can't tell if you're joking."

"Granted, I'm a bit rusty, as it's been at least thirty years since I completed my degree, but it's true. I do, or did, know my way around a basic physics lab."

"Of course. Well, it's the first real thing we have in common. I minored in physics as well. Between us and what's available equipment-wise, we should be able to look for trace elements of a cloaked ship."

"You're wrong." EiLeen's suddenly heated tone, coupled with the fire that burned in her eyes, shocked Dana.

"What about?" Folding her arms over her chest, she waited for whatever mistake EiLeen would pounce on now.

"That's not all we have in common. Surely I don't have to drag you back to bed to remind you?" The words left EiLeen's lips like dripping honey.

Gasping, Dana trembled at the passionate words and the outrageously sexy way EiLeen spoke. Sitting there, only half a meter away, devouring Dana with her eyes, she looked every bit the regal, self-assured woman who had boarded the *Koenigin* some thirty-six hours ago. Now they would have to get inside the less-than-spacious area of the shuttle where the LABKIT was located. She wished they could conduct the test at the table, where they'd have more elbow room. Suddenly remembering EiLeen's question, she felt the color rise on her cheeks. "Um, no. No, you don't have to remind me. I don't think I'll ever forget."

CHAPTER SEVEN

Jitters traveled up and down EiLeen's spine as she sat in the co-pilot/navigator seat again. "The initial findings after retrieving a space sample are bothersome. They're not close, but more than ten hours ago, someone decloaked for a few moments, probably just enough to determine our position. They're cloaked again and closing in." EiLeen sighed and pinched the bridge of her nose. "We have no way of knowing how close, only that it's uncomfortably so."

"There's a way to reach the space station faster, but it'll blow the whistle for all ships within the sector as to our presence. I didn't really see that as an option, but if they've already made us we should consider it."

"So we tear in there, guns blazing, and steal another ship. That defies the purpose of going there in the first place, doesn't it?"

"Not if we obtain a faster ship."

"*If* being the operative word." EiLeen looked out the view port. The star pattern whisked by them, as Dana was using every single resource the propulsion system could produce. "I'm going to have to sacrifice myself in order for you to get away. They're not really interested in you."

"What?" Dana stared at her, clearly aghast. "What the hell are you talking about?"

"Oh, calm down. I don't mean literally. Do keep up." EiLeen barely stopped a chuckle. "I meant, let them think I've sacrificed myself." She grew solemn. "I'm sure they realize the importance of what I'm about to take to the unit on Revos Prime. I would indeed sacrifice myself rather than let it fall into enemy hands. But if it did, it might reignite the war, with almost all the advantages on the enemy side."

"I won't let that happen," Dana said, speaking through her teeth.

"Oh, trust me, I don't feel like cutting my existence short by any means." She locked her gaze on Dana's. "Especially now."

Suddenly looking flustered, Dana busied herself with the controls. "So how do we fake your demise then, my Queen?"

Narrowing her eyes at the facetious way Dana used her former title, EiLeen spoke rapidly. "I have an idea, but we need to be on the space station for it to fool anyone. Can you get us there faster, *Captain*, or were you just bragging?"

"Oh, just for future reference, I never brag." Dana laughed, suddenly sounding reenergized. "I deliver."

It was EiLeen's turn to feel her cheeks warm. Damn it. Every time she thought she had the upper hand with this woman, Dana did or said something to put her in her place. EiLeen returned her eyes to the stars. Normally, such behavior would frustrate her, but truth be told, she rather liked it.

❖

Dana felt quite proud that she got them to the infamous space station so quickly. As soon as it showed up on short-range sensors, EiLeen had gotten up and started walking back and forth between the bathroom and the sleeping area.

"We'll dock in ten minutes," Dana said, working the controls. "Care to tell me your plan?"

"Sure, since you're going to have to do all the acting."

Dana flinched. "What the…what acting?"

"Easy, really. We're going to set the self-destruct sequence on mute and leave the ship. I'll sneak off among the riffraff populating this station wearing a disguise, and you'll put on the best act of a lifetime when our shuttle explodes into smithereens. In the commotion, we steal another ship and take off."

"You make it sound so easy," Dana said weakly. "Disguise, by the way. Disguised as what?"

"As this." EiLeen stood and pulled on a large piece of fabric, looking suspiciously like *Koenigin*-issue bed sheets. Letting it cover half her face and all of her signature gunmetal-gray hair, EiLeen hunched over and moved with difficulty. "I'm your servant, Moi, remember?"

"Stars and skies, EiLeen. You've missed your calling." Dana gawked. In less than a few seconds, EiLeen, former queen and the most regal person in the universe, had disappeared, and in her place stood a hunched-over, meek-looking old woman. "If that doesn't pull it off, nothing will."

"Thank you. Now, your job is to set the muted self-destruct and act heartbroken when I'm dead."

Even though the words were spoken with irony, the meaning of them still sent cold shivers throughout Dana's system. "All right."

A gentle hand on her shoulder made her look up at EiLeen's violet eyes. She was still in character, but her eyes were...hers. "Better not look too closely at anyone. Your eyes are stunning—and very special."

"Noted." EiLeen caressed Dana's cheek quickly and then went to sit down as they approached the space station.

❖

Dana watched EiLeen scurry between the people crowding the gate areas. She looked exactly who she intended to emulate: a lowly servant, running an errand for her intimidating boss. Dana walked through the gate at a slower pace, checking her chronometer as she handed her information to the gatekeeper. The walkway leading to the ship was two hundred meters long, which should keep the station and surrounding ships safe. Should. With explosions you never knew.

Counting backward in her head, Dana kept the gatekeeper busy, not wanting him to go down the walkway to check on the moorings. Some gatekeepers did, even at run-down gambling joints like this.

"Nature of your business?" the gatekeeper asked, sounding utterly bored.

"Just to place a few bets and have our propulsion system cool off. It's been acting kind of weird lately."

"How many on your ship?"

"Just three. A friend, myself, and a servant."

"So one still onboard—" The man was thrown forward at the blast and clung to his desk.

As prepared as she was, Dana felt herself go pale. "No, no! EiLeen!" She tried to think how it would've felt if EiLeen really had been on board the shuttle. It wasn't hard to force the tears; in fact, they streamed freely as she sank to her knees. She was fully aware that even the most run-down stations kept state-of-the-art surveillance equipment. These cameras and sensors were directed at her and their gate right now. "Oh, stars, no…no…" She hid her face in her hands and cried. "What the hell went wrong? What happened?"

"Lady, are you all right?" A man to her left grabbed her by the shoulders and pulled her to her feet. "That your ship?"

"Yes. And my, my friend. She was resting…I have to find my servant."

"Here. Sit down and catch your breath." The man seemed kind, but Dana knew better than to trust anyone at a station like this. He had patted her down pretty well already, no doubt looking for something he could get his hands on. She played along, keeping her hands in her pockets, curled around her muted communicator and her weapon.

The man looked soulfully at her. "This must be so horrible for a young thing like yourself. My name is Boransh. I have a small shuttle a few gates down. Why don't you allow me to give you a place to stay?"

"Yeah? A ship where I could perhaps…rest?"

"Exactly." He beamed. "You have a servant?"

"Yes. Could she come too?" Dana widened her gaze deliberately, hoping she wasn't overdoing it. Either Boransh wasn't used to sly women or he was a sucker for tears, even if he was nothing but a thief.

"Absolutely. As long as she wouldn't mind waiting on me as well. Is she young? Like you?" He actually licked his lips at the thought. His teeth had seen better days and his divided tongue suggested he came from Hioros One, a small desert planet mainly known for its metal ores. The indigenous population was hardened and lived a tough life unless they managed to emigrate to any of their prosperous, lush neighboring worlds. Clearly Boransh hadn't gotten out fast enough. His skin and teeth carried the evidence of the heavy metal–infused atmosphere.

"She's mature, but a hard worker. I have to find her and tell her about EiLeen. It's important." Dana trembled visibly, which wasn't hard. She hated not having EiLeen in her sight. What if she'd run into even bigger trouble here than what they fled from?

"You do so. I'm docked at the fourth gate from here, that way." Boransh pointed to the left. I'll be there to greet you, beautiful."

Nearly gagging at the man's leering expression, Dana hoped she looked sufficiently teary-eyed and grateful. "You have no idea what this means. I'd be stuck here forever and unable to pay my way—"

"Oh, we'll find a very easy way for you to pay your way." Boransh chuckled. "Very easy."

"Thank you." Dana stood. "I'll be back as soon as I find my servant."

"Good." Boransh nodded and strode toward his ship.

The gatekeeper had found his bearings and was now looking for Dana with rage on his face. "Where the hell's that woman?" he bellowed as she hurried around the corner. "I demand she reimburse us. Her damn ship destroyed the whole walkway. Where is she?"

It was a good thing that everyone on the station was most likely looking out for themselves and no one else. Unless they offered a reward, nobody would put any effort into locating Dana and handing her over. She ran between the people populating the run-down station. Most of them looked like they were there as a last resort, hoping to win some credits, and others looked wealthy but desperate for a juicy adventure. Dana was only desperate to locate EiLeen.

Her pocket buzzed and she stopped, stepping into a dark alley-like corridor. "Yes. Where are you?" she hissed into the communicator.

"I saw you just now, but not anymore." EiLeen spoke fast. "I'm outside an interesting-looking establishment called Royal Laser Tattoos. Sounds like something for me, right?"

"I think I saw that sign. I'm in the alley just ahead of it on my left."

"What a cute little thing, in search of a real man, right?" someone rasped behind Dana. "I'll pay you ten credits for your hand. Just your hand."

"Get lost." Dana gave the burly man a disdainful look. "Not interested."

"Fool of a woman. I would've paid you. Now you get nothing and I still get what I want." He grabbed her by the shoulders and shook her.

Dana pocketed the communicator and growled impatiently as she hit the man on his larynx and then kicked him between his legs. He was already going down after the first blow but actually fainted after she kicked him.

"I can't leave you alone for a moment." EiLeen's voice from a few meters away made Dana pivot and run up to her. Throwing her arms around her, she closed her eyes for a moment.

"Thank the stars. I acted out the bloody scene so well I nearly believed myself. It was disturbing."

"Hush. I'm fine and so, I can see, are you. He doesn't look too happy, though. I think his testicles are forever fused to his tonsils. Sucking his thumb could be the only pleasure he requires from now on."

Shocked, and suddenly rather giggly, Dana pulled EiLeen with her, making sure her bed-sheet-turned-shawl covered her properly. "I have a ship for us. No idea about its crew or status, but I have a new protector who, and I quote, 'will find a very easy way for me to pay my way.'"

"Is that so?" EiLeen spoke icily. "I look forward to meeting this honorable individual."

"Damn. Don't blow our cover. I can handle myself, you just saw that."

"I know, but that doesn't mean I enjoy you having to humor yet another sleazy character." The distaste was evident in EiLeen's voice. "Guess we shouldn't keep your enamored shipowner waiting."

"Cute. Really." Dana glanced around the corner, making sure nobody was paying attention to them. The odds that someone would among this motley crowd were pretty high, but she'd rather be sure. "All right, *Moi*, time to go find our ride."

"Yes, ma'am," EiLeen said with sugary meekness. She followed two steps behind Dana, her head bowed. Dana regarded their image in one of the shop windows, thinking how alien this undercover role-play had to be for EiLeen. Granted, for all she knew, EiLeen could have been involved in even more humbling covert operations, but somehow she doubted it. Surely SC intelligence used this woman primarily for her contacts among the high and mighty?

Locating the gate was the least of their problems. Making their way without alerting the gate official who might recognize Dana as the captain of the exploded shuttle was the first challenge. Dana did a quick detour around the gate area, with Moi right behind her, wondering if there was another route to the ship they intended to steal. "Damn, how am I supposed to walk right by this fool?" she muttered under her breath, unprepared when EiLeen tugged gently at her hair. "What are you doing?"

"Let it down. Right now. He's moving through the crowd this way with two grim-looking fellows flanking him. Your hair transforms you completely. Come on!"

Not sure it would work, Dana did as told, wrapping her hair around her in the same manner as EiLeen wore her shawl, covering most of her face. They strode past the shouting crowd and nobody even as much as glanced at them.

The gate walkway leading down to Boransh's ship smelled increasingly worse as they neared the docking doors.

"Oh, this is bad." Dana moaned. "I have a feeling his ship will be even more insufferable."

"I'm sure it's nothing a sprinkle of perfume can fix. Show some courage, Captain."

"Hey, no insolence permitted, Moi." Dana glanced over her shoulder, knowing her quick grin gave her away. "As for sprinkling perfume, we'll need a damn perfume factory."

"No kidding."

As they reached the airlock, the doors opened with an ear-splitting screech.

"Hello, Boransh, how about some oil on those tracks, eh?"

The man just stared at her, looking speechless. "Excuse me?"

"The sound? That noise that renewed my tinnitus for the next decade?" Dana tilted her head, frowning. "Boransh?"

"Fuck, it *is* you. I didn't recognize you at first. I…you took down your hair. I never could've dreamed—" He reached out for her, but the mere thought of him touching her, especially as he hadn't cleaned his hands, or nails, in a long time, made her shudder.

Forcing a smile, Dana acted coy in a playful way. "Uh-uh. I'd like to see our quarters."

"You'll be set up fit for a queen, don't you worry your pretty head. Your servant will bunk with the rest of the crew." Boransh licked his lips.

"She'll stay with me. I'm used to having her around." Dana followed as he motioned for them to walk behind him along the narrow corridor. Corrosion and leaking hydraulics made even the air taste of metal. Mindful of slick oil puddles, she memorized what she could of the ship's layout.

"That may be, but I don't want some old woman breathing down my neck."

"Don't tell me that you want a setup fit for a queen too," Dana said sweetly. Boransh looked like he wanted to either object or merely swat her. She was fairly sure he wouldn't physically hurt her, as that would lower her going price. "How big is your crew?"

"Just me and four other guys."

Finally some good news, if he was indeed telling the truth. "Am I expected to…entertain them as well?"

"No!" Now Boransh looked angry for the first time. "You're my catch. You owe *me*, not them. They're simple men, all fugitives with a price on their head. Nothing for a queen such as you."

Dana heard EiLeen huff behind her.

"You're so right, Boransh. I used to be accustomed to the finer things in life." Dana swallowed against the bile at having to touch even his clothes, but took his arm and looked admiringly at him. "So these simple men, do they join you, the captain of this fine vessel, on the bridge?"

"You're joking?" Boransh patted her hand, making her stomach turn over. "They're in engineering in shifts of two. I have a fully automated bridge that I easily operate myself without any input from those fools."

"Sounds like you have it figured out here aboard the—the…What is the name of your ship?" Dana infused admiration in her voice.

"The *Quistamajar*."

Noting the information, Dana continued. "Now, about those queen-like quarters of yours? I really need to freshen up."

"I'll show you. Your maid—"

"Will help me. Freshen up." Donning a broad smile, Dana nearly chuckled at how this man swallowed her every word. He really was full of himself if he thought a woman like her would ever find him the least bit appealing. Even if he'd bathed and had basic dental procedures, she couldn't see anything redeeming about him.

As Boransh punched in the command to get inside the captain's quarters, Dana gazed pointedly at EiLeen, who in turn pushed her shawl aside enough for Dana to see the long, greasy pipe in her hands. *Now, that's what a real queen would be. Proactive.*

Inside the quarters, which were marginally cleaner than the corridor, Dana circled Boransh and tossed her hair provocatively over her shoulders. "This isn't bad," she said, beaming. "I can see myself being quite comfortable here."

"Excellent—" Boransh's expression was a strange mix of blankness and surprise as he fell forward on the floor.

"Damn. I think I broke a nail." EiLeen poked the large man with the pipe before letting it go, making a disgusted face. "If he'd leered at you one more time, I swear—"

"Yeah, yeah. Let's find something to tie him up with." Dana scanned the room. An assorted set of ropes and other bindings close to the bed made her stomach curl. "Something tells me it will be poetic justice to tie him with those. Wonder how many not-so-willing women he's strapped to his bed?"

"Quite a few, if you take into account that he has had rings welded to the bulkhead for that purpose." EiLeen pointed. "Poetic justice indeed."

They managed to drag the man onto the low bed and secure his arms and legs spread-eagle to the wall and the footboard. Dana wanted to make sure he couldn't give any audio commands to override the ship's computer, even though she doubted the small vessel actually boasted such a feature. She pushed a sock she found on the floor into his mouth and secured it with a gag she fashioned from EiLeen's "shawl."

"There. He looks comfy." EiLeen smirked. "Better get to the bridge before someone misses him."

Dana regarded the man who'd planned to use her and then sell her to others, no doubt. He looked rather pathetic tied up on his own bed, but she was fresh out of pity for the likes of him. "Come on."

Working their way back, they didn't run into any of the men who worked on the lower decks. No doubt they were intimidated by Boransh and kept to themselves. Hopefully they would find him intimidating enough to never question where he decided to steer the ship.

Two decks up they found the bridge. Dark and dingy like the rest of the ship, it was still an average bridge that seemed functional enough. Glancing to her right, she spotted a rusty plate that confirmed Boransh had provided the correct name for the ship. "Okay, here goes," Dana said, muttering. "The *Quistamajar* to flight control. Departing ahead of schedule."

"You won't get any credit refund," a gruff voice said, sounding as bored as the gatekeeper had. "Let me make sure you're not in debt at any of the tables." A few nervous minutes passed. "Disengaging security lock. Propulsion system start allowed."

Dana punched in the commands to take them to a safe distance from the station before she engaged maximum speed, not caring what limitations this flying bucket had. "Bye-bye," she muttered as she cleared the inner perimeter. "I think it's safe to say this was the first and last time I'll set foot in such a place without backup."

"I found the place very educational," EiLeen said matter-of-factly.

"Oh, yes? What on earth did you learn?" Dana glanced over at the woman who now looked like herself again.

"That I'm prepared to do anything to keep you safe. If I hadn't known it wouldn't go down well with you, I would have hit that despicable man in the captain's quarters hard enough to end his life. All for placing his filthy hands on you." She shrugged but gazed cautiously at Dana.

"As a matter of fact, if the roles had been reversed, I would've reacted the same way. I was furious when he tried to suggest I'd put you down with the unhappy foursome below."

EiLeen relaxed marginally, her body no longer ramrod. "That's reassuring." She smiled. "Let's get out of here, then, Captain."

"Certainly, my Queen."

CHAPTER EIGHT

"This ship is in deplorable condition," EiLeen said, regarding the bridge. "How can people live like this?"

"Oh, you'd be surprised." Dana made a wry face. "My aunt struggled to clean, but every surface in our house always had a thin layer of the dust from the mining operation. I couldn't wait to leave. The only sanitary place was the cleaning tube. As soon as I walked out, all I did was rub more grimy dust onto my skin from the towels."

"Where did you grow up?"

"In a mining district with my aunt and uncle. We moved onto a space station when my uncle got a new job at an asteroid mining company. I wasn't too thrilled with my aunt, even if I owe her for taking care of me after my parents died. She tried to keep me from joining the fleet academy since she wanted me to become a teacher on the station and...well, I guess, she wanted me to stay. I ended up leaving at sixteen."

"Ever go back?"

"No." Dana blanched and turned around. "Nothing to go back to. Pirates destroyed the space station after they cleaned out everything of value." She paused and then looked at EiLeen with dull, gray eyes. "I have nothing personal left to return to."

"Darling." Not concerned about the small ship's dirt any longer, EiLeen maneuvered over to kneel next to Dana. "I can't bear to see you like this. Once we're out of range of any potential followers, I'll make sure you know you're not alone anymore." Hesitating briefly, she touched Dana's chin. "Or do I assume too much?"

"No." Only her trembling breath betrayed the emotional storm inside Dana. "I'd say you're spot-on."

"Good." EiLeen's stomach unclenched and her heart mellowed its wild movements. "Good."

"Can you pull up the specs of this piece-of-crap can?" Dana straightened and focused on the helm console. "I have a feeling we're going to need any and all advantages we can think of. We also need to make sure the basement quartet stays put."

Understanding that Dana was trying to hold it together despite lack of sleep and emotional turbulence, EiLeen patted her shoulder and then walked over to what she surmised was the operations console under all the dust. She punched in commands that would allow them to relax some.

"I've sealed the doors from the lower decks," she said calmly, "and deployed perimeter beacons around us using regular lasers. A little trick one of my friends in the intelligence service showed me."

"Sounds good. Is this your way of saying we might just rest a little?"

"As long as we do it right here on the bridge. Rest a little, I mean." Annoyed at herself for the warmth on her cheeks and earlobes, EiLeen busied herself by taking what was left of her "shawl" and wiping off two chairs placed together at the far right. "These look like they actually recline a bit."

"Fantastic. I'm all for relaxing and reclining at this point. Wonder if they have something to eat on this bridge?"

"Eat?" Aghast, EiLeen looked around them. "You've seen the deplorable state of this vessel, which is a very forgiving way to describe this flying soup can, and you suggest we feed off *anything* that individual we just strapped to his bed has touched?"

"Um. When you put it that way…Will you stop looking around as if you think some Golibedarian ham will round the corner and eat *us*?" Dana ran her hand over her face. "Stars and skies, you're right, but I'm famished."

"I'm hungry too. I suppose I could venture out of here and find the galley. If there's actual canned stuff, we might risk it."

"I'm not too fond of the idea of you going alone."

"I'll be fine. Just keep your eye on the stars and I'll be back in a few moments. I have my communicator."

"Good." Dana looked half-placated.

EiLeen passed Dana and pressed her lips to her cheek briefly. "See you soon."

"All right. Be safe."

The ship was ghostly when it was void of any other sound than her own steps. She walked briskly, checking her position with the help of small charts at each intersection. There was a logical structure that had worked well for the ship once, and soon she found the galley. The smell of something musky and old made her nearly turn and go back to the bridge instantly. Instead she poked her head in, hand on her communicator, but all she saw was the huge mess left by whatever crewmember had cooking on his schedule.

She opened cabinets one after another and was about to despair when she found four cans of something that reminded her of her childhood's vegetable soup. She was looking around for something to open them with when the ship lurched, sending her careening into the bulkhead. She dropped the cans, which rolled away from her. Tearing at her communicator, she hung on to the small preparation table that was attached to the deck. "Dana! Talk to me, what's happening?"

"Damn it, they're right on top of us, and below for that matter." Dana's voice sounded pressed. "They've taken out our weapons array, not that this damn ship had an array to speak of."

"I'm on my way back. Are these the same ones as before?"

"I think so, from what I can see on the security-station console. They showed up out of nowhere so they must have cloaking ability. Sounds like the same—ow!"

"Dana!" EiLeen ran down the corridor that sometimes disappeared under her feet. She clung to the hand railing on the wall but knew the ship was losing its inertial dampening. "Damn it, Dana, what did you do? Are you all right?" As she pulled herself forward it was like climbing the Imidestrian chain of mountains where she kept a summerhouse.

"Just fell over the helm and put a crack in Boransh's lovely view screen with my head. Damn, what a bump." Dana's moan propelled EiLeen forward. Her palms burned as she slid along the wall and later the deck. She fell hard onto her knees twice, and the second time she heard the fabric rip in her pants, and her skin as well. Wanting to use the most obscene of Imidestrian swear words, she bit her lower lip and forged on.

"EiLeen, the alarm you set? The perimeter beacons? They're blaring all over the port side."

"Which deck?"

"Decks four and five."

"I locked the guys in the lower decks, one and two, out. Decks four and five are still within reach." Now the ship was nearly stalling, which in itself was impossible in space, but that was the best way to describe the insanely steep climb she would have to make to reach the bridge.

"We're losing pressure on deck five. Trying to seal it."

"They're boarding us!" EiLeen pressed so hard with her feet now, she heard her bones creak. *Damn legs. Maybe I* am *too old?* She climbed, calling out Dana's name every few meters.

"We're being boarded, EiLeen. Get a move on. I can see them passing bulkheads, as Boransh is clearly big on inner sensors. They're two decks below you."

"At least we know they have to climb too. That'll slow them down."

"And you." Dana sounded composed, though her voice sounded faintly tinged with desperation.

"Hey, I'm all right. I'll be with you on the bridge in two minutes. You haven't failed your mission."

"I don't give a damn about the mission. I just want you back here now."

"One. Minute." Nearly losing her breath, EiLeen pulled herself up along the handrails, using the soft soles of her shoes to push her way upward. She could see the double doors leading to the bridge. "Figure out. A way to. Seal the doors, Dana. Or. We will have to. Abandon the bridge."

"On it!"

Eventually, EiLeen pulled herself almost over the edge of the doorway to the bridge. Inside she saw Dana clinging to the command chair. "How's the boarding team doing?"

"Struggling, but doing better than you. They were evidently ready for this turn of events and brought arti-grav boots."

"Brilliant." Artificial-gravitation boots would give them the edge as the ship carried on like an untamed ghazellia. EiLeen was about to flip over the edge of the doorway and join Dana when something hit her head. She cried out and clutched at the pain above her ear. "Scets!" Cursing in Imidestrian helped some, but the gesture had made her lose her grip and she was now bouncing across the sloping floor toward the other side of the corridor.

"EiLeen, what happened?" Dana yelled from the bridge.

She opened her mouth to say she was all right when she saw something move in the outer part of her field of vision. Four individuals were stomping their way toward her. They looked surreal, like they were defying gravity by walking on the wall. Arti-grav boots indeed.

"Dana, we've got company. Four of them. I need a weapon. Something!"

"Do not move." A dark male voice thundered from the comm system.

"What the hell?" Dana called out. "Did they tap into the whole system? Who has such technology?"

"I'd say that's the last piece of the puzzle, Dana. The Onotharians."

"What? In SC territory?" Dana's voice faded. "Stars and skies, this is bad."

"No kidding." EiLeen pushed at the wall, trying to get back through the door to the bridge. Perhaps they'd find a way to block it from inside.

"Seize that female. She's our main objective." The closest figure in a black space suit pointed at EiLeen. "Do you have the extraction device ready?"

"Aye, sir. I have to locate which lobe they've used."

"Just cut her head open. We have no use for her once the implant is extracted."

"There's no need to kill her—"

"*Enough!* Follow orders or merely decapitate her. Then you can explain to our superiors why you insisted on bringing back such a bloody mess."

"Understood, sir."

"EiLeen, did you hear that? You have to get away from there." Dana's voice echoed. She had switched from Premoni to English, probably hoping the thugs didn't understand.

"I'm trying," EiLeen said, moaning as she pushed for her life.

"Damn ship...I can't..." She mobilized what was left of her strength and managed to get hold of the door frame. Sobbing out of sheer fury, she pulled herself up, kicking her legs to gain momentum. Finally sitting on the door, which was now effectively the floor, she was just about to move her feet up when she felt a strong, gloved hand around her ankle. It pulled at her, squeezing so hard, she feared the man would fracture it. She looked down and saw the man in the black space suit just below the doorway. Her reflexes sent her free foot down in a hard kick, hitting his narrow helmet at the temple. Clearly he hadn't seen that coming, as he swore loudly over the comm system and loosened his grip. EiLeen pulled her leg free and scooted backward.

"EiLeen, here!" Dana called out. She threw something rather large and bulky toward her.

EiLeen reached up before the object passed her and broke yet another nail as she grabbed what turned out to be some strange-looking alien sidearm. She frowned at the settings but merely turned it on, relieved when it hummed reassuringly in her grip.

Suddenly the two hands were on her both her legs as the man heaved his way up toward her. Behind her the other three were making their way up through the door opening.

"EiLeen, fire! Shoot them!" Dana's voice was filled with panic. "I'm trying to get over there, but—"

"Surrender, woman. Your days of espionage are over. The Onotharian Empire will rise again." The man growled as he pulled EiLeen toward him.

Not hesitating a second longer, EiLeen aimed at him and fired. The man threw himself sideways and the beam from the alien gun hit the one behind him. The person fell motionless through the door and disappeared out of sight without a sound. EiLeen fired at the one to the left and then at the horrible person with the damn lobotomy kit. They went through the door just as silently. The man in charge of the operation against her grabbed the metal bag from the unconscious or dead lobotomizer, then turned his attention back at EiLeen, this time also with a weapon directed at her.

"As I said, you might as well surrender. I will make it painless."

EiLeen thought fast. What if she let him really close and then took advantage of his nearness by firing at close range? Clearly he hadn't fired at her yet because any disruptive weapon might kill the implant, rendering it useless. It needed to be extracted properly or, as gross as it sounded, cut out.

The ship lurched again.

"…come in, Begoll vessel. Are you present, Captain Rhoridan? The *Koenigin* to Begoll vessel…"

"*Koenigin*, Rhoridan here. We have intruders and need immediate assistance. What's your position, Commander L'Ley?"

"We have you on our screen. ETA ten minutes. Bringing friends."

"Step on it, L'Ley."

"Aye, Captain."

EiLeen was trembling so hard now she could barely keep hold of the weapon. Edging toward the ledge framing the bridge, which now acted as a partial roof, she hoped to climb onto the other side. Just as she shifted her grip on the weapon, the old ship rolled and sent her flying like a projectile. A railing passed her lower arms, and she grabbed it with her free hand. A dark shadow shot past her, and then hard hands tugged at her legs. She almost let go. Excruciating pain shot through her arm toward her shoulder, and she couldn't suppress a deep moan. Then soft, but strong hands gripped her arm and helped her not to fall. She looked up into Dana's stormy dark eyes.

"Shoot him, EiLeen. Hurry!"

EiLeen raised the heavy gun, its handle so thick in her hand she was afraid she'd drop it. Pointing it toward the furious face of the hateful man wanting to kill her, she pressed the sensor and kept her finger on it.

CHAPTER NINE

Dana pulled EiLeen up on the ledge and held her close. Sobbing from sheer relief, she pressed her face against her silvery hair. "You're safe. I've got you. You're safe."

"Calm down," EiLeen said, "I'm fine." Her shaking voice belied her attempt to sound flippant. "I really am." Her tone changed and sincerity laced her words.

"Thank the stars."

"Can we perhaps dock with the *Koenigin* and get off this disgusting barge?" Sitting up, EiLeen crinkled her nose, which made her look close to adorable.

"Absolutely." Dana let go of EiLeen reluctantly and peered over the ledge. "He sure looks out cold. You sure that weapon was set on stun?"

"Stun?" EiLeen gave a one-shoulder shrug. "How would I know? The markings were in some weird alien language. That man wanted to turn my brain into mush. For all I know it could have turned them all into condrusliaci fruits."

"You impossible woman. What the hell is condrusliaci fruit?" Dana's shoulders began to shake as a slightly hysterical laugh started to bubble up through her chest.

"Green, small, round, and with thorns on their shell. If you prick your fingers, nasty warts will appear within a few hours. The inside is delicious."

"You're crazy. I know it now. I'm in…" Dana took a deep breath and steeled herself against the knowledge she might be rejected. "I'm in love with a certifiably insane woman."

EiLeen's expression changed. She gazed intently, her eyes unwavering and unreadable. Then they began to shine and crystal-clear tears shimmered, but didn't fall. "I would argue that you're the one who might need a psychiatric evaluation for saying that, feeling like that."

"It might be foolish, but it feels perfectly sane to me." Daring to hope now, as EiLeen was clutching at her, pulling her even closer on the dirty ledge, Dana cupped her face. "I love you, my Queen."

"You're in big trouble, Captain. You might end up regretting ever telling me, because I love you too. I was prepared to live my life on the memories of these days and nights with you, so sure that letting you go on to live your life was the best thing. Now when I know you love me—oh, damn. For the love of the Creator." She wiped at the now-escaping tears.

"I can't imagine life without you, EiLeen. You're amazing. You're easily the most exasperating woman I've ever met, as well as the most courageous, brilliant, funny, beautiful, cute—"

"What?" EiLeen flinched. "I am *not* cute."

"Ah. Normally you're not, no. Just every once in a while." Dana tried for a placating smile. "And you're dangerous. To my peace of mind, to my poor stampeding heart."

"And you're the woman I never thought even existed—the one who tore down my defenses and saw through the royal mask. Not sure why that is. Not even sure this is fair to you, since being with me will end your anonymity forever. Once in my life in the public eye, you're there to stay, even if you leave me."

"Leave you?" Startled, Dana began to get up and tugged EiLeen with her. "I could never leave you. How can you even think—"

"I don't. I mean, I don't want you to."

"I—"

"L'Ley to Rhoridan. Come in. L'Ley to Rhoridan and Maxio. Do you read me?"

Koenigin! Dana tore at her communicator. "Rhoridan here. We're doing fine but need extracting. Send a shuttle to the dock, Commander."

"Will do, Captain. Thing is, your vessel is drifting too close to the asteroid belt. Its faint gravity is pulling you in. You might need to locate some space suits, ma'am."

"Not sure there are any on this rust bucket. How long do we have before we reach the belt?"

"We estimate eight minutes."

Dana winced. That was barely long enough for the shuttle to reach them. "Keep an open comm signal, Commander. We're going to the main airlock to see what we can find." She motioned for EiLeen to follow her as she took off down the half-smoke-filled corridor.

❖

EiLeen coughed as she stumbled behind Dana, who shoved some containers aside and pushed on. Her deceptively slender body didn't betray her strength, but it was impressive.

"Don't fall behind. We only have a few minutes to find some space suits."

"Calm down, I'm right here." She wasn't about to show how exhausted she was and how her body still ached from the fight with the Onotharian agents. Being slammed into the bulkhead was never a good thing, but having that happen when you were not as well trained as you used to be was even worse. She would definitely sport some interesting bruises if they made it out of the Begoll freighter alive.

"Here. Main airlock." Dana dived into the smaller area and began opening one cabinet door after another. EiLeen started at the other end, hoping to find the suits right away. When she'd gone through six cabinets and still no space suit, she began to tremble. This couldn't be the end. They'd fought so hard to stay alive, to complete the mission. To lose the woman she loved before they even got the opportunity to make this new scenario work made her want to scream.

When the cabinets turned up nothing, Dana looked ashen as she sank down on a chair, drawing deep trembling breaths. "Where the hell do these people store their suits?" She checked her chronometer. "Three minutes, EiLeen. Oh, stars." Her eyes burned nearly visible tracks in the air between them. "I'm so sorry."

"No. No! Don't you dare give up—on us or on life. There must be someth—" EiLeen squinted as something caught her eyes. "What is that? That sign?"

"Where?" Dana leaned forward and pushed what looked like some hoses away. "This?"

"Yes? It's in Begollian, I believe, but doesn't it say craft and tunnel or something?"

"Tunnel?" Dana suddenly stood up, energized, pushed the hoses aside, and felt around the edges of the large sign. "It might not mean tunnel. It could mean chute."

"Shoot? Shoot whom?"

"No, *chute*, as in a tunnel to slide through to something. Preferably to where they keep space suits and such." Dana jumped back. "Oh, gods. Yes!"

A dark hole opened up, totally void of light.

"No time to waste." EiLeen sat down and pushed her way through the hole. Then she was free-falling. Knowing how important it was to not let her arms flail, but instead tuck them into her body and pull up her knees somewhat, she curled up to try to protect herself from a rough landing.

"EiLeen!" Dana cried out from above just as EiLeen dropped through something with hard edges and landed with a thud on the bottom of it. The air was pressed out of her lungs and she barely had the good sense to roll to the side when Dana came plummeting down. She landed with the same eerie sound.

"For the love of the stars, did they have to use such a hard surface to land on?"

EiLeen could hardly make out Dana's contours in the dark, whatever it was they had landed in. Still she could see Dana bolting for what looked like a console. "Close the hatch!"

Automatically looking up and feeling the low ceiling with her hands, she found the handle and pulled. Something came toward her but stopped just within reach, and she pressed the handle every which way until it locked.

"What the hell is this?" She felt before her toward Dana's voice, only to flinch as the light suddenly came on.

"A life raft of the old kind. A tiny space shuttle used by civilians long ago." Dana glanced at her chronometer. "One minute. No time for preliminaries." She virtually hammered and stabbed with her fingers at the dirty console before her. The mini shuttle began shaking and a loud hum reverberated around them. EiLeen threw herself into a torn, dusty seat. She couldn't find any harness or belt, but clung to the armrests as the shuttle began to hover.

"How do we get out of here?" EiLeen shouted over the nearly deafening rumble. "Any idea?"

"Not really. From what I can see, this old heap of junk has a rudimentary weapons array. Guess that's our only option."

"You're going to shoot our way out of here?" She could hardly believe Dana's intent, but they were only seconds away from hitting the outer part of the asteroid belt.

"Yes!" Slamming her palm onto the console, Dana fired. Explosions erupted all around them and then they were hurled forward, actually pulled, and tossed into space.

"Stars be praised, I hope this thing has no major hull issues. Micro fractures we can deal with, but larger things—"

"Will kill us." EiLeen found she didn't have to yell anymore, which was a blessing. She tried to make out the surrounding space through the view port, but it was nearly impossible because of grime stemming from ages of disuse.

An explosion to their port side made them both jump.

"There goes that sorry excuse for a ship." EiLeen shook her head.

"Which helped save our lives this far."

"Point taken. Any signs of either the Onotharians or your ship?"

Tapping the sensors, Dana scrutinized the readings. "As far as I can tell, the *Koenigin* is still en route and should be here in two minutes. How much can go wrong in two damn minutes?"

A loud bang sent the small vessel tumbling, and EiLeen flew across the ship and landed across Dana's legs, hitting her head on the bulkhead. "Holy Creator, you *had* to ask, didn't you? It's the Onotharians. It has to be." She sat up and realized she was nearly straddling Dana's lap. Hurriedly, she managed to stand up before another bang resonated and inertial dampeners went offline. Clinging to Dana's right arm, EiLeen tried to stay where she was. All around her, mayhem broke loose as anything that wasn't bolted to the floor hovered and shifted around them.

"I've got you. Can you press the three red sensors at the top right?" Dana yelled. "We have to return fire or we'll be space dust when the *Koenigin* finds us."

EiLeen pivoted in midair. The only thing keeping her from floating helplessly from one bulkhead to the next was Dana's white-knuckled grip on her left sleeve. Stretching herself to the limit, she reached for the upper right corner of the helm console. Three red octagon-shaped sensors blinked at her, just barely out of reach.

"Push me farther up. Hurry!"

Dana pushed and actually let go of the chair with her left arm. EiLeen tried again. Only a few centimeters away, she yanked her hand loose from Dana's grip and pushed her body toward the elusive sensors. Slamming her fingers against them, she felt the connection in the tiny tremor, and then she was pushed back with such force that everything became black. The last thing she heard was Dana's communicator and its scratchy transmission.

"*Koenigin* to Captain Rhoridan. That was some shot, ma'am. We brought backup and we're ready to tow you."

❖

EiLeen opened her eyes with a soft moan. Something was missing. The ceiling was a soft gray color instead of the corroded, stained mess she'd shuddered at aboard the Begoll freighter. Inhaling the air, she found it clean, with a faint, familiar scent to it.

"EiLeen." An equally well-known voice spoke close to her left.

EiLeen turned her head slowly, for some reason expecting the movement to cause excruciating pain. When it didn't, she relaxed and then she saw Dana. Dressed in her captain's uniform, her hair combed in the usual austere bun, she didn't look at all like *her* Dana. Not until she focused on the light in her eyes and the tears that trickled down her pale cheeks. "Dana."

"You're awake. Thank the stars."

"The shuttle freighter?"

"Space dust."

"The escape pod?"

"Actually it's in the shuttle bay." Dana leaned closer and pressed her trembling lips against EiLeen's forehead. "I thought I'd lost you this time. You had a nasty concussion, but Dr. Irah took care of that. He said all you need is rest."

"He scanned my head?" EiLeen became rigid. "Dana?"

"Yes. We saw the implant. You truly do carry the information within you. I thought you meant it as a metaphor at first."

"Yes. As you saw. Only the intended recipients on Revos Prime headquarters can extract it safely. I didn't enjoy the idea of the Onotharians lobotomizing me in order to get to it."

"But what happens once the information is extracted? And why carry it in your damn brain? That's got to be dangerous to you."

EiLeen slid over and tugged at Dana to lie down next to her. "You're too far away. I'm getting permanent neck damage looking over at you like this. Come here." It was gratifying to feel how quickly Dana moved onto the bed and hugged her. "Now, if you do that, I won't be able to focus."

"Sorry." Not sounding contrite at all, Dana pulled back a little. "Go on."

"Thanks to Guild Nation's most accomplished scientists, once the information is uploaded to the Revos Prime mainframe, this device will disintegrate and become a harmless substance that will leave my body the…um, natural way."

"And now you can't go there without full military escort, as we know that they know that we know."

EiLeen exhaled audibly. "Yes. I had hoped to be able to keep working undercover, but I assume those days are over. I'll talk to Admiral Jacelon about it. I've had Plan B figured out for some time, but I need to run it by him and Marco Thorosac." Thorosac, the Supreme Constellations' civilian leader and the one with the political power as chairman of the planets' representatives, would be the one voicing objections. He didn't know her the way Ewan Jacelon did, and no doubt he didn't trust someone who was more famous for what she wore and whom she knew than what she did. Hopefully Ewan would persuade Thorosac—they were close friends, after all—to see things her way.

"Can you tell me about Plan B?"

"Not yet. Let's go to Revos Prime and deliver the goods. I'm assuming we're on board the *Koenigin*, as you mentioned your physician?"

"We are. In my quarters, as a matter of fact. Commander L'Ley transported all the civilian passengers to the closest space port before going after us." She drew a line along EiLeen's arm. "I need—I needed you here with me, but I'll understand if you want to go back to your quarters. In a day or so, we'll transfer to an SC cruiser with armed assault craft escort and expedite your arrival at Revos Prime."

"I want to stay with you no matter what ship we're on." EiLeen didn't realize how tense Dana had become until air gushed from her lungs and she slumped against her. "We have so much to talk about that can't wait. Or *I* can't wait."

"Agreed. I'm rather impatient myself." Dana pushed herself up on her elbow. "Should I go first?"

"Sure." Lifting her hands, EiLeen began to remove the pins from Dana's hair. "Just let me do this."

Dana's eyes glimmered in the sultriest of ways as her hair slowly tumbled down around her shoulders. She cupped EiLeen's cheek and then leaned in for a gentle kiss. "Just a recap first. I love you, EiLeen."

Bolts of happiness chased through EiLeen's chest and headed for her extremities. "And I love you."

"I don't want to be without you, even after this mission. I can't imagine my life without you in it. Somehow. Anyhow."

"Oh, darling, I feel that way too." Her insides molten with love and affection, EiLeen placed her hand against Dana's, holding it closer to her cheek. "I'm not sure how we'll make it happen, but we will. I—I need you. I adore the way you make me feel and I want to have you with me, to protect you, to hold you, to make love to you, and to have you do all those things for me."

"So eloquent," Dana murmured against her lips. "So very astute."

"I'm always astute."

"I won't argue." Parting her lips, Dana pressed them against EiLeen's. "Mmm. Mine."

And she was. No matter how independent, how ex-royal, and how famously infamous she was, she was Dana's now, and Dana was hers. It really was that easy after all. Love existed in this universe, this galaxy. No matter how jaded she'd been about such things, she knew now that she'd been extremely misguided. All she had to do was dare to grab for her good fortune and hold on. Easier said than done, but the alternative, to never be with Dana, or hold her, or even talk to her about mundane things, was completely out of the question. The mere thought made her heart twitch in agony, as if the idea of a solitary life made her heart threaten to go into full coronary. "Yes. I'm yours. And vice versa."

"Goes without saying." Dana wrapped her arms around EiLeen

and kissed her. Her tongue, slick and eager, parted her lips and requested entrance.

Immediately so turned on she lost her ability to speak, EiLeen met Dana's tongue with hers. The kisses were so many and close together, it seemed like an eternal caress.

CHAPTER TEN

D ana rolled on top of EiLeen. "Are you sure you're all right? No residual headache or anything?"

"None. I feel wonderful." EiLeen's smile widened. "And I think it's only fair to warn you. I've become accustomed to getting what I want over the last decades."

"Oh, yes?" Dana asked innocently. "Is that so?"

"It is. And now I want you."

"Mmm. Sounds good to me." She closed her eyes as EiLeen nipped at her collarbone through the uniform. "Mind if I lose some of these clothes?"

"It boggles the mind that you have to ask." Glittering irises surrounded star-shaped pupils as EiLeen pushed into a half-sitting position. "Do carry on, Captain."

Her jaw going slack for a second, Dana stared. "You're expecting me to put on a performance, my Queen?"

Now looking positively feral, EiLeen shook her head. "Normally I'd even pay to watch you do just that, but I think I'd rather you hurry. No finesse expected. Yet."

Dana chuckled, her nerves jumping at the last remark. Finesse. How could she possibly make love with any sort of skill when it had been so very long ago? Removing her clothes, she found herself hesitating, not because she was reluctant, but because her nerves were getting to her.

"Dana, look at me," EiLeen said, her voice as demanding as ever.

When Dana looked up, her insides contracted because of the onset of nerves and the sight of the extraordinary woman who wanted her. To her surprise, EiLeen's eyes had softened to a warm, loving glow.

"Yes?" Dana swallowed as she removed her shirt and stood there in just her camisole and briefs.

"You know I love you, right?" EiLeen's voice was so soft, so honey-golden, it made Dana's heart clench until she could hardly breathe.

"Yes." Before she decided to act any more like a bashful youngster, Dana got rid of the last pieces of clothes. She stood there naked for a few moments, EiLeen's eyes scorching her as they scanned her from her head to her feet.

"Come to bed. Come be with me, lindelei." EiLeen extended her hand.

Taking it and climbing onto the bed, Dana pulled the covers back and began to unfasten the clasps that held EiLeen's nightshirt together. "What does that mean? Lindelei?"

"It means 'most beloved.'"

"Am I?"

"Yes." EiLeen gasped softly and tugged her closer. Her nightshirt fell open as their bodies aligned.

"Lindelei. I like how it sounds and how it makes me feel." Dana closed her eyes briefly and absorbed the feeling of EiLeen's silky body. "And I *adore* how you feel."

"Then touch me."

"Yes." Dana opened her eyes and let her gaze roam across EiLeen's face and then down to her breasts. So beautiful, with puckered, rigid nipples. The sight of the naked expanse of skin made the area between her legs clench, a sensation that bordered on pain. "Stars and skies, EiLeen, it hurts." Dana moaned and pressed her lips against the side of EiLeen's neck. She licked a hot trail down to her left nipple and sucked it into her mouth.

EiLeen's cry was a mix between pain and pleasure. "Yes! Yes... more..."

Eager to devour her lover, her beloved, Dana moved her mouth back and forth between the two nipples, charmed by the small freckles that described rings around them. Perhaps that was an Imidestrian trait or perhaps just EiLeen. "I need more of you." Dana panted as she let go of a nipple.

"Anything, just don't—don't stop. Don't. Please." EiLeen whimpered and arched beneath Dana, who recognized she was much further along than she'd realized. Perhaps EiLeen was as hungry as she was?

"Open your legs for me, then. I need you just as much. I need you to be mine." Dana cupped the swollen labia between EiLeen's legs with as much care as possessiveness.

EiLeen arched her back further and reached for Dana as she complied. "I need to hold you. Dana. Dana." She was undulating against Dana's hand as she chanted her name. "Dana."

"I'm here. I'm not letting go." Dana caressed between the slick folds, searched for the opening, and hovered there, merely touching the entrance very lightly.

"Inside. Oh, please, please. Inside. Dana!"

As Dana pushed two fingers into EiLeen, she just knew this was right, this connection that stole her breath away and this urge to create pleasure for the wondrous woman in her arms; it was right. She curled her fingers, looked and hoped to find that special spot Earth women had but perhaps Imidestrian women didn't. "Tell me. I want you to feel really, really good, darling."

"I do. I do." EiLeen's hips had begun to jerk.

Then, Dana found a slightly rough patch that she carefully rubbed with her fingertips. EiLeen grew rigid and whimpered so loudly she almost howled. She clutched at Dana, held her tight against her, and the whole time she murmured under her breath, "Lindelei, lindelei…"

"Oh, stars, that's…you're beautiful, you're amazing." Her heart thundered and she knew without a doubt there could never be another like this woman. To have someone like EiLeen give herself so trustingly made her eyes glaze over with tears, and she crushed her lips to EiLeen's once more. "I love you," she said, murmuring the words as caresses in their own right against EiLeen's lips.

"And I you." EiLeen clung to her—husky, wild-eyed—and then she slumped back, melted, and flushed the most beautiful pink all the way down across her chest. Her hips rolled in long, slow waves, and inside, she squeezed Dana's fingers in an exquisite grip.

Dana held EiLeen, her lover—her *lover*—closer and withdrew her fingers gently. Her own sex was throbbing with need, but she was still more interested in providing a truly pleasurable experience for EiLeen.

As it turned out, her soft approach was thwarted because it took EiLeen only a short while to recuperate. One moment Dana was curled around EiLeen, caressing her back slowly, and the next, she was on her back with EiLeen gazing down at her with smoldering, all-pupil eyes.

"My turn to love you, don't you agree, Captain?" EiLeen's smile was part feral, part tenderness. "Do I assume you would enjoy something similar to what you bestowed upon me?"

"Mmm?" Dazed, she looked up at EiLeen, her eyes unfocused. "Sure?"

"You don't sound sure. I might have to experiment." Looking positively evil for a moment, EiLeen then smiled a very happy smile, her lips soft as she kissed Dana's lips, down her neck, across her collarbones, and across her to her left nipple. There, sharp teeth nibbled, pulled, and then EiLeen's tongue soothed ever so gently.

"Again?" Dana whispered. "Oh, again!"

"My pleasure."

The caress kept going until both of Dana's nipples were red, aching in the sweetest of ways and nearly too raw to touch. Too close to orgasm to stand the onslaught of sensual caresses any longer, Dana rubbed her sex against EiLeen's thigh, her movements jerky and desperate.

"It's that bad, is it, Dana?" EiLeen whispered hotly in her ear. "Then let me help you. Dana." EiLeen's hand was suddenly between her legs, her slender fingers sliding deep inside and filling her with the sweetest of needs.

Shaking uncontrollably and gasping for air so fast she felt her head spin, Dana clung to EiLeen, her only safe harbor right now. "Now. I'm so close. Oh, now, now." Convulsing, she pressed her lips against the damp skin of EiLeen's neck. Groaning deep in her chest, she bore down on EiLeen's fingers, ground herself against her ever-caressing hand.

"So good, so good," EiLeen murmured in her ear. "So beautiful to watch, so amazing to touch."

"You...you're incredible." Dana curled up against EiLeen, who carefully pulled her fingers out. The river of moisture between her legs was close to embarrassing, but the memory of how wet EiLeen had been against her fingers made her shrug and choose to not let it faze her. Leaning her head on EiLeen's shoulder, she drew a slightly unsteady pattern across her chest. "You sure we didn't hurt your head?"

"You're joking, right?"

"No?"

"I'm perfectly fine, lindelei." EiLeen tugged her closer. "Don't worry about me. I'm a tough old broad."

Dana couldn't help it. The comment was so haughtily expressed and so ridiculous, she burst out laughing. Giggling helplessly, she clung to her lover. "Old broad? Now, *that's* funny."

"You really never struck me as the giggly type." EiLeen shook her head but smiled indulgently. "Actually, it's rather refreshing."

Dana closed her eyes and let the happiness simmer just beneath her skin. She couldn't believe how safe and how gloriously wonderful it was to be in EiLeen's arms. Running her hands through the short, silky gray hair, she inhaled the special fragrance that was EiLeen. It was tinged with the scent of their lovemaking, which made it even more alluring.

"Will you stay with me in my quarters for the remainder of this journey?" Dana's heart painfully beat double-time at the thought of what lay ahead once they reached Revos Prime. Afraid to ask, but with careful optimism, she waited for EiLeen's answer.

"Yes, lindelei, yes."

EPILOGUE

A dmiral Jacelon. It's been too long. How's Dahlia?" EiLeen stood
just inside the door of the main ballroom aboard the *Koenigin*.

"She's visiting our daughter and her family on Gantharat. Do
call me Ewan, like you used to." The distinguished admiral bent over
EiLeen's hand and kissed it gallantly. "She hates being separated for
more than a couple of months."

"Of course. I've followed your daughter's success. Being an
admiral as well as a protector of the realm is quite the undertaking."

"Not to mention mothering the young prince."

"Yes, that too." EiLeen turned and motioned toward the woman
to her right. "May I introduce Captain Dana Rhoridan, Ewan? I believe
you know her by reputation."

"I sure do," the admiral said, and smiled benevolently at the
ramrod-straight woman next to EiLeen. "At ease, Captain."

"Thank you. It's an honor to meet you, sir."

"Likewise, Captain. As we're in a civilian setting, how about if
you allow me to call you Dana? I'm Ewan."

"Thank you." Dana glanced over at EiLeen, her eyes softening
and her stance changing from a military at-ease to a comfortable pose.
"May I bring you something to drink from the bar, EiLeen? Ewan?"

"I think we should have some Imidestrian sparkling wine, darling."
EiLeen smiled inwardly at how the woman she loved winced at the term
of endearment. Dana still wasn't used to them being a couple in public.
Four months of bliss in private, officially a couple for two weeks after
returning from Revos Prime.

"Certainly. Excuse me." Dana escaped after a quick, wide-eyed glance at EiLeen.

"Do tell me to shut up if I'm meddling. Did I just hear you call the captain of the *Koenigin* 'darling'?" Ewan stroked his becoming white beard.

"You did. I'm a very fortunate woman. She's quite the catch."

The look of consternation on the admiral's face was hilarious, but also something of a concern. "I seem to recall that Captain Rhoridan applied to be reassigned to active overt duty."

"She did after my cover as ex-royal playgirl fell through. Now that I'm planning to assume a more behind-the-scenes role for SC intelligence, I'll be able to work from a multitude of locations. We're hoping she'll be placed fairly close to Earth, or at least one of SC's sub-headquarters."

"I know Captain Rhoridan would balk at any special favors, but after what the two of you went through to reach Revos Prime, I think you deserve a break." Ewan's pale-blue eyes glittered. "Also, I've learned from my female family members how women can move mountains when teamed up with the one they care about. It's unfortunately a little too exciting for an old man."

"Old man? Hardly." EiLeen tilted her head. "Thank you, Ewan. Let's not tell Dana about any special favors, though. She'd be very embarrassed."

"What favors?" Ewan winked before focusing on something behind her. "Ah, here's Dana now with our drinks. Perfect timing."

As they sipped their sparkling wine, Ewan excused himself and began to mingle with other SC leaders.

"So, he's going to help us, is he?" Dana asked casually.

"What?" EiLeen felt the wine enter her nose from her throat. Coughing and sneezing discreetly, she glared at Dana. "Are you trying to drown me, lindelei?"

"No, no." Dana's laughter was mirrored in her glittering eyes. "Not even in a glass of sparkling wine. Imidestrian or not. I still think I'm right, and judging from your not-so-controlled reaction, I'd say I hit on the head."

"Hit what on the head?" Dabbing her nose delicately, EiLeen frowned.

"The nail."

"A nail? I have no clue what you're talking about. Then again, you don't always make sense, but I love you anyway."

"Ouch." Dana grinned. "And you're stalling, my Queen."

EiLeen breathed out in a huff. "Very well. Yes. Ewan Jacelon is going to help us. Pull some strings, and before you get all I-don't-need-any-favors on me, Captain, be assured, he's not only doing it out of the goodness of his heart. They'll be able to pair us up and use us, one way or the other. Just so you know."

Dana seemed to ponder this remark for a moment. "Then that's all I need to know. In fact, it sounds pretty damn good to me."

"I agree."

Pulling EiLeen with her in behind a lush Cormanian palm tree, Dana kissed her thoroughly. "I love you. And this way I get to keep an eye on you so you don't disappear on me."

EiLeen blinked a few times. "Disappear? Never. Never, never, never." She rested her head on Dana's shoulder. Whether aboard the *Koenigin* or any other ship, a space station, or planetside somewhere, this woman was her home. Dana was where she belonged.

Exodus
The Dawning

CHAPTER ONE

S he's a cold-hearted, manipulative, insane know-it-all!" Meija Solimar stormed into the foreman's office and threw herself into a chair. "She thinks we're dealing with bloody cattle and not humans who require a damn *life* aboard these mastodon ships she's building. The specs aren't even fit for livestock, come to think of it. A cow requires certain things to produce milk fit for human consumption. She'll end up producing hundreds of thousands, if not millions, of people gone space mad!"

Gessley Barr, normally a soft-spoken, authoritative man, regarded Meija with obvious caution, as if trying to figure out how to defuse her. This wasn't the first time she'd exploded while trying to deal with the woman in charge of building the ships that would save the Oconodian people, but now Meija knew if she had to lay eyes on the infuriatingly stubborn Chief Engineer Korrian Heigel, there was likely to be bloodshed.

Gessley eyed her tentatively. "This has to be a record. It's the third time this week alone that you've been in here tearing your hair out over the boss."

"She's not my *boss*." Meija spat the words but then relented. This wasn't Gessley's fault. He carried out Heigel's orders like everyone else, civilian or military, because it was his job. But Meija was an independent contractor working for the Social and Cultural Department. She didn't take her orders from Heigel but from the minister of her department alone. Her job was to make sure life was sustainable aboard the massive vessels being constructed in orbit around Oconodos, from a social-anthropological point of view. This task sent her on a perpetual collision course with Heigel.

"Barr, I need more engineers working on—" As if conjured up by Meija's rage, Korrian Heigel flung the door open, spitting orders before she was even inside Gessley's office. Spotting Meija, she pressed her lips into a fine line. "Ah, so this is where you come to get your bruised ego patted."

"Now there's a sign of an enormous ego if I ever saw one. Why would you assume that I'm bruised? Regardless of your lack of manners, I'm tougher than I look."

"I would hope so if I were you." Heigel sauntered over to the desk and rested her hip against it, effectively towering over the two of them, who were sitting down. She was as sexy as she was intimidating, not to mention frustrating. "I don't know how many times I have to explain to a civilian just what's at stake here. We can't humor your romantic ideas of 'generational space cities.' We have to make sure we have enough bunks for close to two million individuals before this curse, or plague, turns us into something our species won't survive. We have less than twenty years to do this. You *know* this, Meija."

"I know the facts and the figures as well as you do." Meija had never heard Heigel use her first name before. Normally she called her Solimar or, on even worse days, "you there." "That doesn't mean you can ship people like they were less than cattle. If you were to do this, you'll have stark-raving-mad people after only a few years, maybe just months. Unless the scientists have developed cryo-sleep that won't actually kill you, racking and stacking the people on the ships won't *work.*"

"See what I have to listen to every single day?" Heigel flung her hands into the air. She was a stunning, tall woman with warm-toned, chocolate-colored skin. Black hair in ringlets tumbled out from the cap of her uniform. Adorned with silver trim around the edges, it was the first obvious sign of her rank as a senior officer.

Stark, icy gray eyes looked at Meija with barely concealed annoyance. Her straight, wide nose with delicate nose wings that often gave away the fact she was about to explode was contradicted by the fullness of her curvy lips. Normally, Meija would find such a mouth a hard-to-resist temptation, but when all the words that came across them were disdainful, impatient, and frustrated—hell, Heigel was still damn attractive, no matter her lack of manners or ability to cooperate. It was disheartening to know that no matter what, Heigel would never regard her in any other way than with cold exasperation.

"If you could at least try to spell the word 'compromise,' then we could have a slim chance of producing a prototype of a ship that our leaders can agree on. As it is now, Heigel, you're creating more problems than you're solving." Meija crossed her arms.

"Have you listened to yourself? Can't you hear how condescending and overbearing you sound? And my name is Korrian. You constantly point out that I'm not your boss, so stop referring to me as Heigel. I keep looking for my father when you do that."

This sudden trace of humor was so unexpected, Meija blinked and merely stared. "All right. Korrian. I'm Meija."

Nodding curtly, Korrian relaxed marginally and sat down on Gessley's desk. "How the hell do we work together to keep Ms. Desomas happy?"

"I don't really care how happy or unhappy Desomas is. I worry what would happen to the population if they're suddenly imprisoned and confined to less space than the inmates in the current prisons are."

"The ships will save them, not imprison them!" Korrian slammed her palm onto her thigh.

"What will they do in their spare time, day after day, year after year?"

"Survive."

Jumping to her feet, Meija glowered at Korrian, trying desperately to reach her and not antagonize her further. "Surviving isn't enough. It never is. You have to live. Laugh. Love your family, your spouse, your parents. Spend time with them. Play. Especially the children need to play, but the adults too. The youngsters will need places to meet and socialize, and learn the skills they need to navigate through relationships. If they're confined to your tiny cubes, yes, we will get more people aboard each vessel, but we'll see morale deteriorate very rapidly, probably within months after the novelty wears off."

"What do you think of this type of reasoning, Barr?" Korrian whirled to face the man who clearly tried to look inconspicuous behind his desk.

"Both of your standpoints have merits. We need to save as many as possible, so compromising the size of the quarters is prudent." Gessley cleared his throat and studied the ceiling. "I'm trying to picture myself aboard one of the Exodus ships, and the idea of being kept, fed, and stored is not very appealing."

"Every basic need will be met," Korrian said, frowning.

"We have other basic needs than merely surviving." Meija made sure her tone was even. "People need a purpose, something to strive for, to play with, and to imagine. If we place them in tiny cubes with no options but to eat and sleep, soon you'll have riots and downright mutinies."

"Your job isn't going to be easy, Commander Heigel." Gessley laced his fingers and rested his chin on his hands. "I know Meija is coming on strong here, but she has a point. Our leaders have initiated Project Exodus, and soon the advance team will leave orbit to explore and reconnoiter a new home for us. I can't even imagine the burden that lies on your shoulders, but don't let our leaders' anxiety attacks steer you off target. The ships will carry our people for decades, maybe even longer, to a new home."

Korrian opened the top button of her uniform jacket and sat down in the chair next to Meija. "I have lived, breathed, and dreamed these specs and my prototype for five years now. Ever since the so-called plague became public knowledge, this has become my reason for existing. I have daily messages from politicians and different governmental departments demanding I squeeze beds and cots into every possible area of the ships. Don't either of you have the audacity to claim I don't give this enough thought."

Meija hadn't realized how much pressure Korrian must be under. She'd only seen the woman's pigheaded, opinionated approach. Her own frustration—she willingly admitted to be something of a hothead as well—had probably done very little to help Korrian see reason.

"I'm not saying that. Ah, well, I guess that's what I've been implying, isn't it?" Meija grunted. "If we can compromise, you should be able to come up with a prototype that allows for maximized passenger numbers and still make it the home it has to be—what?"

Korrian sat up straight, her eyes narrow slits. She didn't look angry or annoyed, though, merely focused. "What did you say?" she asked slowly.

Suddenly nervous, Meija cast a glance at Gessley. "A prototype that can maximize—"

"No, not that. You said, make it a home." Getting up from the chair, Korrian began pacing, a familiar sight by now. "A home. Not merely transportation." She muttered under her breath as she pulled out a computer sheet and tapped it. She drew new lines, punched in commands, and it was as if she had completely forgotten she wasn't alone. "Use the light-sensors to propel…add extra output…less need for propulsion energy." Korrian stopped and looked at Meija and Gessley as if she'd forgotten who they were. "Meija, you've been on my case since day one. Now's your chance to get some of your ideas through. That means you're going to have to reside in the engineers' quarters rather than the space station."

Meija tried to follow Korrian's thought process but failed, mostly. "You—are you saying suddenly you want my input?" What had happened the last few minutes?

"Won't it thrill you that some of your outlandish ideas might have merit?" Korrian gave a crooked smile. "I would've thought so, as I have no problem recollecting your endless chatter about quality of life and areas to *breathe* in."

"Of course I want you and the authorities to listen."

"We have two days to get the first blueprints and model done. This will take some unconventional problem-solving."

"Why can't I stay at the hotel on the space station?" Meija had lived in the hotel for two months now and didn't mind the short shuttle trip between the station and the space-dock where the prototype vessel was being built.

"I have to have access to you and your input around the clock, and I can't wait for the shuttle to carry you back and forth. If you're going to contribute, you're going to have to forfeit the luxuries and share a room here."

Meija had just begun to consider the idea of living at the local crew quarters but hadn't counted on that last part. "Share a room? With whom?" She knew, of course, since Korrian looked a tad ill at ease. "Share your quarters?"

"As chief engineer, my quarters are more spacious than the others." Korrian shrugged. "I can't come up with a better solution, can you?"

Meija thought fast. On one side, she would finally have a chance to influence the design of the ships that would save the Oconodian people, and on the other, she'd have to stay in such close proximity to the woman who had made her life living hell for so long. Meija looked down at her hands, so tightly clasped her fingertips were white. "All right," she heard herself say. "I'll have my things sent over. I trust you'll give me some closet space?"

"Sure." Did Korrian sound relieved, or was Meija's imagination playing tricks on her?

"Excellent," Gessley said, and rounded his desk. "This will work very well, I can feel it."

"We'll see." Korrian buttoned her jacket and adjusted her cap. "Go sort your things out, Meija. I'll be at the drawing board in the main studio. Barr, get me four more engineers, at least. I don't care who you have to schmooze. Just do it."

Meija merely nodded, still a little shell-shocked at what had been decided so hastily. She watched Korrian stride out the door and cross the main walkway, heading back to do her job. How was it possible that she suddenly was in this position of power and influence? Going from frustrated consultant to working closely with the brilliant woman in charge of constructing the only way for their people to survive boggled her mind.

CHAPTER TWO

Korrian gripped the laser pen and began working. Using the old draft as a template, she tried to remember all the things Meija had said that she had blown off as utter nonsense. Had she been so blinded by her own ambition to succeed and the desire to prove herself to her superior officers? As she'd told Barr and Meija, she'd lived and breathed this project for years on end, and at the rate the population changed and spread in some parts, they couldn't complete it fast enough. Physicians and geneticists had declared they'd lose control of the situation if the planet-wide evacuation didn't take place within two decades.

Now, for the first time in ages, she found herself reenergized and motivated to look at the project from a new angle. She couldn't quite pinpoint why she'd resisted even trying a new concept, other than that she'd been stuck—and fatigued after working with hardly any days off for too long.

Meija Solimar had blasted into the space-dock, a strange and rare bird among the homogenous group of engineers and ships' mechanics. Dressed in her very new Oconodian uniform adorned with insignia rank of provisional non-commissioned officer, she'd looked fresh-faced and idealistic. Korrian wondered if Meija's ethereal beauty, which made her look younger and unseasoned, had made her not listen to her opinions.

"So this is where the magic happens." As if conjured from Korrian's thoughts, Meija showed up to her left, smiling carefully. "I don't pretend to know anything about blueprints or technical drawings, but even I can understand that this is top-of-the-line technology. Our leaders spare no expense."

"Nor should they if they want to save the Oconodians."

"Some of the Oconodians." Meija's light-green eyes darkened. "The changed ones are still Oconodians." Something, a catch, in Meija's voice made Korrian stop what she was doing and put her laser pen down.

"These changes they're going through, whether called the plague or the curse, puts them on a collision course with the rest of us. As they're growing in numbers and the incidents where normal—"

"Normal." Meija's lips tensed. "An interesting word. Especially when wielded against something we don't understand and which is much bigger than us."

"Are you saying I'm prejudiced? Or merely uneducated?"

"No. There have been far too many incidents where Changed individuals have used their superior strength or mental powers to injure unchanged Oconodians. I just don't want to believe that all those instances happened deliberately or with malice."

"I see. Evidently someone close to you has Changed." Korrian pushed a tall stool closer to the work area. "You don't have to respond to that. It's really none of my business. Take a seat. We have work to do." Looking up at Meija, she could see that her words had struck a nerve. Meija, paling slightly, merely nodded and climbed onto the stool.

"Very well. You seem to have altered the original plans a bit already." She pointed at the images on the sheet. "This looks like a strange sort of bicycle wheel."

"Just a rough sketch. Something you said about the ships becoming the passengers' home. I suddenly saw the design in my mind. Twenty ships altogether. Average one hundred thousand individuals on each vessel. Two in the center, eighteen others in a circle around them, all connected with the center ones by roads in the shape of spokes on a wheel, so to speak. Magnetic locks will keep the ships together in this shape, and the two in the middle will hold the propulsion system. By constructing the ship this way, I can make the other vessels in the outer ring much larger without compromising speed or wasting resources. In fact, it will actually be beneficial in the long run." Korrian again watched Meija's expression change—from grave to curious to excited.

"You're serious?" Meija leaned forward and her unruly ponytail landed on the drawings. "Oh. Sorry." Smiling broadly, she tucked the strawberry-blond tresses into her cap. "So, what am I looking at here?" She pointed at the part of the drawing Korrian had just changed.

"That's the addition. I can add about twenty-five percent of space to each ship without compromising speed or structural integrity. The bridge will be located here, in the middle, directly connected to both of the center ships."

"And this?" Meija tapped with a perfectly manicured blunt nail on the sheet. "These areas running along—"

Ear-splitting thunder rolled through the dock toward them. Korrian looked up and went cold at the sight of loose objects being hurled through the air. "Down!" She tugged frantically at Meija and pulled her onto the floor. Covering the slighter body with her own, she closed her eyes and held on to Meija, who in turn hid her face against Korrian's shoulder.

"What's going on?" Meija called out, then coughed as dust whipped at them. "What the hell was that?"

"Damn if I know." Korrian struggled to get up; the floor was still trembling because as the inertial dampeners had not yet recovered. "I have no one working on anything remotely explosive or combustible. Stay here." She pushed away from the table and began walking on the still-unsteady floor toward the door leading to the space-dock.

"No way. I'm going with you." Meija caught up with her. "Your temple is bleeding." She reached into her pockets and pulled out a tissue. "Here."

Grudgingly, Korrian accepted it and pressed it to the side of her head, which throbbed badly. Examining the tissue, she saw that the cut was worse than she'd expected. "Guess I might need repairing."

"You're not dizzy, are you?" Meija placed a gentle hand at the small of Korrian's back.

The touch elicited a shudder that traveled up her spine and down the back of her legs. Korrian sucked in her lower lip between her teeth. "I'm fine. Let's go."

They moved carefully between tipped-over cabinets, tables, and chairs. In the distance the alarm klaxons blared consistently. Finally they reached the tall doors leading into the vast hall that contained all the equipment, tools, and doors to the different airlocks. The doors leading out to open space, where they were building the prototype while outfitted with space suits and mini tool-shuttles, had several backup systems. As long as the reason for the explosion was unknown, she couldn't assume the safety systems hadn't been compromised.

"I see two guys over there, on all fours, but moving at least." Meija pointed to the left. "And one more behind them. How many were working in here?"

"Six, unless they were fetching something from storage or"— Korrian motioned with her head toward the airlocks—"or outside. I have to reach the comm system over there by the main computer console. Do you think you can help the guys and look for the missing ones? I'll be right there to help you."

"Sure." Meija narrowed her eyes and focused on Korrian's temple. "The bleeding's stopped for now. Just keep that tissue handy. You're going to need to see a doctor."

"Later." Korrian nodded briefly and turned to make her way through the rubble. She walked a few paces then turned. "Meija? Be careful."

"You too."

Shuffling through the mess of tools and other equipment toward the computer, she saw increasing activity outside the view ports and hoped nobody had to pay with their life for whatever had caused the mayhem around them. Reaching the console, she opened the emergency communication channel. "Emergency, emergency, this is Chief Engineer Korrian Heigel. What's going on?"

A female voice replied. "Dispatch here. What's your status, Commander Heigel?"

"So far no fatalities. I have Meija Solimar here and she's searching our facility looking for my staff. I've seen three of them move but don't know the extent of their injuries. Any idea what caused the explosion?"

"Not yet, ma'am. We've deployed rescue teams as one of the airlocks on the lower decks disengaged. We think that was the origin of the explosion."

"Is Colonel Rayginnia there?"

"Ma'am, the colonel is among the injured. She was conducting a tour of the space-dock for some members of the Main Ministry."

"Oh, damn. We have ministers roaming around the facility and *this* happens?"

"Yes, ma'am."

"All right. Dispatch emergency personnel to my location. I'll help Ms. Solimar conduct a search-and-rescue until they get here. Heigel out." Hurrying back to where she'd left Meija, she found the first man, one of her engineers, sitting on the floor with a makeshift tourniquet around his thigh. A metal bar had perforated his calf and now he was grayish and pale.

"Belonder, how are you doing?" Korrian knelt next to the young man.

"Not too bad, Commander. Ms. Solimar is very capable."

"Help's on the way. Just stay put and they'll take care of you." Korrian moved to the other two. A woman was cradling the head of a man lying on the floor next to her. Korrian recognized two junior engineers, fresh out of a prestigious university in Conos, the capital. The man's head was a bloody mess.

"Commander…" The woman looked up, wide-eyed and pale. "The cabinet fell, and, and, Toimi, he, the tools just—"

"Shh. Just stay with him. Help's on the way. Do you hear me, Reeva? Emergency personnel are coming." Korrian knelt and felt for Toimi's pulse. Fast and thin, but it was there against her fingertips, and he was breathing. "Call out for me if you need me. I have to check for the others. Were all six of you in here?"

"No. Just Chassine. The others went off duty an hour ago." Reeva kept caressing Toimi's cheek. "That new woman, she went over there. Chassine's station." Sobbing quietly, Reeva pointed to the far left of the hall.

"I'll go and check on them. Hang in there." Korrian made her way, not without difficulty, as this was where they kept the large disks for the mainframe computers. Made of metal-infused glass, they had shattered and left sharp edges everywhere. She hoped some had survived with the backup plans and blueprints intact, but that wasn't her main concern right now. Rounding two overturned desks, she gasped as she saw two uniformed legs sticking out from under a third desk, which in turn was buried under a large shelf.

"Meija?" Korrian bent down and tried to see what was going on.

"Korrian! Chassine's in here. She's stuck."

"Vital signs?"

"Pulse is very weak and her breathing is shallow. I've managed to support her head enough to help her breathe every now and then. I think she has bruised or broken ribs. We're going to need the portable crane."

"Got it. Help's on the way. I'll go see if the ceiling crane is working. Will you be all right?"

"Sure, I will. I just ho—" Another explosion, this time farther away, shook the facility. The bookcase slid toward Korrian, who realized it would end up on Meija's legs if she didn't stop it. Throwing herself at the shelf with all her might, Korrian looked around for something to prop up against it. Anything. Her eyes fell upon a canister of metal bars, but there was no way she'd be able to reach it. "Meija, you need to back out as fast as you can."

"I can't leave Chassine."

"And I can't hold the shelf up away from your legs much longer. You have to get out. Now!" Did this woman argue about absolutely everything?

"All right." Meija shimmied out from under the desk and jumped to her feet. "Oh, hell, what do you need?"

"Grab some of the metal bars over there." Grunting, Korrian braced herself against the slipping shelf. "Hurry!"

Pushing through the rubble, Meija reached the canister and took several of the heavy bars, which she carried back and pushed against the shelf and wedged against the floor. Korrian had to admit she was impressed, a feeling that didn't decrease when Meija dived back under the desk as soon as the last metal bar was in place.

"Korrian, she's not breathing!"

"Will I fit in there?"

"I...don't think...so." Meija was clearly breathing with Chassine. "Just get help."

Korrian glanced over her shoulder. "They're here. I'll go find the damn hoist."

Korrian worked tirelessly for the next two hours. The emergency personnel had taken care of the wounded, with the exception of Chassine, right away. Meija, of course, refused to surrender her spot under the desk. She didn't emerge until Korrian and Gessley managed to lift the shelf and then the desk away from the unconscious woman. The emergency personal had given her equipment to help keep breathing for Chassine when the young woman stopped, which she did every four or five minutes.

"You all right?" Korrian said, and quickly steadied Meija when she wobbled. "Easy."

"Just a bit light-headed."

"Hardly surprising since you've been cramped in there for so long."

"Chassine is so young. She'll be all right, won't she?" Meija wiped at her wet lashes.

"No matter what, she has you to thank for stabilizing her." Korrian pushed her hair out of her eyes. "Now that we've evacuated everybody, we need to get cleaned up before LEO wants to interview us. Crime scene investigators are waiting to take over as well." Korrian had dealt with Law Enforcement Orbit before and knew they wouldn't leave anything to chance.

"So we're sure this was manmade and not an accident?" Meija rubbed at her lower back and frowned.

"No, not sure, but two explosions in totally unrelated places, nearly at the same time?" Shrugging, Korrian guided Meija through the rubble. "You hurt your back, didn't you?"

"No, I'm fine. Just need to clean up a bit, like you said."

"My, or should I say *our,* quarters are on deck ten. Come on." Not quite thinking, she wrapped her arm around Meija's shoulders. "We need a break."

Chapter Three

Meija regarded Korrian's quarters and knew she couldn't hide her feeling of utter shock. Every possible surface held drawings, blueprints, models, and literature. She glanced at the en suite bathroom, wondering if she would find as much work-related clutter in there. Her luggage had been delivered and sat just inside Korrian's outer door, but she didn't see anywhere to unpack. "You've got to be kidding."

"I know. It looks pretty bad." Korrian actually colored, which highlighted her chocolate-colored complexion with a lovely golden-pink hue. "Why don't you hit the restroom and have a shower, and I'll clean out some drawers and so on?"

"A shower. I'd kill for a shower, so why not?" Meija grabbed one of her bags and closed the door behind her. Regarding her reflection in the mirror she moaned inwardly in silent horror. Dusty, grimy, her hair stuck out in all directions, half braided and half a total mess. Her eye makeup had smudged and her shirt was shredded all along her left arm. "No wonder she wanted me to clean up. I could scare sensitive individuals or be cast as everyone's favorite monster bride in a horror flick." Groaning, Meija removed her torn clothes and stepped into the shower stall. She'd gotten used to the constantly recycled water rarely being more than lukewarm on the space-dock, and this was also true for the showers. Still, it was refreshing to get clean and she reveled in the sensation of soft towels against her skin. Digging through her bag, she pulled out underwear and a new uniform. She doubted her dirty clothes were salvageable and planned to recycle them at the closest recyc-station. This would give her enough points to use in the space-station shops.

She towel-dried her hair and didn't bother to style it, merely fashioned a loose sort of side braid. After adding some makeup to take away the paleness and dark circles, she felt ready to join Korrian. The poor woman was probably dying to use her own shower by now. Returning to the living area, she saw Korrian had been as efficient in removing the clutter as she was in her work at the drawing board.

"I've made room for you here," Korrian said, and pointed at two open drawers, "and over there." She pushed open a sliding door to a closet. "Judging from the size of your bags, you'll be able to fit your things in here."

"Thank you. Bathroom's all yours."

"All right." Korrian stood, and only now did Meija see how stiffly the other woman was moving. "Make yourself at home. When I'm done, we can get something from the dispenser to eat."

"Sure." Meija watched surreptitiously as Korrian limped to the bathroom. "Did you hurt yourself?"

"I'm fine." Korrian glanced at Meija over her shoulder. "Thank you."

Once she was alone, Meija unpacked her things and placed the bag with the destroyed uniform by the door. Looking back at Korrian's quarters, she realized they were quite large compared to the tiny cubes that junior officers squeezed into. Korrian had two single beds in a bedroom away from the main living area and a small kitchenette that made simple cooking possible if she grew tired of the dispenser. Normally a food dispenser had pretty good selections, but some people still enjoyed old-fashioned cooking. She couldn't tell if Korrian ever cooked; in fact, the living area was devoid of any of the personal belongings such as photos, art, or knickknacks that most people gathered.

Korrian suddenly stood next to her, also dressed in a fresh uniform. "All settled?"

"Yes. Thank you." Why hadn't she noticed until now just how devastatingly beautiful Korrian was? Perhaps because she used to wear a perpetual scowl as soon as she saw Meija? Right now, with her hair in soft, damp curls, her eyes even darker as if shadowed by what had just happened, and a little more off guard, she was stunning. There was still something dangerous, almost wild, about her, sort of simmering under the surface. No doubt, if challenged, or agitated, or heaven forbid, attacked, this woman could explode.

"How about some stew?" Korrian said as she rounded Meija and walked up to the dispenser. "Not even a dispenser can screw up a regular stew."

"Sounds good. I mean, I'm not really hungry, but—"

"Me either. We have to eat, though. Once we go back, they'll keep us for quite a while, and then we need to clean up the mess and continue working." Korrian punched commands into the dispenser. "You acted very selflessly today." Her voice sank to a low murmur. "In fact, I thought we'd lose both you and Chassine under there."

"I couldn't leave her. She stopped breathing every five minutes. At least." Uncomfortable at the praise, Meija sat down in the cleared dining area.

Korrian placed a bowl of stew in front of her. "Utensils in the drawer under the table. What would you like to drink?"

"Just water, please."

Soon they were both seated, eating in silence. Meija discovered she was actually famished and devoured her food without even looking up. She gulped down her water, and only then did she notice that Korrian had put down her spoon and regarded her with half a smile.

"So, I was hungry after all. I had no idea."

"Glad you could eat." Glowering down at her own bowl, Korrian merely drank her water and then began to clear the table. "Want more?"

"No, no, thank you. I'm full." Meija watched Korrian put the dishes into the cleanser unit. "I want to say something." She looked at her laced fingers and then back up at Korrian, who had stopped what she was doing. "I realize you're an intensely private person. I mean, I don't know you, but it's not like I'm totally blind. So for you to offer to share your quarters, just so this project doesn't stall, is pretty fantastic. I appreciate it, and I'll do my best to not get in your way."

Korrian avoided her eyes for a moment but then met Meija's gaze head-on. "You don't have to feel you're intruding. Not at all. I'm not the easiest person to get along with, and most of my staff would agree that I'm hard to please. You, however, have some good ideas that I hadn't allowed myself to consider quite the same way before." Frowning, Korrian rubbed her temple. "Which is not usually how I function at work either, strangely enough."

"So we're really off to a new start?" Meija hoped this was true.

"Looks like it. The fact that neither of us has yelled at the other in hours must be a good sign."

Meija laughed. She had to since this was the first time she'd noticed Korrian showing any trace of a sense of humor whatsoever. "Guess we should get down to the mayhem."

"Yes. They should be done with the security sweeps of our part of the space-dock. As the senior officer among the engineers, I need to be there."

"And where you need to be, so do I." Meija only realized how that might sound when the words left her lips. "I mean, workwise. Not on your free time. So. Well." *Stop talking!* Meija adjusted her uniform and placed a new cap on her unruly hair before she looked briefly at Korrian.

Korrian actually smiled. Not the disdainful smirk that Meija had seen countless times before, but a small, bashful, and rather endearing smile. Genuine-looking.

"Let's go," Korrian said, and held open the door. "Hey, wait. Let's get your handprint logged in for the inner door." She opened a small door to the right of the door. "Place your palm here." She pointed to a silvery square inside. As Meija held her hand against it, Korrian entered her code and finished by confirming the entry with her own handprint.

The elevator was out of service, as it had to be scanned by the safety teams, so they had to hurry down the stairs and reached their offices and main engineering just in time to catch Gessley as he walked out of the conference room.

"Good timing," he said, looking tired. "They're waiting to grill you. Especially you, Meija." He shook his head.

"What's that supposed to mean?" Korrian asked before Meija had a chance.

"Just that they've heard about the way Meija's been complaining about the Exodus project." Gessley shrugged. "I told them they're totally off track, but from looking at them—"

"Ms. Solimar. Perfect timing." A tall, gangly woman stood in the doorway to the conference room. "Why don't you join us first, and my colleague will interview Commander Heigel in the room across from here?" Her black bangs framed a face consisting of sharp planes and narrow, dark eyes.

"Sure, why not?" Meija swallowed her sudden onset of nerves. Glancing at Korrian, she shrugged and followed the LEO officer.

Three men sat around the table and looked at her in a non-expressive way similar to the woman's. "I'm Inspector Nacqui. These gentlemen are on my team." Nacqui didn't introduce them by name but merely gestured for Meija to take a seat. Leaning against the table next to Meija, Nacqui towered above her, pursing her lips for a few moments before she spoke. "So, Ms. Solimar, we hear that you're not a fan of the Exodus project?"

CHAPTER FOUR

K orrian waited impatiently for Meija to emerge from the conference room. Her own interview had only taken twenty minutes, a mere recounting of what she remembered from the first and second explosion. It bothered her that some questions seemed to indicate an interest in Meija's whereabouts as well as her opinions. Could they seriously suspect her of sabotaging the Exodus project? Meija was driven and convinced that her ideas about how the generational ships should be constructed had merit.

"Looks like they think they're onto something with Meija." Gessley Barr showed up and handed her a cup of tea. "I mean, I like the kid, I do, but she's been stirring things up ever since Minister Desomas commissioned her. Not smart when you want to change something from within. I tried telling her that."

"I thought you agreed with her?" Korrian held her mug but didn't drink. Instead she paid attention with her entire system to the man who'd listened to her complaints regarding Meija so many times.

"Some of her thoughts about not treating our people as cattle—her words, not mine—were correct," he said. "She's young, of course, and idealistic. She doesn't know when to back off, when to compromise."

"You're joking, right?" Korrian didn't like that Barr was selling Meija short this way.

"No, I'm not. I'm devastated that people got hurt today, and it sure pains me that someone among us would resort to such methods."

"I must be more exhausted than I realized. Who are you accusing, exactly?" Korrian put her mug down, untouched.

"Oh, nobody in particular. You know, the person responsible might not have realized how severe the blast would become. She—they might just have tried to make a stand for what's right. You know, these fools and the way they demand righteousness and sacrifice and so on. Idiots."

"I don't think I've ever heard you talk like this, Barr. They might oppose the project, but everyone is entitled to their opinion." Was Barr the type that was only too ready to distance himself from someone who looked like they might drag him down? "You're not suggesting Meija could be behind the attack, are you?"

"I wouldn't presume to have an opinion as to who the saboteur is." He shrugged. "All I know is she's the newest one here, and she's sure brought some serious critique to the table. She's probably nothing more than a young, idealistic do-gooder. Who knows?"

"If she's anything, she's brave, bordering on foolish." Korrian shook her head and strode over through her office to where the maintenance staff had now put back her desk. She ran some diagnostics on her equipment, relieved that everything seemed intact. "Computer. Pull up latest schematics."

"Affirmative." The last blueprints lay spread over her large desk sheet. Korrian grabbed her laser pen and went to work. Her mind was still jumbled with thoughts of Meija and what might be going on behind the door to the conference room. The passionate Meija, who'd risked her life for someone she hardly knew a few hours ago, would never sabotage the Exodus project. *Would she?* An evil voice tried to spread doubt in the back of her mind. Would Meija go to such extremes to get her way, and the way of the minister who placed her on the space-dock?

But when would she have placed the devices, and how? Granted, Meija could have come and gone as she pleased within the facility, but only during the times when she was logged in to be there. She had stayed in the space-station hotel nearby until today and had to take the shuttle over, which was recorded. What if surveillance cameras could place her in the places where the explosives had been placed? Granted, lots of contractors and personnel visited several of the units in the dock, but in Meija's case, which was already on the LEO's radar, her presence there could be potentially very damning.

She heard the door open down the corridor and slowly shifted so she could peer outside. Meija stepped out and closed it behind her. She stood leaning against it for a few moments, a trembling hand covering her eyes. That was enough for Korrian. She walked toward Meija, who looked up and smiled faintly, her lips tense and pale.

"Now, that's right on the top of my list of things to never do again, but I'll probably have to repeat it tomorrow." Her voice was as hollow as her eyes. "I was outraged and angry at first, but they kept going on and on, and now I'm just scared, Korrian. Looks like you're getting rid of the thorn in your side when it comes to the design of the Exodus ships, anyway."

"What did they do to you? Weren't you offered a lawyer, for heaven's sake?"

"They said it was just an interview—not a hearing."

"Sounds like complete garbage. If that were the case, you shouldn't have to come out of there practically in tears." Korrian's blood began to heat up. If she allowed it to reach the boiling point, she'd march right in to the smug LEO officer and end up getting arrested herself. "We're going to get you legal representation, just in case."

"I need to call Minister Desomas. She shouldn't hear this from someone else. I can't afford to lose her confidence in me." Wiping at her eyes with furious flicks of her fingertips, Meija squared her shoulders. "I'm not taking the fall for this, just because they need someone to pin it on quickly. That means whoever is trying to sabotage the program might succeed since they can operate without—what? Ow, you're pinching me."

"Oh, sorry." Korrian hadn't realized how firm her grip of Meija's upper arm was. "You said whoever is trying to sabotage will be able to operate...undetected. That's what you meant to say, right?"

"Yes."

"So, knowing what a gossip mill this is, we can assume that the individual, or individuals, that are responsible for this have relaxed somewhat since LEO homed in on you."

"You say that like it's a good thing." Meija's eyes darkened.

"It is, well, not for you right now, but in the long run it can work to our advantage." Korrian tugged at Meija. "Come on, we need to go to my office. Too many eyes and ears can spy here. My office is my domain. Nobody goes there without my say-so."

"I know." Meija followed her. "Not if they value their lives. That's the first information they gave me on my very first day here, on my introduction tour. Stay out of Heigel's office."

"Seriously?" Korrian couldn't tell if Meija was joking or not.

"Said sort of tongue-in-cheek, but those of us on the tour knew it was true."

"Excellent." Korrian pressed her palm to the sensor by her door. It opened and she motioned for Meija to step inside. She closed the door and then pulled a small, bullet-shaped scanner from her belt. Scanning the entire room, she put it back after reading the results carefully. "No sign of unauthorized surveillance equipment or explosive components."

"You always check for such things?"

"Only the surveillance, since we construct sensitive technology here. I'm probably as naïve as everybody else here, because it never dawned on me that someone would dream of destroying the only chance we have to save our people."

"Clearly someone has a big problem with this concept. I know there's a politically controversial force that says the Change is the natural way for our people to develop."

"And the scientists aren't helping by bickering about why some people are changing and others aren't. And why this started happening in the first place." Korrian sat down by her drawing sheet and engaged her laser pen. "Use my private line to contact the minister. You will find the link-address to Viasan Jigher there as well."

"Viasan—*that* Viasan Jigher?" Meija stared at her. "You know her?"

"Not privately, but in her capacity as one of Oconodos's best lawyers."

"One of them? Try legendary and *the* best." Meija looked dazed. "And you mean I should just call her up and say 'Korrian Heigel told me to call you,' just like that?"

"Yes. When she learns what this is about, I promise you, it will take precedence over all her other work."

"I see." It was clear that Meija doubted Korrian's certainty in the matter, but she still walked over to the computer and used the communication link.

Korrian drew the outline of the ship that the Oconodian government had approved of. They wanted each ship to harbor 200,000 people, but taking Meija's plans and standpoint into consideration, that was impossible. Half as many was a more realistic number, and with space to accommodate new generations taken into consideration. She remembered suddenly something her mother used to say. "When someone tries to tell you that 'life isn't just about fun and game,' that usually means they've lost the ability to play, to be joyous." How was it she had only remembered that just now? Her mother used to say that quite often, and in a way it summed up the point Meija was trying to make. If people weren't allowed to play, enjoy life, even fight for it, to some extent, what was the use of living? She could hear how Meija had shouted at her earlier that morning. "Merely living isn't enough!"

How could she have been blinded so badly by the ones panicking over the Change—the politicians that had wanted the ships as basic as possible to have them ready long before it was doable. She'd been swept away by their reasoning, and now when she understood this, she knew exactly where she needed to start. The two ships in the center of the wheel-like formation would hold the propulsion system, the government facilities, and the military installations. Each ship in the outer circle would have to be a self-contained city with backup systems to make independence possible, should they accidentally be severed.

She could hear Meija's voice at their previous meetings, which she'd once viewed as hours of frustration while trying to deal with an unrealistic dreamer. Meija had insisted that the people on the ships would need shops, theaters, gyms, restaurants, coffee shops, bars, game rooms, etcetera, and that those who by default lost their profession, such as farmers, should be given the chance to work in the vast hydroponic bays where most of the oxygen would be produced. The more Korrian remembered from Meija's lecturing, the more she was impressed, and sheepishly embarrassed, which she would never admit to, of course.

"You were right." Meija interrupted Korrian's thoughts. "And, oh, look…that's stunning. You've improved on that first sketch already. Look at that, will there be—are those trains?" Her exuberance had returned, which made Korrian think Viasan Jigher had accepted her case.

"And? What did she say?" Korrian looked at Meija's face, noting the glittering eyes, now shiny for all the right reasons, it seemed. "Meija?" She touched Meija's arm gently.

"Yeah. That. Yes, she'll be here in two days. Her current case is almost over. The jury is supposed to give their verdict within twenty-four hours, and then she'll shuttle here. Quite eager to dig into this, to quote her. She seems—feisty."

"Putting it mildly." Korrian rested her head in her hand. "You seem to have regained your confidence."

"Not entirely. I mean, yes, of course, she was very confident and so on, but I don't feel better just because this stellar lawyer is on my side...but because you are. For whatever reason you don't seem to doubt my innocence. Or if you do, you don't show it." Meija tilted her head, her disheveled ponytail falling over her shoulder.

"I know it's not you." And suddenly she did, without a doubt. One second before, she might have had a grain of uncertainty, but now, after voicing her confident trust, it was there, cemented.

"Thank you," Meija whispered. She looked at Korrian with eyes that seemed to fill her face, shimmering with sudden tears. "That's quite the journey, isn't it? Going from 'you foolish, frustrating, idealistic, and unrealistic bitch' to 'I know you didn't try to sabotage and kill innocent people.'"

"Not really." Korrian stood and cupped Meija's shoulder. "Someone who's frustratingly idealistic would hardly be a callous murderer, would they?"

"Guess not." Meija sniffled. "And even more extraordinary is that you seem to embrace some of what I've been trying to say. That's incredible."

"Not really." Korrian smiled at her own repetition. "Common sense."

"Hmm. Right." Meija shuddered. "What time is it?"

"Actually, it's getting late. Usually I work till midnight or thereabout, but I think we need to get some rest. Something tells me tomorrow will be another challenging day."

"Yes." Meija looked toward the large view ports overlooking the dock where the spaceship prototype was taking form. "Look. See all those security patrol shuttles? Guess we can sleep reasonably safe tonight."

Korrian saw small two-seat shuttles with LEO markings scurry around the dock. "Well, at least there are enough of them to disturb the saboteur. They claim to have swept the entire space-dock for explosives and similar devices. I'm not too impressed with LEO right now, so I hope they're on top of things."

"Yes, me too."

"Ready to retire for the evening?" Korrian let go of Meija's shoulders. She logged her entry into the draw sheet and powered off her laser pen.

"Yes. Now that you ask, I'm exhausted and sore."

"I have some liniment that our old doctor on the dock gave me. It's rather strong and makes you feel a little woozy, but it really helps."

"Sounds great."

They walked out of Korrian's office and took the elevator to deck ten. Several other officers were doing the same, but she wasn't interested in exchanging "who do you think..." comments. It took her less than ten seconds to notice the way the others looked at Meija. Cold disdain amd unbridled curiosity combined with skepticism radiated from several of them. Korrian shifted, making sure she stood between Meija and the other engineers and mechanics.

"We should call the infirmary and check on Chassine," Korrian said out loud, making sure she sounded matter-of-fact.

"Yes, I've been thinking of her the whole time today." Meija looked questioningly at Korrian.

"I still wish you'd get them to check you for injuries as well, having kept her breathing under the rubble for so long."

"Korrian, what are you up to?" Meija mumbled the words under her breath. "I'm fine."

"Hey, I was there, remember, the whole time when you refused to leave a member of our team. The desk and shelf could've collapsed and crushed you at any second, and still you stayed."

Meija glanced around Korrian and colored slightly. "Stop it," she whispered hotly. "They're staring."

Good. "Anyway, that's all I'm saying." Korrian smiled broadly at the flustered Meija.

The elevator stopped at the deck ten and they stepped off together with five others. Just as they were about to walk toward their quarters, one of the young men spoke up.

"Ms. Solimar, ma'am?"

"Yes...sorry, I don't know your name?" Meija squinted at his nametag. "Ensign Frolck?"

"Yes, ma'am. I apologize." He looked so unhappy that Korrian nearly took pity on him.

"Whatever for?" Meija looked nonplussed.

"For jumping to conclusions. I know Chassine, and I visited her in the infirmary. She didn't know who kept her safe while she was stuck under the rubble, but she said she owed this woman her life. I didn't know it was you, Ms. Solimar. Sorry for being such an idiot. Should've known the LEOs would get it all wrong."

Her tears spilling over now, Meija stepped closer to Korrian, who placed a hand at the small of her back. "Thank you for telling me she's all right. She is, isn't she?" Meija asked Ensign Frolck.

"Yes, she's going to make a full recovery once her ribs and other fractures heal."

"Good. Excellent."

"I hope you discourage any other gossip you hear, Ensign," Korrian said sternly.

"Aye, Commander. Count on it." He saluted both of them. "Good night, Commander. Ms. Solimar."

Meija wiped at her tears as they walked to their quarters. "That was...intense. How did you know?"

"I saw how they acted. I thought I'd better deal with the situation before the rumors got out of control."

"Thanks." Meija placed her hand on the sensor to open the inner door. "I have to admit I'm ready to use a painkiller dropper."

"I have a medicine dispenser." Korrian pointed toward the bedroom. "Right next to my bed. The right one."

"Thanks." Meija stopped on the threshold and walked back to Korrian. "There's a secret sweetness to your nature that you keep hidden from most people."

"Surely you're mistaken." Korrian couldn't stop herself from smiling nervously, no matter how she tried. "That observation could ruin my whole reputation if it got out."

"I won't tell." Standing on her toes, Meija kissed Korrian's cheek. "Thank you." She disappeared into the bedroom.

Korrian raised her hands and slid her fingertips across the skin on her cheek. Meija's lips were incredibly soft. The chaste touch of them against her cheek was enough to make her tremble, which of course was ridiculous. Meija was being appreciative, that was all.

CHAPTER FIVE

Meija placed the dropper under her tongue and clicked twice on the sensor. It would only take a few minutes for the medication to take full effect, for which she was grateful after such a horrific day. She decided to change into sleepwear before she returned to the living area. The mere thought of wearing her uniform a minute longer nauseated her. She pulled on soft blue pajamas and then joined Korrian. "There. Much better." Meija's smile turned into a slight frown as Korrian merely stared at her. "What's wrong?"

"You—look different." Korrian sat at the dining table with her portable work sheet and a laser pen in her hand. "I've only seen you in uniform."

"Likewise. I just wanted to be comfortable. I hope it's all right?"

"Oh, sure. Absolutely." Korrian colored at the tips of her ears and turned to the drawing on the table. "You up for doing some more work?"

"Yes. Painkiller's kicking in." Meija pulled up a chair and sat down on Korrian's left side. "You have to fill me in on what I'm looking at here."

"This is a schematic of one of the residential decks. As you can tell, I've opened up several areas where we can plan for just about anything. Playgrounds, stores, restaurants, schools…"

"Library, theater, game rooms…"

"Yes. Here's another sketch where I've implemented the biologists' and physicists' calculations when it comes to how big the hydroponic bays need to be in order to provide the oxygen as well as food."

"That's pretty brilliant." Meija leaned over the blueprints. "What do those lines represent?"

"Steam piping for watering. As you know, we have to recycle absolutely everything on the Exodus ships. Nothing can leave the ships as we would lose too much energy if we needed to start up again. Once we reach our ultimate speed, we can steer and navigate, but we can't stop until we reach our destination."

"What if we run out of essentials? Water? Food?"

"We can't. That's why everything needs to be recycled. I assume our leaders will write new laws that everyone aboard the ships will need to abide by or face severe punishment. It's for everybody's survival, so I assume they'll enforce this particular law rather harshly."

"Hmm. What else is new? They seem pretty harsh already." Meija made a face. "Sorry. Go on."

Korrian surprised her by patting her leg and then yanking her hand back as if she'd burned it. "Um. So, here's the irrigation system. Any condensation, spill, or superfluous water will be recycled through the filter system that we put in place on every deck throughout the whole fleet." Pulling up yet another sheet, she then slid it over to Meija. "This is where we need to brainstorm. You say we need to have stores. What will we sell and where will the merchandise in question come from?"

"I've thought of that. As you say, recycling is key, so that makes for a thriving secondhand market. Bartering, or performing services, as payment. This will keep people at a balance with each other."

"What do you mean?"

"A society like ours is now, hierarchal in nature and with rather large gaps between the richest and the poorest, the powerful and the powerless, is dangerous on a confined place like a generational ship. You see?"

"Yes, I think so." Korrian leaned her chin into her hand, her eyes entirely focused on Meija.

"So, we need to at least start out evenly. No doubt the shrewder and more enterprising individuals will find ways to get ahead. That's the nature of the beast, so to speak. The fact that nobody lives in luxury and some in deplorable houses, like they do now, will sort of push the reset button. I imagine there will be restrictions regarding how much luggage people will be allowed to bring, so even if *what* they bring will differ, it's what they do with it once they're aboard that matters. A suitcase full of designer-label outfits is all fine, but once those clothes are worn out, or recycled, you're going to need something else. Perhaps your favorite designer is aboard one of the ships and setting up shop. The designer will use the reproduce computers to make new fabrics and other design elements and in turn will barter their designs for things they want or need."

"I see what you mean, and I can buy into this concept. But you also talk about restaurants. Why? Everyone will have a dispenser available in their quarters."

"Yes, of course. But just as some will most often choose to eat at home with their family, some will prefer to eat out, with others, either because they enjoy it or because they're alone or even lonely." Meija tried to not inject too much feeling into what she was saying, since she didn't want Korrian to think she was talking about herself.

She forced herself to not allow her voice to tremble as she continued. "Life will go on, in some ways just like it always has done, but in other ways, along completely new tracks. Some will be able to remain in their chosen profession, but some will have to adjust and work with something entirely different. Not everyone reacts the same way to change. Some thrive, and some go under. It's up to us, as the originators, as the think tank, if you will, to foresee this and come up with strategies and alternatives."

"What about the age rule the politicians are bickering about? I see that as potentially disastrous."

Korrian was referring to the debate currently raging among the Oconodian rulers. Some argued it was no use to take anyone over the age of sixty since the journey to find a new world would take from fifteen to thirty years. Others spoke of the callousness of such reasoning and argued that people were worth saving regardless of age.

"I have no answer," Meija said. "People who have to leave someone behind will carry with them an immense sense of loss and guilt, two destructive emotions that can potentially derail a person. To be honest, I think it's not comparable with any practical issues about resources."

"I hear you. So far, the ones in charge of making that decision haven't altered the number of passengers. Perhaps if I show them the new and improved specs, we can help them not be too practical and not swerve toward thinking heartlessly." Korrian regarded her table filled with work sheets. "I can't believe how I managed to work on this, merely thinking about irrigation and square meters rather than what this is."

"And what is that?" Meija scooted close and touched Korrian's shoulder gently. Something about the sadness on Korrian's face made it possible to enter her personal space.

"It's the future. It's us. Us, as in Oconodians. Whether the perceived threat of the Change is as devastating as they claim or not, the decision is made. We're leaving Oconodos. Forever." Her voice low, Korrian looked like she had a problem breathing.

"So I take it you're going? I mean, for sure?"

"If the ships depart in my lifetime, yes. How could I not? I've lived and breathed these vessels for years on end. I have no close family."

"Nor do I, anymore." Meija didn't know where she found the courage, but the desolate tone in Korrian's voice made her run the back of her curled fingers down her cheek. "I do want to go, though. I think I can be useful, and apart from that, I'm curious about what's out there."

"You afraid of the Changed ones?" Korrian didn't flinch or jerk her head back. Instead, she took Meija's hand and held it gently against her skin.

"Not as a rule. I've met a few of the incarcerated ones. One of them was responsible for the collapse of the sports-arena ceiling. I was there when it happened, so when given the chance, I opted to meet this particular man. Did you know he's just fourteen?"

"No." Korrian looked shocked. "Fourteen? Hardly a man."

"Exactly. I met a frightened boy who kept asking about his parents and little sister. Neither of them had Changed at the time, but later his little sister did. She's kept in one of the camps with her parents. They volunteered to go with her there."

"Camps, huh? That's one inventive way of labeling yet another form of prison."

"So you don't agree that we need to keep the Oconodians safe?" Meija turned her hand within Korrian's grip and laced their fingers together.

"Yes, I have no problem that our law enforcers lock up whoever's committing crimes—but mainly those who do it to harm or cause damage. A fourteen-year-old kid, an even younger little girl, both transforming into something unknown, something they can't stop or help. Yes, I have a problem with that."

"I agree. I'm torn about what's going on and the way it's escalated the last decade. It used to be a random thing, but something is making people change, and since our best minds and our leaders claim the only way is to leave our planet…I feel I have to believe they do know what's best."

"I'm not so sure they do, but I've been assigned a task, and since I have sworn an oath of allegiance to my people and leaders, that's what motivates me."

"Yes. Still, the Changed ones are Oconodians too."

"That they are." Korrian gripped Meija's hand harder. "Today's been strange in more ways than one."

"Talk about an understatement." Meija had to chuckle. "We argue and fight as usual. Then the attack with all that drama. Suddenly I'm a suspect of said attack. And now…here we are."

"Yes." Korrian's eyes darkened and she ran the thumb of her free hand along Meija's lower lip. "Are you sure you're all right? It's been such a turbulent day for you."

"I can't say I'm not shaken. I am. Right now, here with you, I'm actually fine."

"I promise I won't let anyone pin this on you." Korrian suddenly stood and pulled Meija into her arms.

Meija inhaled deeply the by now so-familiar fruity scent that she associated with this enigmatic woman. She had never even dared to entertain the idea of approaching Korrian this way, mainly because until today, she'd found her extremely intimidating. Now, this close to Korrian, she felt the warmth of her body, so reassuring. "I believe you," Meija said, whispering. "And even if you can't persuade anyone to see the truth, I'll have known that you tried. That you believed I could never hurt anyone."

Flinching, Korrian pulled back, her eyes suddenly narrow, a more familiar look. "No. Not an option. If they end up charging you with any ridiculous accusation, I'll prove to them—" Korrian clasped her forehead. "Which is something I should've thought of right away. We can't wait to see if they charge you with anything. We need to find out who did this and prove your innocence way before it gets that far. While you still can move around the space-dock."

Meija clung to Korrian's upper arms. "Korrian. I don't want you to get dragged into this. You're far too important to this project. If they slow you down, they'll slow the Exodus project down and that way—"

"It's not up for debate. I don't know why you can't see this, but you're just as important for this project." She drew a deep, unsteady breath. "And for me."

"For you?" So sure she'd misheard, or misunderstood, Meija tried to read the truth in Korrian's eyes.

"Yes. I know it seems sudden, but it really isn't. We've worked together for a while now, and despite the fact that we've bickered worse than our esteemed politicians, sometimes I've quieted down my ego and just looked at you. Those are the times when I've acknowledged very briefly that I'm attracted to you. I'm not being conceited, but there have been times when I've noticed you looking at me as well."

Was it possible to blush until you fainted from lack of oxygen to your brain? Meija was pretty sure she was a candidate for such an event, if the heat in her cheeks was anything to judge by. Still, here Korrian stood and exposed the way she felt, not knowing how she would be received. "I have. I mean, I do. Look." Meija smiled nervously. "Can't help it."

"I'm rather relieved. I hoped I hadn't imagined it."

Meija knew she had to be honest. "I always found you even more sexy than infuriating, but never thought you'd ever see me like that. Or even like me in any capacity."

"If the brass hadn't shoved you down my throat, using you as their pawn, I wouldn't have been as rude, but that's no excuse. I should've listened more from the start. Perhaps…I can't help but feel that has something to do with how you were treated today."

"No. No, I can't believe that." It was crushing to see the recrimination on Korrian's face. "I don't know who whispered in their ears, or what they whispered, but it has nothing to do with you. Us." Meija stepped back into Korrian's embrace. "I rather like this, though."

Korrian chuckled, if a bit shakily. "Yes?"

"Absolutely." Tipping her head back, Meija smiled. "So, Commander, should I be concerned about any ulterior motives on your part for asking me to live together?"

"What? No! Live together?" Korrian looked entirely shocked for a few moments, then she scowled and laughed at the same time. "You're teasing me." It looked like Korrian actually didn't mind the banter.

"Good. Because my next line is 'I'm on my way to bed now, because I'm bushed,' which could be misconstrued." Meija winked.

"Good suggestion. I'll just make a few notes of what we talked about so we can start from there tomorrow."

"All right. If I'm already asleep when you go to bed, I'll see you tomorrow morning."

"Yes." Korrian let go but then pulled Meija back into her arms. "Sleep well." She kissed her cheek softly.

Meija couldn't keep from taking it one step further. Having stared her own mortality in the face while under the rubble with Chassine, she suddenly had the courage to turn her head and capture Korrian's lips with her own. She didn't deepen the kiss, but the mere sensation of the silky soft mouth against hers made her tremble. Finally she let go and took a step back, her breathing uneven. "Sleep well too," Meija said.

"You kiss me like that and ask me to sleep well?" Korrian pushed her hands into her pockets. "Cruel woman."

Meija laughed and walked toward the bedroom. She didn't know how well she'd sleep, but the idea that she was going to be resting in Korrian's quarters, less than a meter away, was reassuring.

CHAPTER SIX

Korrian sat up in bed, her heart hammering painfully. Cold sweat ran between her breasts and down her spine as she whipped her head to the side, searching for Meija. As her eyes fell upon the still form of the woman who was stubbornly sneaking her way into her heart, she slumped back against her pillows. So relieved she could hardly breathe, Korrian watched the slow, steady movements of Meija's chest. She was asleep and nothing bad had happened to her.

Korrian stood on slightly unsteady legs. She took a new uniform into the bathroom and went through her usual morning ablutions. Following her routines normally helped ground her, but whatever dream had put her in this state must have been deeply disturbing, as she found it difficult to shake.

Checking the time, she walked back into the bedroom and placed a gentle hand on Meija's shoulder. "Meija? Time to wake up."

"Mmm? Korrian?" She stretched like a lazy cat. "Already?"

"Yes. You sleep well?" Korrian had to smile at Meija's confused, sleepy expression. Her hair lay in complete disarray all over the pillow, and she had wrapped both arms and legs around the sheets and the duvet during the night.

"Mmm-hmm. Didn't think I would, but I did. Can't remember you even coming to bed."

"No, you were out cold once I was ready."

"No kidding." Meija sat up. "So, another day."

"Yes, and a lot to do. If you'll get up, I'll make us breakfast."

"All right. Sounds good." Stretching, a long and luxurious pull that left a gap between the pajama jacket and pants, Meija yawned.

Korrian's mouth became dry, and she hurried into the kitchenette and programmed tea and buttered bread. Then she busied herself with her work sheets, standing at the table with her tea mug. Her heart rate had nearly returned to normal when slender arms wrapped around her waist from behind. Damp, shampoo-scented hair tickled her arm as Meija placed her head on her shoulder.

"Thanks for making breakfast. Next time my turn, all right?" Meija let go and fetched her mug. "Korrian?" she asked wonderingly when she returned. "Am I crowding you? You're all flustered."

"No, you're not. I—I like that you feel free enough around me to touch me. I know I'm not easy to like." Did the smile she attempted looked as stiff as it felt?

"Not easy to like? Whoever told you such a vicious lie?" Meija put her mug down. "It's not true. Yes, when I thought you detested me, I was frustrated, but mainly because no matter what, I liked you anyway." Cupping Korrian's cheek, she tilted her head and squinted, a look typical for Meija. "I confess to being somewhat of a touchy-feely type of person, if you'll let me be. That said, I'm quite picky when it comes to who I touch and feel." She crinkled her nose.

"That's a relief." Korrian chuckled, completely charmed by Meija's flirtatious side. "Let's eat. We need to get out of here."

"Yes! Food." Winking, Meija ran her fingertips along Korrian's arm. "My next favorite thing."

❖

"Minister Desomas, please…" Meija tried again, but the woman on the view screen merely shook her head impatiently. In her late fifties, her blond hair in a severe bun, she glared at the screen with cold blue eyes.

"Ms. Solimar, I'm sure nobody would ever dream of accusing you of anything. Everybody knows you're there as my representative to try to talk some sense into that stubborn, ill-mannered woman running the project."

Meija cringed, as Korrian was standing behind the desk holding the screen, hearing everything. "The LEO officers did seem to home in on me, ma'am, and—"

"Ridiculous. If anything, they were probably thrilled to find someone who could give them an insight regarding whom to target. Why would they think you, a mere speck of a girl, would blast the entire space-dock to bits? That doesn't make sense."

In a way Desomas's blunt words could be interpreted as a complete vote of confidence, but then again, Meija didn't find being called "a speck of a girl" in that condescending tone a compliment.

"Minister Desomas," Korrian said, and rounded the screen. "I think you need to listen to Ms. Solimar with a little less disdain. You should also know that she, and she alone, has managed to reach this 'stubborn, ill-mannered woman' and convince her to listen to her expertise."

"Excuse me? *Her* expertise? I'll have you know, Commander Heigel, that Ms. Solimar is at the space-dock voicing my opinions, doing my bidding."

"I had no idea that you hold a degree in social anthropology, Minister. I'm impressed." Korrian's tone clearly stated she was nothing of the sort.

Meija tried to step on Korrian's toe, to get her to stop goading Minister Desomas, but she was out of reach.

"I have had enough of this insolence, and frankly, Ms. Solimar, I expect you to handle little hurdles like this on your own. Good day." Minister Desomas spoke curtly and then the screen went black.

Korrian shrugged. "Touchy."

"I wonder why." Meija sighed. "Korrian, that's my boss. I'm going to have to live with her—Stop laughing, I don't mean *with* her. I mean—oh, you know what I mean. Once my assignment is done, I'll have to either have a working relationship with Desomas or at the very least get good references."

Korrian's teasing smile waned. "Ah, so, once you're done with the prototype, you'll move on. I see."

"Now you're putting words into my mouth. And besides, with my profession, what can I work with at a space-dock?"

"I was hoping—never mind."

"No, go on. I want to hear." Meija couldn't take it when she saw Korrian begin to shut her out. "If there's even a remote chance for me to work near you, you have to tell me."

Korrian relaxed a little. "I'm being an idiot. I'm sorry." She leaned her hip against the desk and looked down. As she slowly raised her head, her eyes were darker and the skin around them tense. "I see myself working this project until the ships are launched. If that happens before I'm too old, I hope to be on them, hopefully in some kind of useful capacity. I can't set an exact date, but I strongly recommend that Minister Desomas find another punching bag, because I'm going to need your expertise for the foreseeable future."

Meija smiled, and her aching cheeks told her it was one of her wide beaming grins. "That sounds perfect. Now I just have to convince that Nacqui woman to direct her hounds toward the scent of the right prey."

"*We*. We have to convince the Nacqui woman." Korrian chuckled. "And I think our future plans sound pretty damn perfect."

CHAPTER SEVEN

Yes, just like that!" Korrian glanced up at Meija, who actually did a twirl before she placed her elbows on the work sheet. "That's damn awesome. If you make every partition between the bulkheads that way, you can easily adjust the cabins from singles to doubles. Large families can even have triples."

"Of course they can have triplets, that's how they get those big families."

The way Meija's jaw lost cohesion and she burst out in a proper belly laugh made the silly joke worth everything. Korrian shook her head and smiled. They'd been working on the blueprints for hours, and it was time for lunch. She didn't want to stop working too long, which gave her an idea. "Can I ask a favor? Can you go to the break room and run the dispenser for us and bring something back here? I'd like to keep working and not lose momentum."

"Naturally. What can I get you?"

"Just punch in Heigel lunch special four. And some tea, please."

"I'll be right back." Meija made a production of looking around them. "We're alone in here."

"Yes?" Turning her head around, Korrian confirmed this. "So?"

"This, funny lady. Just this." Meija pressed her lips against Korrian's, very sweetly and far too quickly. "Lunch special four coming up." Twirling—again—Meija hurried from the room.

Korrian gazed down at her sketches. To an outsider, it might look like a mishmash of technical specs and three-dimensional drawings, but to her it made perfect sense. It had been such an incredible revelation when Meija had taken only one look and then understood every subtle and clever thought behind it. Not so much from the technical specs that she freely admitted to knowing nothing about, but the three-dimensional drawings together with the floor plans were enough for Meija to grasp everything. What a terrible loss it would've been if they'd let their frustration and anger get in the way of this new understanding. Most of the blame lay with her, but Meija would never agree to that. Meija was convinced that the blame was equal, since they had both spat such disdainful words at each other.

Stretching her perpetually sore trapezius muscles, Korrian studied her plan for the residential area. She frowned and erased a unit in the restroom and replaced it with another that saved space. The more she envisioned herself living aboard one of these ships, the more she came up with compact solutions. She also imagined herself sharing quarters with Meija, and this was yet another motivator that gave birth to new concepts.

Another great idea that Meija had thought of earlier was that they should challenge themselves and make sure every single piece of equipment could do double duty. This suggestion sparked Korrian's imagination and inspired her to find solutions that she normally wouldn't have come up with. She suspected that had been Meija's intention all along.

Meija. Korrian checked the time and realized Meija had been gone forty minutes, which was ridiculous as it took less than ten minutes to prepare the food and bring it back. Frowning, she pressed the communication sensor on her lapel. "Heigel to Solimar. What's keeping you, Meija? Did you burn my lunch?" Smiling at the thought of Meija's scowl at the facetious insult, Korrian tapped her laser pen against the work sheet while she waited for the acerbic comeback.

When her hail was met with silence, she tried again. "Heigel to Solimar. Over." Still only silence. "Meija? Korrian here. Do you read me?" Not sure how often Meija used the communications device, as she normally worked right alongside Korrian and didn't have the need for hailing anyone else, Korrian strode toward the break-room area. She passed two ensigns, each carrying a tray with their lunch. They saluted her slightly awkwardly, trying to balance several bowls and mugs on each tray.

"Commander."

"At ease, and hold on to that before you drop it. You getting lunch for the entire mechanic crew?"

"Yes, Commander." The closest, a young woman, smiled carefully. "May we bring you something, ma'am?"

"No, I'm fine, thank you. Have either of you seen Ms. Solimar?"

"No?" The young woman looked over at the man. "Have you?"

"No. Not since yesterday."

Korrian's heart suddenly twitched with pain, as if stabbed by something very small and sharp. "Very well. If you see her, tell her I'm looking for her."

"Of course, Commander."

Korrian was already hurrying toward the break-room area. She ran into several other mechanics and engineers, but nobody had seen Meija. Something was catastrophically wrong.

❖

Meija blinked and looked up, at first fully expecting to still be in bed. She was rather uncomfortable, though, and where was her pillow? Realizing that she was in fact sitting up, she moaned at the discomfort of something prodding her shoulder.

"Hey. Wake up, girl."

That voice. Hard to distinguish. Whispering the words and yet with a male tone…who was in her room? Meija tried to open her eyes, but her eyelids were so heavy it seemed an impossible task.

"Come on. Wake up." More urgent now, the voice seemed closer.

"Tired." Meija was appalled at how swollen her tongue felt. "Sleep."

"No time for that. Open your eyes."

Meija was about to tell the person they had to wait, that she was too tired, when she heard a muted voice that she did recognize.

"Heigel to Solimar. Over."

Korrian? Prying her eyes open, Meija flinched at the sharp light from above. This wasn't her bedroom. Not the one on the space station and definitely not the one she shared with Korrian at the dock. Squinting to protect her sensitive eyes, she tried to figure out where she was and who the hoarse, whispering voice belonged to. As she shifted, she realized she was on the floor. A very damp, cold, and hard floor.

"Meija? Korrian here. Do you read me?"

"Korrian. Korrian?" Meija tried to find her lapel to respond to

Korrian's hail, but she couldn't move her arms. "Ow. What's going on?" Realizing that her arms were tied painfully tight together behind her back, she bit down hard on her lower lip and forced her eyes wide open.

"There. That's more like it." The hoarse voice sounded closer.

Meija's eyes were finally adjusting and now she saw long rows of piping, leading in all directions. "Where am I?"

"In the basement, I guess you could say. The heart of the dock, in a manner of speaking. All the important manifolds, pipes, fiber tubes, etcetera run through here. Last time was only to get everybody's attention. Also, it led the damn LEO mercenaries to even greater heights of incompetence when they went after you." The stranger chuckled. "After they discover what's left of your body, they'll assume you had a bit of a mishap when you set the timer."

"Timer? What are you talking about? Who are you? Untie me!" Meija pulled at the restraints, but they only dug even more painfully into her wrists. Moaning, she changed her approach and tried to move her legs again. Stretched out before her, they felt numb, but she thought she could wiggle her feet if she tried hard enough. It took her yet another second to understand that her ankles were strapped together as well. Panic started to build, but she forced it down. Her mind was less foggy now, so whatever this person had used to tranquilize her was wearing off.

"Why are you doing this?" Meija moaned, thinking it best to sound weaker than she was. The person was still backlit and, except for their uniform, it was impossible to make out any features. Was the hair blond? Or short and gray? The saboteur looked male, but that could be a clever disguise. Meija wanted to sob at the throbbing pain in her temples, but she refused to give him the satisfaction.

"Why I'm doing this? You're joking, right? Our elitist government decides that the Changed ones are second-rate citizens and dangerous ones on top of that. So they use most of our resources and build these monstrosities to take the rich and famous to some sort of perceived paradise. The road to righteousness demands sacrifice."

"What are you talking about? What elite? Road to righteousness? Are you crazy?" Meija couldn't believe the misguided venom that erupted from the person in front of her.

"No, you have it all wrong, like you've had ever since you set foot here. Still, the way Heigel kept looking at you, I knew you were the distraction I'd been waiting for."

"So, you had this planned all along?" Meija tried shifting sideways to get a better look at this individual. "And when you place a bomb here, you'll take out most of the station. And life support. How the hell will you survive that? Or are you going to sacrifice yourself?"

"Oh, trust me, I've thought of everything."

"A fool's reasoning. Nobody's perfect. You always overlook something, and when it comes to what you're about to do, that something can be fatal, even for you."

"Shut up." The voice sank to a low growl, making Meija 90 percent sure this was a man. He seemed to know her well enough, so this wasn't a stranger.

"Thought you wanted me to talk. You have to make up your mind." Meija disregarded the pain now and kicked her legs out over and over.

"Stop that. You're only hurting yourself." The saboteur leaned over her and placed something on her lap. "Guard this with your life, Meija. I have to go now."

"No. No!" At a distance she saw clearly that he was male. "Come back. No!" She yelled at the top of her lungs.

A resounding tone from the box sitting on her thighs made her flinch. She blinked away tears of pure fear from her eyelashes and saw a small display on the top begin to count down.

CHAPTER EIGHT

K orrian ran along the corridor, having checked all the break rooms and restrooms on this deck. She'd tried the communication channel constantly, but no one answered. Her chest hurt as she ran, and she knew it was from keeping sobs of fear from erupting. Clenching her teeth, she hurried to the elevator that would take her to the bridge. Inside, she nearly gave in to the panic simmering beneath the surface, but the ping alerted her in time to get a grip on herself.

"Commander?" A startled lieutenant about to enter the elevator stumbled backward as she barreled onto the bridge.

"Captain," Korrian barked. "I have reason to think the saboteur is about to strike again. Soon. My social anthropologist is missing and—"

"Commander Heigel. Inhale and exhale and speak in a manner that is distinguishable," Captain Warro said calmly. "Go to red alert." The last directive lowered the light on the bridge and sent everyone aboard the space-dock to their duty station. "Commander?"

"Yesterday, Meija Solimar, assigned to my unit as Minister Desomas's representative and subject-matter expert, was heard by the LEO regarding the attack against the space-dock. This after having risked her life to save another young woman in my unit. Today, she went to retrieve lunch from the dispensers, something that should normally take ten minutes. It's now been at least fifty minutes, and she's not responding to hails."

Captain Warro, a tall, burly man with iron-gray hair and neatly trimmed beard, looked at her with narrowing eyes. "Warro to Nacqui. Report to the bridge instantly."

"Captain—"

"Give me a moment, Heigel. I know it's disturbing information, but I need Nacqui here."

"She's the one who—"

"She's obeying my directives. Take a seat, Commander."

Korrian glared at her commanding officer. He might quiet her for now, but she'd be damned if she'd sit down when Meija's life was in danger.

❖

Meija stared at the display. As far as she could tell she had about twenty minutes before the device exploded and took her and all the vital conduits out.

"Damn it." She had listened with increasing agony as Korrian had kept hailing her, but as she was unable to reach the sensor, she could only listen. She felt a strange mix of complete agony and comfort hearing the voice of the woman she'd come to care so much for, was perhaps even falling in love with.

"Meija, I'm not sure you can hear me, but I'm going to assume you do. I have to." Korrian sounded devastated. "I'm on the bridge. I've informed the captain and we're at red alert. Where are you, Meija? Where *are* you?" Murmuring and unintelligible voices in the background took over, but at least she heard other people.

Her heart ached at the frenzy in Korrian's whispers. If there was a way to press the sensor. If she could press against it for more than two seconds, she'd have an open channel back to Korrian. Suddenly remembering the headband she wore to keep her hair in place, she snapped her head forward. She couldn't do it with too much force or she'd send the headband flying. Four attempts and an increasingly aching neck later, she held the rigid piece of material triumphantly between her teeth. Pushing with her tongue, she moved it until it pointed downward in a semicircle. She had to aim blindly, as the inner part of her lapel was out of her sight. Pushing and pushing, she prayed for the clicking sound that would prove she was in the right spot. She listened so intently she nearly missed it when it suddenly happened. It clicked once and then it was gone. Meija backed up with the end of the headband, and then she could actually feel the tip of it settle in the little groove in the lapel. She pressed and counted to four seconds to be on the safe side. Tucking the end of the headband into her cheek, holding on to it with the back of her molars, she tried speaking.

"Korrian," she slurred. "Korrian, come in. Do you read me?"

"Meija?" Korrian was there immediately. "Quiet, everyone. I think I hear her. Meija?"

"I'm here. I hear you." Meija let go of the headband, her jaws aching so badly now it was impossible to clamp down on it anymore. "A man, I think, a man grabbed me. I woke up here. He placed a bomb on me. A large one."

"Meija, where are you? Tell me where you are."

"I don't know. I think somewhere beneath engineering. It looks like a basement, sort of. Lots of pipes, manifolds, conduits going in all directions. In fact..." Meija forced her head to turn as far it would go to the left and the right. "I think I'm in the center of all these pipes. They lead away from me in four different directions."

"Then I know. I'm on my way. Keep the channel open."

"No problem, I lost the headband." Meija sobbed. "You have to hurry, or not come here at all. The countdown is showing twelve minutes."

"I'll be there in less than five."

❖

Korrian ran across the desk and saw how Captain Warro motioned for his security chief to accompany her before slamming his palm against the console next to the command chair. "All hands, this is the captain. Go to the escape pods and abandon the station. This is not a drill. Abandon the station. Proceed to the closest escape-pod facility. This is not a drill."

The elevator door opened and Nacqui stood there, hands behind her back.

"You're with Commander Heigel, Nacqui," Warro said, his voice short.

"Aye, sir." Nacqui didn't as much as flinch. "What's going on, Commander?"

"The woman you all but accused of bombing the station yesterday is now kidnapped and strapped to an unknown device in the culverts."

"I see." Nacqui offered no explanation but spoke into her communication device. "We have a lead now. Culverts. Deploy units one to four from all directions to converge on the center nexus."

Voices called in confirmations as they stepped off the elevator. Korrian didn't wait. She ran toward the center of the space-dock, where a system of ladders led down to the nexus. "We're on our way, Meija. Can you still hear me?" she gasped as she pushed people aside.

"I hear you. Just hurry, Korrian. I heard the captain just now. Everyone is leaving, and maybe you should too?"

"Damn it. I'm not leaving you." Turning the corner, Korrian saw Nacqui keeping an even pace with her. "If I have my way, I'll never leave you."

"Korrian..." Meija's voice was filled with tears. "Darling."

"One minute and I'll be there."

"Does anyone have a knife or something? I'm sort of tied up here."

"I have my tool belt. We'll figure it out." Korrian reached the junction where a large pillar carried the entire center part of the ceiling. She pressed her palm to the sensor and opened the door. With Nacqui and the security officers behind her, she didn't bother with the steps. She merely squeezed with hands and feet and slid the ten floors down to the lowest level.

"I heard a bang. Is that you, Korrian?" Meija asked, sounding in stereo all of a sudden.

"Yes. I'm here now. Can you yell louder? I'm turning off my communicator now."

"Oh. All right. Hello! Hello! Over here!"

Korrian heard immediately where Meija's voice came from and hurried toward it.

"Commander. Careful! He might have set booby traps." Nacqui yanked her shoulder nearly out of its socket. "Let me scan first."

"Hurry. Meija. We're on our way!"

Nacqui scanned and moved toward Meija's location far too slowly. As much as Korrian realized why they had to use caution, she knew the minutes were passing too fast.

"I think you're good to go, Commander."

"Finally." Korrian pushed past the LEO officer and rounded the corner. Then she saw Meija sitting tied to one of the pipes. A thirty-by-thirty-centimeter box sat on her lap with numbers blinking on a display.

"You're here. We have six minutes." Meija was shaking so badly her teeth were clattering.

"Plenty of time," Korrian lied. "Let me see." She risked a two-second delay by pressing her lips quickly to Meija's temple. "Looks like a simple enough timer, but something tells me it's not."

Nacqui joined them and knelt next to Meija, who stared at the LEO officer with wide eyes. "What's she doing here?"

"I'm the investigating officer." Nacqui scanned the box. "It has two backup circuits. I think our only option is to untie Ms. Solimar, hold the device still while she wiggles free, and then set it down."

"Yes. And cool it to buy ourselves more time."

"Agreed."

Another LEO agent had joined them and was now cutting Meija's restraints off. Korrian and Nacqui lifted the box a fraction of a centimeter, which was barely enough for Meija to shift backward. The agent behind her pulled her out the last bit.

"My legs are asleep after sitting like that for ages. At least it felt like ages." Meija didn't make any attempt to leave.

"Get out of here, Meija."

"No. Don't ask me to do that." Meija's voice showed beyond anything that this was non-negotiable.

Korrian opened her tool belt and chose a small magnetic screwdriver. Inserting it into the side of the box, she carefully pried the side open. "You're right. Two circuits. The first one will set the other two off within an additional few seconds. If we cut the first one with the timer, the delay will be about two seconds. With cooling perhaps ten."

"That's not enough. It will cripple the station and set the Exodus program back several years." Nacqui growled. "No matter what, we're toast since we won't make it far enough even if we cool it."

"Wait. Let me see one thing." Korrian used a small flashlight to shine inside the box. "If I'm not mistaken, this is a fail-safe."

"What? Where?" Nacqui pushed her face close to the floor and looked where Korrian pointed. "I'll be damned—"

"Operated via a communication channel." Korrian yanked her lapel off her uniform. "I think it's this command. Multi-operator. We rarely use it since the sound quality leaves a lot to be desired if a lot of people use the same channel." She didn't wait, since they were virtually out of time. Holding Meija close with one arm, she pressed the sensor six times in rapid sequence and finished with a six-second continued squeeze. "Korrian to engineering staff. You all safely in the pods?"

"Aye, ma'am," several voices replied, with loads of static.

"Look!" Meija pointed at the slowly darkening display. "Is that a good thing?"

Korrian motioned for Nacqui to scan the bomb.

"It's turned off." For the first time Korrian detected emotion in Nacqui. Her voice trembled as she performed the reading twice more. "It's off. Defused."

"Oh, thank the Gods." Meija melted into Korrian. "Oh, thank you."

"I have you. Let's get out of here." Korrian gazed at Nacqui. "Are you comfortable letting your crew deal with that vile thing?"

"Certainly. You go ahead. We still have to figure out who did this. They're most likely on one of the pods or a shuttle."

"Probably trying to figure out how to reach the road to righteousness that demands sacrifice." Meija huffed indignantly.

"What?" Korrian snapped her head toward Meija. "What did you say?"

"The road to righteousness demands sacrifice. That's what the man said before he took off. Sounded really pompous and weird."

"And I've heard someone say it before. I can't believe it, but I know who the saboteur is. He said the exact same words to me yesterday."

"Who?" Nacqui asked.

Korrian helped Meija stand up, keeping an arm around her. "His name is Gessley Barr."

"Gessley? No…" Meija quieted and something very painful passed across her features. "Oh, no. I should've known. But he was, I mean, I thought he was my friend." She sent a pained look toward Korrian. "When I was moaning and groaning over your stubbornness, he always listened, was always sympathetic."

"While he plotted to blow us all to pieces." Nacqui spoke rapidly into her communicator. "No shuttles? All right. Put surveillance on all the returning pods. We cannot let him slip through the net."

More voices confirmed her commands as they walked toward the ladder.

"This time we can take the elevator. No rush anymore." Korrian circled the column and pressed another sensor. After a while a barely visible door opened and the three of them stepped inside. "I think you owe us an explanation of why you were so set on Ms. Solimar being guilty."

"I never thought she was guilty." Nacqui spoke matter-of-factly. "Our tactic worked. We hoped the real perpetrator would fall for it as well. Seems he did."

"And this tactic nearly got Meija killed and the space-dock blown up."

"A calculated risk." Nacqui shrugged.

"You callous bitch—"

"Korrian. Don't." Meija pressed a hand to Korrian's sternum, holding her back. "Let her deal with Gessley and whoever he works for, or collaborates with. Let them deal with it and let's go home. Please." Nearly translucent green eyes gazed up at her.

"Fine. You deal with Gessley and then you stay away from us." Turning to Meija, she worriedly looked her over. "Do I need to take you to the infirmary?"

"Absolutely not. I want to go home."

Korrian smiled at Meija's adorable scowl. "Then home it is."

EPILOGUE

Meija had never been more comfortable. She buried her nose in the strong, yet so soft, column that was Korrian's neck. She had fallen asleep directly after her long, hot shower, exhausted and so relieved she couldn't even eat. Korrian had lifted her up from the dining-area chair and tucked her into bed. Meija had gone to sleep as soon as she felt the soft bedding, only to wake up briefly when Korrian came to bed, she too dressed only in a towel.

Now Meija glanced at the time and shrugged. So, it was the middle of the night. So what? Korrian had put a privacy lock on their door as well as on their communicators. Unless there was another red alert, nobody would disturb them.

Before Korrian had installed the privacy locks, the captain had expressed his admiration as well as remorse for Meija's experience. He also told them that Gessley Barr had been sighted on one of the pods and that an arrest was imminent.

"Mmm, you feel wonderful," Korrian murmured against Meija's hair. "I could get used to this...waking up like this, very easily."

"Me too." Meija shifted and felt the towel fall away. "Oh, my."

Korrian's face softened. "Oh, my, indeed." She ran her hands up and down Meija's back. "I was right."

"You were? How's that?" Meija reveled in the touch.

"You do feel wonderful."

"Your hands are extraordinarily soft. How can you have such hands?"

"I'm used to handling delicate equipment. Maybe that has something to do with it?"

"Korrian!" Meija laughed and kissed the tip of her nose. "That was kind of cheesy."

"Could be. Doesn't make it any less true. You are delicate. Sometimes. Most of the time you're super strong and tougher than anyone I've ever known."

"Hey, you're not exactly a weak kitten either."

Korrian rolled them over, pulling her own towel off. "True." She kissed Meija softly. "I know it's soon—"

"Not soon enough." Meija wrapped her arms and legs around Korrian, much like she'd done with her duvet the previous night. "I may be a little rusty when it comes to making love, but I think we'll be wonderful together."

"I don't doubt it." Korrian pushed against Meija, grinding their hips together. "I need to feel you. Feel your heartbeat, your breath." She pushed a hand between them, cupping Meija. "Yes, and feel how much you want me. I need that too. I want you to know how much this means, of how my heart began to break at the mere thought of losing you."

"I called out for you, I cried for you, and I promised myself if I lived through today, I wouldn't hesitate a moment longer to tell you how I feel." Whimpering, Meija undulated against Korrian's hand. "I'm falling in love with you, Korrian. You're constantly on my mind."

"Meija. Sweetheart." Korrian pushed against her hand with her hips.

Meija couldn't reach Korrian's sex, but her breasts swayed so enticingly just in front of her that all she had to do was reach for them and pull one nipple into her mouth. "Mmm. Yes."

It didn't take them long. Hardly any finesse, just soaring feelings and so much budding love was all it required. Meija's orgasm ignited Korrian's, and they held on so tight to each other that the convulsions seemed mutual. She had never been so in tune with a lover that she couldn't tell whose orgasm happened first or for how long.

Meija giggled and snuggled close. "That was fun."

"Sure was."

"I want to do that again. Soon."

"Me too."

"And I don't regret telling you first."

"You spoke my mind. I'm in love, Meija. Head over heels, which is totally unlike me."

Meija nuzzled her neck. "Trust me, I don't lower my guard that easily either."

"It's more than falling in love, though. The changes you brought with you are far beyond that." Korrian hoped Meija would understand. "Until yesterday, I've often doubted that the project would be a success. Today, I see working together with you, and later with more people with your expertise, as the Exodus project's salvation. Because of you this project will stand a chance of succeeding."

Meija rose on her elbow and ran the back of her curled fingers along Korrian's cheeks. "You flatter me, but with our joined efforts we will one day leave Oconodos and create a new life and a new home for our people."

Korrian gazed up at the fairy tale–looking creature who spoke of love and a future as if it were the easiest thing in the world.

Meija chuckled and pressed her lips against Korrian's. "Mmm. Love you."

Korrian tossed her head back and laughed.

Easy? Yes, maybe it was.

Glossary

ORACLE'S DESTINY

Characters

Dr. Gemma Meyer: CMO in the SC fleet, from Earth.
Dr. Ciel O'Diarda: druid and herbalist healer from Gantharat.
Kellen O'Dal: Protector of the Realm, from Gantharat.
Rae Jacelon: admiral, Protector of the Realm by marriage, from Earth.
Andreia M'Aldovar: leader of the former Gantharian resistance. Also known by her codename Boyoda.
Tammas O'Mea: young woman from Gantharat.
Ilias O'Mea: Tammas's newborn son.
Tenner O'Sialla: a male physician from Gantharat.
Tacrosty: sergeant in the SC marine corps, from Corma.
Lund: corporal in the SC military, from Earth.
Vesmonc: major in the SC military, from Imidestria.
Vollenby: private in the SC military.
Raviciera: displaced young girl of Onotharian descent.
Pomaera: displaced woman of Onotharian descent, Raviciera's mother.
Camol: from Gantharat, Tammas O'Mea's husband and Ilias's father.

Alien Names and Words

Supreme Constellations Unification of Planets: SC. A sector of home worlds and space stations with Earth at its center.
Gantharat: a planet outside of the SC, recently liberated after being occupied for twenty-five years by a neighboring people.

Onotharat: a planet outside of the Supreme Constellation, an all-but-depleted world whose people were forced off the planet they'd occupied and exploited for the last twenty-five years.

Paustenja: a Gantharian city.

Rihoa: a Gantharian city.

G'benka: a Gantharian wild-growing root.

Mirisia: an area of Gantharat.

Ganath: capital of Gantharat.

Singuisa: a Gantharian bush with antibacterial qualities.

Teroshem: a Gantharian rural area.

Premoni: an intergalactic language.

Emres: a Gantharian city.

H'rea dea'savh!: Gantharian curse words.

Sientesh'ta: a Gantharian bush that grows in the wild.

Loc'tialdo: a Gantharian flower.

Siengash: mountains on Gantharat.

Sien Dela: a mountain pass on Gantharat.

Bujjadin: drug dealer.

Henshes: Gantharian word for "darling."

THE QUEEN AND THE CAPTAIN

Characters

EiLeen Maxio: former Queen of Imidestria.

King Reidder: EiLeen's brother, the former King of Imidestria.

Dana Rhoridan: captain of the luxury cruiser *Koenigin*.

Tory L'Ley: commander and next in command of the *Koenigin*.

Mock: EiLeen's footman and assistant.

Ewan Jacelon: fleet admiral in the SC fleet.

Paymé Soth: head chef of the *Koenigin*.

Mr. Ta'Yans: a guest aboard the *Koenigin*.

Marco Thorosac: elected leader of the SC, chairman of the High Council.

Lt. Freya: helms officer on the *Koenigin*.

Saghall: ensign on the *Koenigin*.

Dr. Irah: CMO on the *Koenigin*.

Moi: undercover servant.

Boransh: a criminal for hire.

Dahlia Jacelon: chief diplomat in the SC, married to Ewan Jacelon.

Alien names and words

The *Koenigin*: a luxury cruiser.

Imidestria: a planet within the SC.

Cormanian: from the planet Corma, a planet within the SC.

Revos Prime: small planet on the SC border where the fleet and military train soldiers and civilians in combat and intelligence operations.

Alpha VII space station: a multitude of space stations, Alpha, Beta, and Gamma, dispersed throughout the SC in three rings. Alpha is the ring closest to the center.

Guild Nation: a planet within the SC and its newest member.

Imicaloza: capital of Imidestria.

Sindianah: a mythical Imidestrian water creature said to live in the sea and occasionally claim the heart of a sailor.

MAFE: Masking Feature that makes a ship difficult to detect.

Hioros One: small desert planet known for metal ores.

The *Quistamajar*: Boransh's ship.

Begoll: small mining planet within the SC.

Lindelei: Imidestrian word for "most beloved."

THE DAWNING

Characters

Meija Solimar: social anthropologist.

Gessley Barr: engineer at the Exodus project.

Korrian Heigel: chief engineer at the Exodus project.

Ms. Desomas: minister of the department.

Col. Rayginnia: colonel, stationed at the space station.

Belonder: an engineer at the space-dock.

Toimi: a junior engineer at the space-dock.

Reeva: a junior engineer at the space-dock.

Chassine: a junior engineer at the space-dock.

Nacqui: inspector, head of security at the space station.
Viasan Jigher: famous lawyer.
Frolck: ensign. Mechanic at the space-dock.
Warro: captain of the space-dock.

Alien names and places

Oconodos: a planet. The home world of Oconodians.
Conos: capital of Oconodos.
LEO: Law Enforcement Orbit.

About the Author

Gun Brooke (gbrooke-fiction.com) resides in the countryside in Sweden with her very patient family. A retired neonatal intensive care nurse, she now writes full-time, only rarely taking a break to create websites for herself or others and to do computer graphics. Gun writes both romance and sci-fi. Connect with her on Facebook (gunbach), on Twitter (redheadgrrl1960), and on Tumblr (gunbrooke).

Books Available From Bold Strokes Books

Date with Destiny by Mason Dixon. When sophisticated bank executive Rashida Ivey meets unemployed blue-collar worker Destiny Jackson, will her life ever be the same? (978-1-60282-878-0)

The Devil's Orchard by Ali Vali. Cain and Emma plan a wedding before the birth of their third child while Juan Luis is still lurking, and as Cain plans for his death, an unexpected visitor arrives and challenges her belief in her father, Dalton Casey. (978-1-60282-879-7)

Secrets and Shadows by L.T. Marie. A bodyguard and the woman she protects run from a madman and into each other's arms. (978-1-60282-880-3)

Change Horizon: Three Novellas by Gun Brooke. Three stories of courageous women who dare to love as they fight to claim a future in a hostile universe. (978-1-60282-881-0)

Scarlett Thirst by Crin Claxton. When hot, feisty Rani meets cool vampire Rob, one lifetime isn't enough, and the road from human to vampire is shorter than you think… (978-1-60282-856-8)

Battle Axe by Carsen Taite. How close is too close? Bounty hunter Luca Bennett will soon find out. (978-1-60282-871-1)

Improvisation by Karis Walsh. High school geometry teacher Jan Carroll thinks she's figured out the shape of her life and her future, until graphic artist and fiddle player Tina Nelson comes along and teaches her to improvise. (978-1-60282-872-8)

For Want of a Fiend by Barbara Ann Wright. Without her Fiendish power, can Princess Katya and her consort Starbride stop a magic-wielding madman from sparking an uprising in the kingdom of Farraday? (978-1-60282-873-5)

Swans & Clons by Nora Olsen. In a future world where there are no males, sixteen-year-old Rubric and her girlfriend Salmon Jo must fight to survive when everything they believed in turns out to be a lie. (978-1-60282-874-2)

Broken in Soft Places by Fiona Zedde. The instant Sara Chambers meets the seductive and sinful Merille Thompson, she falls hard, but knowing the difference between love and a dangerous, all-consuming desire is just one of the lessons Sara must learn before it's too late. (978-1-60282-876-6)

Healing Hearts by Donna K. Ford. Running from tragedy, the women of Willow Springs find that with friendship, there is hope, and with love, there is everything. (978-1-60282-877-3)

Desolation Point by Cari Hunter. When a storm strands Sarah Kent in the North Cascades, Alex Pascal is determined to find her. Neither imagines the dangers they will face when a ruthless criminal begins to hunt them down. (978-1-60282-865-0)

I Remember by Julie Cannon. What happens when you can never forget the first kiss, the first touch, the first taste of lips on skin? What happens when you know you will remember every single detail of a mysterious woman? (978-1-60282-866-7)

The Gemini Deception by Kim Baldwin and Xenia Alexiou. The truth, the whole truth, and nothing but lies. Book six in the Elite Operatives series. (978-1-60282-867-4)

Scarlet Revenge by Sheri Lewis Wohl. When faith alone isn't enough, will the love of one woman be strong enough to save a vampire from damnation? (978-1-60282-868-1)

Ghost Trio by Lillian Q. Irwin. When Lee Howe hears the voice of her dead lover singing to her, is it a hallucination, a ghost, or something more sinister? (978-1-60282-869-8)

The Princess Affair by Nell Stark. Rhodes Scholar Kerry Donovan arrives at Oxford ready to focus on her studies, but her life and her priorities are thrown into chaos when she catches the eye of Her Royal Highness Princess Sasha. (978-1-60282-858-2)

The Chase by Jesse J. Thoma. When Isabelle Rochat's life is threatened, she receives the unwelcome protection and attention of bounty hunter Holt Lasher who vows to keep Isabelle safe at all costs. (978-1-60282-859-9)

The Lone Hunt by L.L. Raand. In a world where humans and Praeterns conspire for the ultimate power, violence is a way of life…and death. A Midnight Hunters novel. (978-1-60282-860-5)

The Supernatural Detective by Crin Claxton. Tony Carson sees dead people. With a drag queen for a spirit guide and a devastatingly attractive herbalist for a client, she's about to discover the spirit world can be a very dangerous world indeed. (978-1-60282-861-2)

Beloved Gomorrah by Justine Saracen. Undersea artists creating their own City on the Plain uncover the truth about Sodom and Gomorrah, whose "one righteous man" is a murderer, rapist, and conspirator in genocide. (978-1-60282-862-9)

The Left Hand of Justice by Jess Faraday. A kidnapped heiress, a heretical cult, a corrupt police chief, and an accused witch. Paris is burning, and the only one who can put out the fire is Detective Inspector Elise Corbeau…whose boss wants her dead. (978-1-60282-863-6)

Cut to the Chase by Lisa Girolami. Careful and methodical author Paige Cornish falls for brash and wild Hollywood actress Avalon Randolph, but can these opposites find a happy middle ground in a town that never lives in the middle? (978-1-60282-783-7)

Every Second Counts by D. Jackson Leigh. Every second counts in Bridgette LeRoy's desperate mission to protect her heart and stop Marc Ryder's suicidal return to riding rodeo bulls. (978-1-60282-785-1)

More Than Friends by Erin Dutton. Evelyn Fisher thinks she has the perfect role model for a long-term relationship, until her best friends, Kendall and Melanie, split up and all three women must reevaluate their lives and their relationships. (978-1-60282-784-4)

Dirty Money by Ashley Bartlett. Vivian Cooper and Reese DiGiovanni just found out that falling in love is hard. It's even harder when you're running for your life. (978-1-60282-786-8)

Sea Glass Inn by Karis Walsh. When Melinda Andrews commissions a series of mosaics by Pamela Whitford for her new inn, she doesn't expect to be more captivated by the artist than by the paintings. (978-1-60282-771-4)

The Awakening: A Sisterhood of Spirits novel by Yvonne Heidt. Sunny Skye has interacted with spirits her entire life, but when she runs into Officer Jordan Lawson during a ghost investigation, she discovers more than just facts in a missing girl's cold case file. (978-1-60282-772-1)

Blacker Than Blue by Rebekah Weatherspoon. Threatened with losing her first love to a powerful demon, vampire Cleo Jones is willing to break the ultimate law of the undead to rebuild the family she has lost. (978-1-60282-774-5)

Murphy's Law by Yolanda Wallace. No matter how high you climb, you can't escape your past. (978-1-60282-773-8)

Silver Collar by Gill McKnight. Werewolf Luc Garoul is outlawed and out of control, but can her family track her down before a sinister predator gets there first? Fourth in the Garoul series. (978-1-60282-764-6)

The Dragon Tree Legacy by Ali Vali. For Aubrey Tarver time hasn't dulled the pain of losing her first love Wiley Gremillion, but she has to set that aside when her choices put her life and her family's lives in real danger. (978-1-60282-765-3)